Boonesborough

Massacree!

Pecos Bill

Lucinda Rescues a Friend

William Tell

WITHDRAWN

Tom Plays, Fights and Hides

Moy Castle

The Lady Roxana Picks Her Mate

Cedar of Red Horse Hill

The Broken Note

Two Years before the Mast

Peter Graves

The Burglars

Through Golden Windows

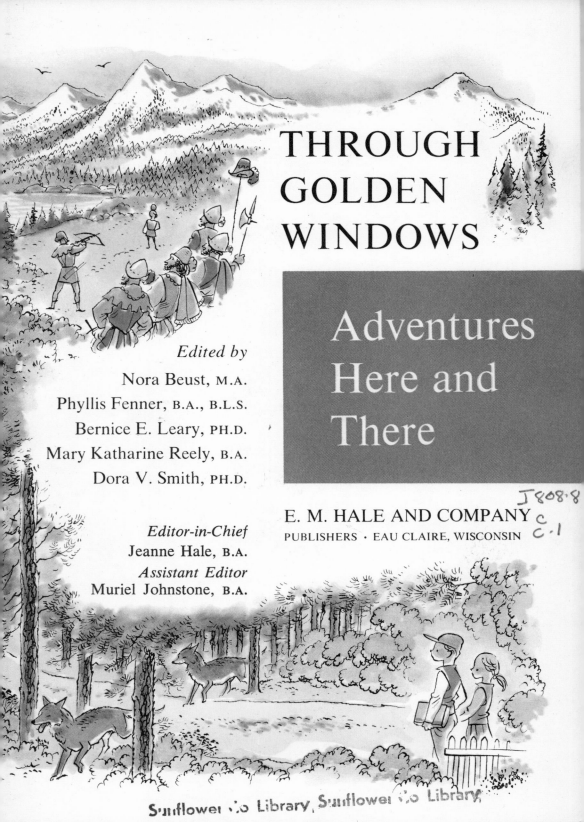

THROUGH GOLDEN WINDOWS

Adventures Here and There

Edited by

Nora Beust, M.A.

Phyllis Fenner, B.A., B.L.S.

Bernice E. Leary, PH.D.

Mary Katharine Reely, B.A.

Dora V. Smith, PH.D.

Editor-in-Chief
Jeanne Hale, B.A.

Assistant Editor
Muriel Johnstone, B.A.

E. M. HALE AND COMPANY
PUBLISHERS · EAU CLAIRE, WISCONSIN

Acknowledgments
and Copyright Notice

Through Golden Windows

In a reading world filled with children's books the addition of one more anthology or set of anthologies leads naturally to the question "Why?" We, who compiled *Through Golden Windows,* first asked ourselves that question almost ten years ago. We are still asking it. Always we arrive at the same answer. "The books are needed."

The power of books has long been recognized. And never more than today when material things are assuming increasing importance, and even the simple act of opening a door is fast getting out of human hands; when global and continental distances are shrinking from weeks and days to hours and minutes, and nearness at home means crowded living, crowded schools and playgrounds, crowded streets and highways; when family ties are weakening and children suffer from want of close, two-parent affection and guidance.

What can books give to a child who is growing up in today's curiously complicated world? Many things, we believe, although the evidence is not altogether conclusive. Facts and information, of course, about almost everything; understanding of himself and others; confidence and security; fun and laughter; friends and friendships; escape from reality at times, and again the courage to face reality—all these are possible results if the right book is used with the right child in the right way.

But suppose the right book is not available? Crowded living means limited space for books, at home and at school. Or suppose parents and teachers do not know the right book? Many, by their own admission, do not know children's books well. Must the child's values in reading be left to chance, while he struggles with his everyday problems, or grows up without feeling the full rapture of a good book?

Through Golden Windows grew out of a fear, on the one hand, that children's needs are not being met well enough through books; and out of a faith, on the other hand, that carefully compiled anthologies, easily accessible, would help teachers and parents do a better job of guiding children's reading.

Such books, we believe, should give children experience—here, there and everywhere. It should give them variety—sober fact and gay fantasy, practical prose and picture-filled poetry, lives of the great and the everyday intimacy of home folks, history of the past and history in the making, high adventure and the small thrills of daily living. It should show them some of the wonders of the earth and sky and the great achievements of great men. It should assure them the safe moorings of home and country, of family and friends. It should give them confidence in themselves and in others, and in a world that, for all its problems, is a wonderful world to grow up in.

To be most useful, each book should be not too large and not too small, not too easy and not too difficult, but "just right" for the child in pre-school

viii

and primary grades or in middle and upper grades. Based on children's interests and reading preferences, it should have not too much nor too little of any one type of material, but a balanced content that would invite all readers.

Through Golden Windows, therefore, was made with an eye on the child and his needs and interests at different stages of development. Bound in ten volumes, each book is attractive to look at, comfortable to hold, interesting to read, and easy to talk about.

Taken together, these books represent five large areas of interest: fun and humor, adventure, children everywhere, the story of America, and science. For each area there are two volumes, one for children of pre-school and primary age, and the other for intermediate grade readers. Hence, as a child grows in reading power, he may move from *Mostly Magic* to *Fun and Fantasy,* and satisfy his need for fun in both. Again, for adventure he may enjoy *Wonderful Things Happen* until he is ready for *Adventures Here and There.* His broadening interest in people finds satisfaction first in *Good Times Together* and later in *Children Everywhere.* Similarly, *Stories of Early America* eventually gives way to *American Backgrounds* and *Wide, Wonderful World* to *Man and His World.*

Within each volume, the selections are loosely tied together into related units, in order that a child may pursue an interest in Pets or Pioneers or Plants, for example, without searching for "more." The obvious overlapping of units and of volumes is not without purpose or benefit. Were it possible to organize reading materials into airtight, dark little compartments, *Through Golden Windows* would defeat its purpose to help "the whole child" to live and grow. On the other hand, a free, less exacting organization allows him to find the same inter-relationships and similarities among his reading experiences as exist in his daily life.

Through Golden Windows, then, aims first to satisfy the child, meet his everyday needs and help him find early the absorbing joy of reading. It aims, also, to acquaint teachers with much of the best in children's books. Used as basic reading in a college course in children's literature, *Through Golden Windows* will help to overcome the limitations imposed by a barren reading childhood and give teachers and parents that first security they need to guide children's reading. Beyond such a course lies a whole world of books that teachers will continue to explore, year after year.

It aims, finally, to help parents by providing a basic home library for their children. Here are stories as old as "Once upon a time" and as new as the children themselves. Here are stories and poems to read aloud and to read to one's self in a quiet corner, "to-go-to-sleep-by" and "to-get-up-with," to laugh at and to learn from, to sing and to act, and sometimes to read for no other reason than the fun of doing something together as a family.

It is to children, teachers, and parents everywhere that these books are affectionately dedicated, in the hope that through the pages they may see, as "through golden windows" the rewarding vista of life itself.

BERNICE E. LEARY

Adventures
Here and There

Everyone enjoys an adventure and what fun it is to sit down with a whole book full of them. You can meet Tony who kept his father's fruit stand and find out how Lucinda rescues her friend in the story from Ruth Sawyer's prize-winning book, *Roller Skates.* Or you can get into a rough and tumble fight with Tom Sawyer who has a hard time keeping his exploits from his Aunt Polly.

Another type of adventure is written and illustrated by William Pène du Bois, who created *Peter Graves.* Peter has a very exciting time with Houghton's invention which might have resulted in an engine that would run without fuel!

Animals provide plenty of action. This is especially true in pioneer days when the wolves were bad because of the cold, snowy winters. Joey and Tommy earn a larger bounty than they expected in *Wolf! Wolf!*

Jim Kjelgaard, whose nature stories are becoming classics, writes a story about a dog tracking a bear; a young girl saves a village in Carol Brink's story, *Massacree!* The western stories, *Pecos Bill* and *Bill Peters, the Stage Driver* and *In a Wyoming Blizzard,* by Frank Dobie are all very exciting adventures. Also included is *William Tell; I Strike the Jolly Roger,* a story of pirates; and *Cadmus Henry,* which tells of the historical balloon ascent during the Civil War.

These are just a few of the thrilling experiences you can have when you find a quiet spot and begin to read.

NORA E. BEUST

Contents

Adventures Here and There

THE Independent Saturday Afternoon Adventure Club had so far been entirely successful. Randy had spent her second Saturday at the Ballet Theatre and was now able to walk on her toes quite easily, and had made a ballet skirt out of five pairs of muslin curtains that couldn't be darned any more. Rush had gone to hear Rudolph Serkin play the piano, and had been practicing furiously ever since in the hours that were not occupied by school or baseball. Mona had seen Katharine Cornell in a play and was very hard to live with as a result. She now moved queenlike and distant through a world of her own.

But this particular Saturday was Oliver's, and they had agreed to stay home. Not that he could go out by himself, of course, as they could; but in order to make him feel like a proper member of the I.S.A.A.C., they respected his Saturday and stayed at home. Also, besides giving him back the three dimes he had lent them, each added a dime of his own.

Oliver Goes to the Circus

BY ELIZABETH ENRIGHT

Illustrated by Susanne Suba

The day passed pleasantly enough. There was lemon pie for dessert at lunch, and afterwards Rush and Randy gave Isaac a bath in the basement washtub. When he was dry, they took him for a walk to show him off. The walk was a great success, and so was Isaac. People stopped them frequently to admire and pat him; and every time they asked what kind of dog he was, Rush gave them a different answer in a polite, serious voice. A Bronx beagle, he might say, or a Central Park setter, or an Interborough Rapid Transit retriever. Randy almost died.

1

When they came back to their own block, they could see Mona hanging out of the second-story window of their house.

"Where's Oliver?" she called, when they drew near.

Rush and Randy looked at her blankly.

"I don't know. Where is he?" shouted Rush.

"Isn't he home?" cried Randy.

"We can't find him anyplace," answered Mona, withdrawing her head and closing the window with a bang.

They ran up the steps and into the house. Cuffy looked pale and distracted. "Rush, you go down the street to the Potters' and see if by any chance he's gone to play with Petey, though goodness knows he's never done such a thing before. Randy, you run round the block. Maybe he's trying out his roller skates again."

"Maybe he's just hiding," suggested Randy.

"His coat and cap are gone," Mona told her. "And anyway I've looked everywhere. In all the closets and underneath the beds. Even in the trunks in the basement."

"Where's Father?"

"Gone to Philadelphia to lecture. He won't be back till five and we don't know where to get him. Hurry up, Randy, run along."

At that moment the object of all this concern was seated comfortably at Madison Square Garden. His knees were crossed, he was leaning back with a bottle of pop in one hand, and watching a lady in spangles hanging by her teeth to a rope fifty feet above the ground.

It had all been very simple, but it was also a well-thought-out campaign. Four weeks ago Oliver had received seven dimes which he had prudently concealed in one of his last summer's sandals. Today he had received seven more, which altogether with the sandal money made fourteen dimes. Untold wealth,

2

but he did not let it go to his head. Everything proceeded according to plan.

Today when he was supposed to be resting he had got up, put on his coat and cap, and walked, faintly jingling, right out of the house. There was no trouble of any kind. When he got to Fifth Avenue he went up to a policeman and said, "Where is the circus, please?"

And the policeman said, "Madison Square Garden. Aren't you kinda young to be out alone?"

Oliver simply said, "No, I don't think so," and went his way. When he came to another policeman some blocks farther on, he went up to him and said, "Where is Madison Square Garden, please?"

"Going to the circus, eh?" said the policeman. "It's at Fiftieth Street and Eighth Avenue. You all alone?"

Oliver simply said, "Yes, I am," and proceeded on his way, leaving the policeman with his hands full of traffic.

At Fiftieth Street he went up to another policeman and said, "Which way is Eighth Avenue, please?"

"That way," said the policeman, jerking a white cotton thumb westward. " 'Bout three block over. Ain't nobody with you?"

Oliver simply said, "No, nobody," and crossed the street with the green light.

It was easy when he got there too. He just stood in a long line of grownups and children and held tight to his dimes and listened to what the people in front of him said when they got to the window. So when he got there he was able to say, "One, please. The kind that costs one dollar," and count out ten dimes slowly and carefully. The man behind the window had to peer down in order to see him at all. Then holding his ticket tightly he followed close behind a large family and tried hard to look like one of them.

"Like to hold your own ticket, eh, sonny?" said the ticket man.

"Yes, I do," replied Oliver, and entered the magic portals. It was wonderful. It smelled of elephants the minute you got in, even before you came to the real circus part. Breathing the smell deeply, Oliver climbed some steps that a uniformed man told him to, and then walked along a corridor that another uniformed man told him to. He thought he heard a lion roar some place, and his feet crunched on peanut shells. It was very exciting. Finally he came to the right door, entered it, and found himself in another world. It was a vast world, carpeted with blue sawdust and walled with thousands of faces. A complicated web of cables and rope ladders and nets rose from the huge arena to misty regions high overhead. On the blue sawdust at the bottom there were three large caged rings, and in each of these rings the most extraordinary things were happening.

"This way, Bud," said the usher, steering the bedazzled Oliver to a seat. Oliver sat down without knowing that he did

4

so. After a long time he removed his coat and cap blindly, never taking his eyes off the ring nearest him. In it three lions, two bears, and a black leopard were climbing ladders, while on high gold stools seven other lions sat and snarled and batted with their paws at their trainer who was the bravest man in the world and wore a red coat. He could make those animals do anything. Before he was through, one of the bears was pushing the other in a huge baby carriage while all the lions, on a bridge overhead, sat up on their hind legs and begged. Oliver sighed deeply: it was almost too much. His only regret was that he was too busy watching his ring to pay attention to the others. The air rang with the crack of whips and the sharp commands of the trainers.

As the cages were dismantled and the animals taken away, Oliver began to notice the men who were going up and down the aisles selling things: jeweled canes, and clown hats, and things to eat. They called their wares hoarsely like a lot of crows. "Hot dogs, hot dogs!" cried one, and "Getcha roasted peanuts here," cried another, and "Icecole pop," still another. But the one Oliver was most interested in was the man who kept saying "Cotton candy. Cotton c-a-a-a-n-dy," as he went by with what looked like a lot of pink birds' nests on sticks. Oliver finally bought one. It was interesting; you bit into a cloud of pink spun sugar and it instantly became nothing in your mouth. He ate it lingeringly, to make it last. All the time fascinating things were going on in the huge arena before him. Clowns came out and did their stunts, a man jumped over three elephants, ladies in spangles rode standing up on the backs of broad white horses, and dozens of tiny taffy-colored ponies, with plumes on their foreheads like the frills on lamb chops, pranced delicately about the rings and performed the most astonishing tricks. Oliver bit into his pink cloud and stared dreamily.

5

The procession was magnificent beyond description; from zebra-drawn coaches to elephants wearing tasseled capes and jeweled howdahs. Oliver watched it raptly while eating a hot dog with mustard. He surveyed the acrobats (whose muscles seemed to stretch like garters) while eating another hot dog, this time with sauerkraut. It was forbidden Paradise. Cuffy didn't believe in hot dogs or mustard or sauerkraut, but Oliver believed in them all. By the time the aerial artists had come along he was quenching a violent thirst with a bottle of pop. (It was at this moment that his entire family was in an uproar about his disappearance.) The act was so exciting that he couldn't finish the pop till it was over, because it made his stomach feel so queer when one of the glittering creatures high overhead leaped from her fragile swing and arched through the air like a bird to the next glittering creature. The climax came when one of the creatures stood on her head on a trapeze without holding on and swung to and fro, shimmering like a

6

dragonfly, far above the arena. It was breath-taking. Oliver felt so weak after watching her that he quickly finished his pop and purchased a bag of peanuts to fortify himself.

What a circus it was! One continual blaze of glory from beginning to end; from the flashing, bounding acrobats to the trained seals clapping their flippers; from the daring tightrope walkers to the fat clown who kept finding live ducklings in his pockets. Oliver did not want to believe it was over and sat for quite a while with people climbing over him and pushing past him, in the hope that they were all mistaken and something new was about to begin in the arena.

"Whatcha waitin' for, Bud?" said the usher, coming up to him. "Don'tcha know you'll get swept up with the trash and fed to the elephants if you wait too long?"

Probably he doesn't mean it, Oliver thought, but he got up hastily.

And after quite a lot of blundering about in the wrong direction (owing to the fact that he didn't understand the meaning of the word "exit") he found himself out on the street. Already it was dusk, and he began to hurry. For the first time the probable consequences of his adventure began to trouble him. It made him especially uncomfortable to think of Cuffy, for some reason.

And now the streets kept turning the wrong way, and he found himself on Tenth Avenue instead of Fifth. The place looked strange; full of high, dark buildings, and big noisy boys who went bowling by him on roller skates, and shouted at him hoarsely to get out of the way. As if that weren't enough, he began to have a terrible stomach-ache. Though he was a calm and resourceful person, Oliver was only six years old after all. So the next move seemed to be to cry. He stumbled and banged along the street, sobbing quietly and wiping his nose on his sleeve, wishing with all his heart that he was at home with Cuffy, and that he had never heard of hot dogs or cotton candy. Dimly he was aware of a clopping of hoofs on pavement but he was too miserable to look up until he heard a voice say:

"Whatsa matter, sonny?"

Oliver saw a big square policeman seated on a big square horse, magnificent as anything at the circus. All his buttons and two gold teeth glittered richly in the light of the street lamp.

"What's eatin' you?" repeated the policeman kindly.

"I'm lost!" wept Oliver, "and I'm sick at my stomach, and I want to go home!"

"What's your name?"

"Oliver M-Melendy."

"Know where you live?"

Oliver told him.

8

"Okay. You quit crying now," said the policeman. "You and me will take a little ride to your house. Think ya can hold out?"

"I guess so," replied Oliver dubiously. His stomach felt awfully unreliable. The policeman got off his horse and hoisted Oliver up on it as if he had been a kitten. Then he got on himself, behind Oliver, clucked at the horse and away they went. Oliver thought gloomily that it was probably the only time in his whole life that he was ever going to ride with a mounted policeman and he felt so sick he couldn't appreciate it.

"I guess I'm going to get a scolding when I go home," Oliver told the policeman. "Maybe I'll get a spanking too." All the shine was gone off the day.

"Why, what did you do?"

"Will you promise not to arrest me?" said Oliver cautiously.

"I doubt if it will be necessary," said the policeman, so Oliver told him.

"Well, I'll let your family take care of the penalty," the policeman decided. "It's a very serious offense all right, but it seems to me you've been punished almost enough as it is."

The traffic cop at Fifth Avenue looked at the mounted policeman, and gave Oliver a pat on the shoulder.

At the Melendy house all was confusion. Randy was in tears. Father (who had returned from Philadelphia) and Rush were still out searching, and Cuffy was saying into the telephone, "Six years old; he has blue eyes, blond hair, and he weighs—" when the doorbell rang, and she dropped the receiver.

"Oh, Oliver darling, where were you?" cried Mona's voice, and Cuffy arrived to see her on her knees beside Oliver, who looked smaller and paler than ever before. Behind him stood the largest, most solid policeman she had ever seen in her life.

Aching with relief, Cuffy hugged Oliver, then she looked up at the policeman and said, "That's the quickest response I ever got from anything. I hadn't no more than just finished describing him to the police this minute—"

"The police force is never at a loss, ma'am," replied the officer with a wink.

Cuffy held Oliver away from her:

"Where in the world have you been?"

"To the circus," replied Oliver wanly.

"To the circus! Alone?" Cuffy was horrified.

"I wouldn't be too hard on him, ma'am," advised the officer.

"Go ahead and spank me if you want to," Oliver said, and was sick on the doormat.

Long, long afterwards, when all the thunder and lightning in his stomach had subsided, and the danger of a spanking

was past, Oliver lay in his small bed with his hand in Father's.

"Why did you go without telling us, though?" asked Father. "You could have gone to the circus. Rush or Cuffy would have been glad to take you. I would have taken you myself if I could have stolen the time."

Oliver sighed. "I did ask Cuffy about it once, but she said, oh, no, there's too much measles around. And everybody else was going out alone on their Saturdays, so I just thought I'd go alone too. I did want to see the circus so badly."

"Didn't you know we'd worry?"

"I guess I didn't think about it till afterwards," Oliver admitted.

"Well, you'll never give us a scare like that again, will you?"

"No, I never will, if I can help it," promised Oliver.

"All right then. That's that. Now suppose you tell me what you liked best at the circus."

"Oh, everything was wonderful. I liked the man on the one-wheel bicycle, and the elephants, and that automobile with all the clowns and the donkey in it, and the lady who stood on her head on the swing, and I liked all the things I was eating, while I was eating them. But the thing I liked best of all wasn't in the circus."

"What was that?" said Father.

"It was when the policeman brought me home on the horse," replied Oliver.

For now, no longer overshadowed by stomach-aches or unhappy apprehensions, the memory of that ride had become a radiant thing. He remembered the horse's two pointed ears that could move independently of each other, and its brawny, arching neck with the tidy black mane; and its strong, healthy smell. It was sort of like riding on a boat, only better because it felt alive, and you were higher up. And behind, immense and gorgeous in his uniform, rode the officer of the law who had befriended him. Oliver remembered how he held the reins in white gloved hands the size of baseball mitts. The splendor of that ride would never die.

A Vagabond Song

BY BLISS CARMAN   *Illustrated by Susanne Suba*

THERE is something in the autumn
    that is native to my blood—
Touch of manner, hint of mood;
And my heart is like a rhyme,
With the yellow and the purple and the crimson keeping time.

The scarlet of the maples can shake me like a cry
Of bugles going by.
And my lonely spirit thrills
To see the frosty asters like a smoke upon the hills.

There is something in October sets the gypsy blood astir;
We must rise and follow her,
When from every hill of flame
She calls and calls each vagabond by name.

IT WAS much too fine a night to think of going to bed at once, and so, although the witching hour of nine P.M. had struck, Edward and I were still leaning out of the open window in our nightshirts, watching the play of the cedar-branch shadows on the moonlit lawn, and planning schemes of fresh deviltry for the sunshiny morrow. From below, strains of the jocund piano declared that the Olympians were enjoying themselves in their listless impotent way; for the new curate had been bidden to dinner that night, and was at the moment unclerically proclaiming to all the world that

he feared no foe. His discordant vociferations doubtless started a train of thought in Edward's mind, for the youth presently remarked, apropos of nothing whatever that had been said before, "I believe the new curate's rather gone on Aunt Maria."

I scouted the notion. "Why, she's quite old," I said. (She must have seen some five-and-twenty summers.)

The Burglars

BY

KENNETH GRAHAME

Illustrated by

Ernest H. Shepard

"Of course she is," replied Edward scornfully. "It's not her, it's her money he's after, you bet!"

"Didn't know she had any money," I observed timidly.

"Sure to have," said my brother with confidence. "Heaps and heaps."

Silence ensued, both our minds being busy with the new situation thus presented: mine, in wonderment at this flaw that so often declared itself in enviable natures of fullest endowment—in a grown-up man and a good cricketer, for instance, even as this curate; Edward's (apparently) in the considera-

14

tion of how such a state of things, supposing it existed, could be best turned to his own advantage.

"Bobby Ferris told me," began Edward in due course, "that there was a fellow spooning his sister once—"

"What's spooning?" I asked meekly.

"O, I dunno," said Edward indifferently. "It's—it's—it's just a thing they do, you know. And he used to carry notes and messages and things between 'em, and he got a shilling almost every time."

"What, from each of 'em?" I innocently inquired.

Edward looked at me with scornful pity. "Girls never have any money," he briefly explained. "But she did his exercises, and got him out of rows, and told stories for him when he needed it—and much better ones than he could have made up for himself. Girls are useful in some ways. So he was living in clover, when unfortunately they went and quarrelled about something."

"Don't see what that's got to do with it," I said.

"Nor don't I," rejoined Edward. "But anyhow the notes and things stopped, and so did the shillings. Bobby was fairly cornered, for he had bought two ferrets on tick and promised to pay a shilling a week, thinking the shillings were going on forever, the silly young ass. So when the week was up, and he was being dunned for the shilling, he went off to the fellow and said: 'Your broken-hearted Bella implores you to meet her at sundown. By the hollow oak as of old, be it only for a moment. Do not fail!' He got all that out of some rotten book, of course. The fellow looked puzzled and said:

" 'What hollow oak? I don't know any hollow oak.'

" 'Perhaps it was the Royal Oak?' said Bobby promptly, 'cos he saw he had made a slip, through trusting too much to the rotten book; but this didn't seem to make the fellow any happier."

15

"Should think not," I said, "the Royal Oak's an awful low sort of pub."

"I know," said Edward. "Well, at last the fellow said, 'I think I know what she means: the hollow tree in your father's paddock. It happens to be an elm, but she wouldn't know the difference. All right: say I'll be there.' Bobby hung about a bit, for he hadn't got his money. 'She was crying awfully,' he said. Then he got his shilling."

"And wasn't the fellow riled," I inquired, "when he got to the place and found nothing?"

"He found Bobby," said Edward indignantly. "Young Ferris was a gentleman, every inch of him. He brought the fellow another message from Bella: 'I dare not leave the house. My cruel parents immure me closely. If you only knew what I suffer. Your broken-hearted Bella.' Out of the same rotten book. This made the fellow a little suspicious, 'cos it was the old Ferrises who had been keen about the thing all through. The fellow, you see, had tin."

"But what's that go to——" I began again.

"O I dunno," said Edward impatiently. "I'm telling you just what Bobby told me. He got suspicious, anyhow, but he couldn't exactly call Bella's brother a liar, so Bobby escaped for the time. But when he was in a hole next week, over a stiff French exercise, and tried the same sort of a game on his sister, she was too sharp for him, and he got caught out. Somehow women seem more mistrustful than men. They're so beastly suspicious by nature, you know."

"I know," said I. "But did the two—the fellow and the sister—make it up afterwards?"

"I don't remember about that," replied Edward indifferently; "but Bobby got packed off to school a whole year earlier than his people meant to send him. Which was just what he wanted. So you see it all came right in the end!"

I was trying to puzzle out the moral of this story—it was evidently meant to contain one somewhere—

At that moment a flood of golden lamplight mingled with the moon-rays on the lawn, and Aunt Maria and the new curate strolled out on the grass below us, and took the direction of a garden seat which was backed by a dense laurel shrubbery reaching round in a half circle to the house. Edward meditated moodily. "If we only knew what they were talking about," said he, "you'd soon see whether I was right or not. Look here! Let's send the kid down by the porch to reconnoiter!"

"Harold's asleep," I said; "it seems rather a shame—"

"O rot!" said my brother; "he's the youngest, and he's got to do as he's told!"

So the luckless Harold was hauled out of bed and given his sailing orders. He was naturally rather vexed at being stood up suddenly on the cold floor, and the job had no particular interest for him; but he was both stanch and well disciplined. The means of exit were simple enough. A porch of iron trellis came up to within easy reach of the window, and was habitually used by all three of us, when modestly anxious to avoid public notice. Harold climbed deftly down the porch like a white rat, and his nightgown glimmered a moment on the gravel walk ere he was lost to sight in the darkness of the shrubbery. A brief interval of silence ensued, broken suddenly by a sound of scuffle, and then a shrill long-drawn squeal, as of metallic surfaces in friction. Our scout had fallen into the hands of the enemy!

Indolence alone had made us devolve the task of investigation on our younger brother. Now that danger had declared itself, there was no hesitation. In a second we were down the side of the porch, and crawling Cherokee-wise through the laurels to the back of the garden seat. Piteous was the sight that greeted us. Aunt Maria was on the seat, in a white evening frock, looking—for an aunt—really quite nice. On the lawn stood an incensed curate, grasping our small brother by a large ear, which—judging from the row he was making—seemed on the point of parting company with the head it adorned. The gruesome noise he was emitting did not really affect us otherwise than esthetically. To one who has tried both, the wail of genuine physical anguish is easily distinguishable from the pumped-up ad misericordiam blubber. Harold's could clearly be recognized as belonging to the latter class. "Now you young—" (whelp, *I* think it was, but Edward stoutly maintains it was devil), said the curate sternly; "tell us what you mean by it!"

"Well, leggo of my ear then!" shrilled Harold, "and I'll tell you the solemn truth!"

"Very well," agreed the curate, releasing him; "now go ahead, and don't lie more than you can help."

We abode the promised disclosure without the least misgiving; but even we had hardly given Harold due credit for his fertility of resource and powers of imagination.

"I had just finished saying my prayers," began that young gentleman slowly, "when I happened to look out of the window, and on the lawn I saw a sight which froze the marrow in my veins! A burglar was approaching the house with snakelike tread! He had a scowl and a dark lantern, and he was armed to the teeth!"

We listened with interest. The style, though unlike Harold's native notes, seemed strangely familiar.

"Go on," said the curate grimly.

"Pausing in his stealthy career," continued Harold, "he gave a low whistle. Instantly the signal was responded to, and from the adjacent shadows two more figures glided forth. The miscreants were both armed to the teeth."

"Excellent," said the curate; "proceed."

"The robber chief," pursued Harold, warming to his work, "joined his nefarious comrades, and conversed with them in silent tones. His expression was truly ferocious, and I ought to have said that he was armed to the t—"

"There, never mind his teeth," interrupted the curate rudely; "there's too much jaw about you altogether. Hurry up and have done."

"I was in a frightful funk," continued the narrator, warily guarding his ear with his hand, "but just then the drawing-room window opened, and you and Aunt Maria came out—I mean emerged. The burglars vanished silently into the laurels, with horrid implications!"

The curate looked slightly puzzled. The tale was well sustained, and certainly circumstantial. After all, the boy might really have seen something. How was the poor man to know—though the chaste and lofty diction might have supplied a hint—that the whole yarn was a free adaptation from the last Penny Dreadful lent us by the knife-and-boot boy?

"Why did you not alarm the house?" he asked.

" 'Cos I was afraid," said Harold sweetly, "that p'raps they mightn't believe me!"

"But how did you get down here, you naughty little boy?" put in Aunt Maria.

Harold was hard pressed—by his own flesh and blood, too!

At that moment Edward touched me on the shoulder and glided off through the laurels. When some ten yards away he gave a low whistle. I replied by another. The effect was magical. Aunt Maria started up with a shriek. Harold gave one startled glance around, and then fled like a hare, made straight for the back door, burst in upon the servants at supper, and buried himself in the broad bosom of the cook, his special ally. The curate faced the laurels—hesitatingly. But Aunt Maria flung herself on him. "O Mr. Hodgitts!" I heard her cry, "you are brave! For my sake, do not be rash!" He was not rash. When I peeped out a second later, the coast was entirely clear.

"TOM!"

No answer.

"Tom!"

No answer.

"What's gone with that boy, I wonder?
You TOM!"

No answer.

The old lady pulled her spectacles down and looked over them about the room; then she put them up and looked out under them. She seldom or never looked through them for so small a thing as a boy; they were her state pair, the pride of her heart, and were built for "style," not service—she could have seen through a pair of stove-lids just as well. She looked perplexed for a moment, and then said, fiercely, but still loud enough for the furniture to hear:

"Well, I lay if I get hold of you I'll—"

She did not finish, for by this time she was bending down and punching under the bed with the broom, and so she needed breath to punctuate the punches with. She resurrected nothing but the cat.

Tom Plays, Fights, and Hides

BY MARK TWAIN

Illustrated by Louis Slobodkin

"I never did see the beat of that boy!"

She went to the open door and stood in it and looked out among the tomato vines and "jimpson" weeds that constituted the garden. No Tom. So she lifted up her voice at an angle calculated for distance, and shouted:

"Y-o-u-u Tom!"

There was a slight noise behind her and she turned just in time to seize a small boy by the slack of his roundabout and arrest his flight.

"There! I might-a thought of that closet. What you been doing in there?"

"Nothing."

"Nothing! Look at your hands. And look at your mouth. What is that truck?"

"I don't know, aunt."

"Well, I know. It's jam—that's what it is. Forty times I've said if you didn't let that jam alone I'd skin you. Hand me that switch."

The switch hovered in the air—the peril was desperate—

"My! Look behind you, aunt!"

The old lady whirled round, and snatched her skirts out of danger. The lad fled, on the instant, scrambled up the high board fence, and disappeared over it.

His aunt Polly stood surprised a moment, and then broke into a gentle laugh.

"Hang the boy, can't I never learn anything? Ain't he played me tricks enough like that for me to be looking out for him by this time? But old fools is the biggest fools there is. Can't learn an old dog new tricks, as the saying is. But my goodness, he never plays them alike, two days, and how is a body to know what's coming? He 'pears to know just how long he can torment me before I get my dander up, and he knows if he can make out to put me off for a minute or make me laugh, it's all down again and I can't hit him a lick. I ain't doing my duty by that boy, and that's the Lord's truth, goodness knows. Spare the rod and spile the child, as the Good Book says. I'm a-laying up sin and suffering for us both, I know. He's full of the Old Scratch, but laws-a-me! He's my own

22

dead sister's boy, poor thing, and I ain't got the heart to lash him, somehow. Every time I let him off, my conscience does hurt me so, and every time I hit him, my old heart most breaks. Well-a-well, man that is born of woman is of few days and full of trouble, as the Scripture says, and I reckon it's so. He'll play hooky this evening, and I'll just be obleeged to make him work, tomorrow, to punish him. It's mighty hard to make him work Saturdays, when all the boys is having holiday, but he hates work more than he hates anything else, and I've got to do some of my duty by him, or I'll be the ruination of the child."

Tom did play hooky, and he had a very good time. He got back home barely in season to help Jim, the small colored boy, saw next-day's wood and split the kindlings before supper —at least he was there in time to tell his adventures to Jim while Jim did three-fourths of the work. Tom's younger brother (or rather, half-brother), Sid, was already through with his part of the work (picking up chips), for he was a quiet boy, and had no adventurous, troublesome ways.

While Tom was eating his supper and stealing sugar as opportunity offered, Aunt Polly asked him questions that were full of guile, and very deep—for she wanted to trap him into damaging revealments. Like many other simplehearted souls, it was her pet vanity to believe she was endowed with a talent for dark and mysterious diplomacy, and she loved to contemplate her most transparent devices as marvels of low cunning. Said she:

"Tom, it was middling warm in school, warn't it?"

"Yes'm."

"Powerful warm, warn't it?"

"Yes'm."

"Didn't you want to go in a-swimming, Tom?"

A bit of a scare shot through Tom—a touch of uncomfortable suspicion. He searched Aunt Polly's face, but it told him nothing. So he said:

"No'm—well, not very much."

The old lady reached out her hand and felt Tom's shirt, and said:

"But you ain't too warm now, though." And it flattered her to reflect that she had discovered that the shirt was dry without anybody knowing that that was what she had in her mind. But in spite of her, Tom knew where the wind lay, now. So he forestalled what might be the next move.

"Some of us pumped on our heads—mine's damp yet. See?"

Aunt Polly was vexed to think she had overlooked that bit of circumstantial evidence, and missed a trick. Then she had a new inspiration.

"Tom, you didn't have to undo your shirt-collar where I sewed it, to pump on your head, did you? Unbutton your jacket!"

The trouble vanished out of Tom's face. He opened his jacket. His shirt-collar was securely sewed.

"Bother! Well, go 'long with you. I'd made sure you'd played hooky and been a-swimming. But I forgive ye, Tom. I reckon you're a kind of a singed cat, as the saying is—better'n you look. This time."

She was half sorry her sagacity had miscarried, and half glad that Tom had stumbled into obedient conduct for once.

But Sidney said:

"Well, now, if I didn't think you sewed his collar with white thread, but it's black."

"Why, I did sew it with white! Tom!"

25

But Tom did not wait for the rest. As he went out at the door he said:

"Siddy, I'll lick you for that."

In a safe place Tom examined two large needles which were thrust into the lapels of his jacket, and had thread bound about them—one needle carried white thread and the other black. He said:

"She'd never noticed if it hadn't been for Sid. Confound it! Sometimes she sews it with white, and sometimes she sews it with black. I wish to geeminy she'd stick to one or t'other—I can't keep the run of 'em. But I bet you I'll lam Sid for that. I'll learn him!"

He was not the Model Boy of the village. He knew the model boy very well though—and loathed him.

Within two minutes, or even less, he had forgotten all his troubles. Not because his troubles were one whit less heavy and bitter to him than a man's are to a man, but because a new and powerful interest bore them down and drove them out of his mind for the time—just as men's misfortunes are forgotten in the excitement of new enterprises. This new interest was a valued novelty in whistling, which he had just acquired from a Negro, and he was suffering to practice it undisturbed. It consisted in a peculiar birdlike turn, a sort of liquid warble, produced by touching the tongue to the roof of the mouth at short intervals in the midst of the music. Diligence and attention soon gave him the knack of it, and he strode down the street with his mouth full of harmony and his soul full of gratitude. He felt much as an astronomer feels who has discovered a new planet—no doubt, as far as strong, deep, unalloyed pleasure is concerned, the advantage was with the boy, not the astronomer.

The summer evenings were long. It was not dark, yet. Presently Tom checked his whistle. A stranger was before him —a boy a shade larger than himself. A new-comer of any age or either sex was an impressive curiosity in the poor little shabby village of St. Petersburg. This boy was well dressed, too—well dressed on a week day. This was simply astounding. His cap was a dainty thing, his close-buttoned blue cloth roundabout was new and natty, and so were his pantaloons. He had shoes on—and it was only Friday. He even wore a necktie, a bright bit of ribbon. He had a citified air about him that ate into Tom's vitals. The more Tom stared at the splendid marvel, the higher he turned up his nose at this finery and the shabbier and shabbier his own outfit seemed to grow. Neither boy spoke. If one moved, the other moved—but only sidewise, in a circle; they kept face to face and eye to eye all the time. Finally Tom said:

"I can lick you!"

"I'd like to see you try it."

"Well, I can do it."

"No you can't, either."

"Yes I can."

"No, you can't."

"I can."

"You can't."

"Can!"

"Can't!"

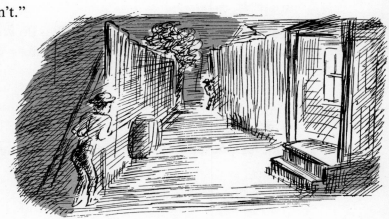

An uncomfortable pause. Then Tom said:

"What's your name?"

" 'Tisn't any of your business, maybe."

"Well, I 'low I'll make it my business."

"Well, why don't you?"

"If you say much, I will."

"Much—much—much. There, now."

"Oh, you think you're mighty smart, don't you? I could lick you with one hand tied behind me, if I wanted to."

"Well, why don't you do it? You say you can do it."

"Well, I will, if you fool with me."

"Oh yes—I've seen whole families in the same fix."

"Smarty! You think you're some, now, don't you? Oh, what a hat!"

"You can lump that hat if you don't like it. I dare you to knock it off—and anybody that'll take a dare will suck eggs."

"You're a liar!"

"You're another."

"You're a fighting liar and dasn't take it up."

"Aw—take a walk!"

"Say—if you give me much more of your sass I'll take and bounce a rock off'n your head."

"Oh, of course you will."

"Well, I will."

"Well, why don't you do it then? What do you keep saying you will for? Why don't you do it? It's because you're afraid."

"I ain't afraid."

"You are."

"I ain't."

"You are."

Another pause, and more eying and sidling around each

other. Presently they were shoulder to shoulder. Tom said:

"Get away from here!"

"Go away yourself!"

"I won't."

"I won't either."

So they stood, each with a foot placed at an angle as a brace, and both shoving with might and main, and glowering at each other with hate. But neither could get an advantage. After struggling till both were hot and flushed, each relaxed his strain with watchful caution, and Tom said:

"You're a coward and a pup. I'll tell my big brother on you, and he can thrash you with his little finger, and I'll make him do it, too."

"What do I care for your big brother? I've got a brother that's bigger than he is—and what's more, he can throw him over that fence, too." (Both brothers were imaginary.)

"That's a lie."

"Your saying so don't make it so."

Tom drew a line in the dust with his big toe, and said:

"I dare you to step over that, and I'll lick you till you can't stand up. Anybody that'll take a dare will steal sheep."

The new boy stepped over promptly, and said:

"Now you said you'd do it, now let's see you do it."

"Don't you crowd me now; you better look out."

"Well, you said you'd do it—why don't you do it?"

"By jingo! for two cents I will do it."

The new boy took two broad coppers out of his pocket and held them out with derision. Tom struck them to the ground. In an instant both boys were rolling and tumbling in the dirt, gripped together like cats; and for the space of a minute they tugged and tore at each other's hair and clothes, punched and scratched each other's noses, and covered themselves with dust and glory. Presently the confusion took form and through the fog of battle Tom appeared, seated astride the new boy, and pounding him with his fists.

"Holler 'nuff!" said he.

The boy only struggled to free himself. He was crying—mainly from rage.

"Holler 'nuff!"—and the pounding went on.

At last the stranger got out a smothered "Nuff!" and Tom let him up and said:

"Now that'll learn you. Better look out who you're fooling with next time."

The new boy went off brushing the dust from his clothes, sobbing, snuffling, and occasionally looking back and shaking his head and threatening what he would do to Tom the next time he caught him out. To which Tom responded with jeers, and started off in high feather, and as soon as his back was turned the new boy snatched up a stone, threw it and hit him between the shoulders and then turned tail and ran like an antelope. Tom chased the traitor home, and thus found out where he lived. He then held a position at the gate for some time, daring the enemy to come outside, but the enemy only made faces at him through the window and declined. At last the enemy's mother appeared, and called Tom a bad, vicious, vulgar child, and ordered him away. So he went away, but he said he " 'lowed" to "lay" for that boy.

He got home pretty late, that night, and when he climbed cautiously in at the window, he uncovered an ambuscade, in the person of his aunt; and when she saw the state his clothes were in, her resolution to turn his Saturday holiday into captivity at hard labor became adamantine in its firmness.

THERE was one more new friend to come that September. Lucinda skated herself straight to him. Miss Peters had told her to take her laced shoes over to Eighth Avenue and have the cobbler there put on new toe-pieces. She had left the shoes and was skating back when the affair took place. At the corner was a fruit-stand—a very nice fruit-stand. Lucinda had often admired the gloss on the apples, the straightness of the pyramids of oranges and lemons, the good condition of the bananas. And once she had stopped and bought a Bartlett pear—they looked so nice. The Italian who owned the stand looked nice, too. As he was an Italian, and as her parents had gone to Italy, it had seemed right to Lucinda that she should cultivate his acquaintance. The Bartlett pear had seemed a good beginning but it hadn't taken her far. The man spoke little English, Lucinda no Italian.

But on this afternoon a boy was tending the stand, a straw-thin, undersized boy, with a mop of curly, black hair and eyes like the picture of the young Michelangelo that hung in one of the classrooms at Miss Brackett's. Public school had been let out, and the children were filling the streets on their way home. A fattish boy and a lantern-jawed one came swaggering along with evil in their eyes. Lurching suddenly they fell against the stand, and being none too secure on its wheel and two legs, it was shaken, spilling the fruit into the street. The boys grabbed what fruit they could and were off down the street, thumbing their noses back at the Italian boy.

Lucinda Rescues a Friend

BY RUTH SAWYER

Illustrated by Valenti Angelo

31

Lucinda skated to his rescue. Silently they picked up what fruit was left, wiped it clean, a cloth between them, replaced each on its own pyramid. Then Lucinda lifted a face of true compassion, and the boy nearly cried. It told how much of a boy he was that he didn't really cry, Lucinda thought; for he must be mad as the dickens. Ironing his lips hard against white even teeth he said: "What can I do? My father says I must not let them steal the fruit that way. But there are always two— and bigger than I. If I stand to protect one end, they fall against the other. Wait until I grow big, then . . ." He gave a dispirited shrug to his shoulders. So many years to wait.

Lucinda was boiling with indignation: "You mean they've done it before?"

"Three times!"

"I call that mean. Two against one and stealing, I call that mean! Jumping Jupiter, I wish Patrolman M'Gonegal had this beat! He'd lick 'em good."

Lucinda was using her best street vernacular. Like Nature in Thanatopsis she spoke a various language and used it unfailingly.

Flushed with anger and mortification, the boy smiled at Lucinda as at a miracle performed by a patron saint. "They are bad boys, cowards. They never try it when my father is here; he is big, strong. It is only when I am left in charge."

True to form Lucinda asked his name and all about his family. The family name was Coppino, his father's was Vittore; he was Tony. In her turn Lucinda dwelt heavily on the joys of being an orphan. She explained away all conscientious scruples by saying that she expected Italy was an elegant country to be living in, that her mama was undoubtedly getting well and strong there, and that both parents were prob-

ably enjoying themselves as much as she was. "Happy all 'round, you see."

Tony Coppino pressed an apple into her hand at parting. "Please take it. We are friends now. Come again."

For the two remaining afternoons of that school week Lucinda skated to Eighth Avenue and found Vittore, the father, in charge. Each afternoon she left written on the pad: "I am going around to see if my friend Tony Coppino is having any more trouble with his fruit-stand." So did the Misses Peters learn of Tony. On Saturday morning Tony was left again in charge. She was on her way to reclaim her mended shoes from the cobbler, and it was pure luck that she arrived just after the worst catastrophe that had yet occurred. A third boy had joined the original two. This time they had brought a paper bag for their loot and almost upset the stand. Oranges, lemons, apples, tangerines—the gutter ran with them. The boys had made away with dozens, and Lucinda found Tony explaining in rapid Italian to his father what had happened.

She understood him perfectly—having seen it happen once before. Tony's gestures completed the story for her: three fingers held aloft and shaken in defiance, arms rotating to convey the avalanche of fruit that fell.

When Vittore, dejected, returned to the Coppino living and storing quarters to replenish the pyramids, Lucinda accompanied him. She skated slowly, the better to explain in words of one syllable and carefully separated, how great was her sorrow. To her delight she not only made herself understood, but won a smile from Vittore's grim lips. She was equally delighted to find where they lived. In a cellar! She had never known anyone before who lived in a cellar. In the front, dark end of it the fruit was stored in crates, or barrels or hung from the ceiling in bunches. The back, light end of it was where the family lived. It opened on a sunny backyard, which made a pleasant room, Lucinda thought. The kitchen-parlor-dining-room had two bright windows looking out on it. The garden was planted to herbs and a few flowers, and there was a heavenly smell about the whole place made up of apples, citrus fruits, garlic, and cheese. Lucinda sniffed the air, her nose wriggling like a rabbit's. What a place for goblins! She wondered if there were any there, and if Tony had seen them.

But the family were as exciting as the smells. There was Mrs. Coppino looking very smiling and bulgy. She bobbed up and down and said "Grazie—grazie," over and over. On the floor was a very small Coppino shoving itself about on its very plump and bare bottom. "Oh, it's a real bambina!" Lucinda shouted with joy. She had never seen one alive before, but her adored Cousin Lucinda Wyman had brought back pictures to her from Italy. And at this very moment, probably, her mama and papa were looking at bambinos loose in the streets.

34

She threw herself, skates and all, down beside the smallest Coppino, patting its cheeks, asking Mrs. Coppino: "What is its name? Name?" Then she patted herself and said, "Lucinda." Then she patted the bambina and said again, "Name?"

Mrs. Coppino caught on. She laughed and bobbed some more and said: "Girl—Gemma."

Lucinda got up reluctantly. "Ask her if I can come back to see the bambina some other day?" she said to Vittore.

Put into Italian it brought another bobbing response, "Si-si-si!"

"She say," said Vittore, "any time come please." On the way back to the stand he managed to confide a good deal to Lucinda. Tony was a good boy, but what could he do? Soon there would be ten-twenty boys against him. He, Vittore Coppino, had to go to market, two times the week, to buy the fruit for his stand. What could he do?

Lucinda agreed with him. It was a difficult situation. She skated home slowly, much perturbed, thinking hard. But it was not until Monday and another school week had begun that a way out of the difficulty came to her. "Good-bye, Miss Peters!" she shouted upon leaving her at the curb. "I've got a perfectly elegant idea. I'm going to see if it works."

It was a complicated idea. It called for connivering, as Johanna would have said. She had no time to skate to Bryant Park that morning. She waved to Patrolman M'Gonegal and passed him at breakneck speed. She was bound for a friend made during lazy summer hours at Narragansett, where she had been allowed to run fairly free. He had a confectionery shop on Fifth Avenue at Thirty-Seventh Street, and his name was Louis Sherry. Lucinda had had many occasions to taste the excellence of his confections. Louis Sherry liked children and he was a very giving person. She was hoping now with might and main that he would be in his shop at that time in the morning.

Luck was with her. Louis Sherry was inside and busy with the day's business. He greeted Lucinda with pleasure: "And the good mama and papa—how are they?"

Gone, said Lucinda, with a wide sweep of the hand. "I'm an orphan, a temporary orphan."

She was smiling too broadly to allow for sympathy. If she did not need sympathy what was it? Being a very keen man Louis Sherry guessed. "Let me see—it was the French curls that you always liked so much, and the chocolate nougats. Am I right? A little bag of them for consolation?"

Lucinda's smile grew. "How did you guess? They are not for myself. I want them for a bribe."

"And whom will you bribe?"

"Patrolman M'Gonegal; he has a sweet tooth."

"But don't you know it's wrong to bribe the police force? There's a law against it." The Frenchman, who was born in Vermont and was fast becoming one of the famous caterers and men of New York, was trying his best to look serious. But while he was covering his amusement he was moving behind the counter, reaching for a small white paper bag with Louis Sherry in gold on it.

"Dear me!" said Lucinda. "You see it's this way," and she proceeded to go carefully into the affairs of the Coppinos.

Louis Sherry handed over the confections with twinkling eyes. "I hope the bribe works. If you get into trouble come to me."

School over, Lucinda stood not upon the order of her going. She almost bowled Ferguson down in front of the stoop he was sweeping. Ferguson was Miss Brackett's colored man and almost as important as Miss Brackett herself. She found Patrolman M'Gonegal at the corner of the Avenue and Forty-Second Street. She beckoned him frantically to the curb and presented the bag. "From my friend, Louis Sherry."

"A friend of yours—think of that!" Patrolman M'Gonegal was impressed.

"I have a good many friends. Just now I have one suffering lots of hardships."

"As bad as that!"

"You'd be surprised how bad it is, Mr. M'Gonegal." Lucinda braced herself for the next moment. Her words came like hurrying feet: "Mr. M'Gonegal—I think you could help."

"Professional—or as a man?"

"It's this way." And again Lucinda went into the affairs of the Coppinos. She even told about the bambina named

Gemma. "I thought if you knew the policeman on their beat—Eighth Avenue and Forty-Ninth Street—he might do something."

Patrolman M'Gonegal considered: "It would be Jerry Hanlon."

"Is he nice?"

"As nice a lad as you'd find in uniform."

"There's no time to waste," said Lucinda. "I expect they are losing a dollar's worth of fruit this very afternoon."

Patrolman M'Gonegal responded like a true New York policeman of the nineties. He would make a point of seeing Jerry Hanlon that night. He would fix it up with him. After school, was it? It wouldn't take five minutes for Jerry to put the fear of God in all the boys that wanted trouble.

The next morning Lucinda was tipped off by Patrolman M'Gonegal as to arrangements. The time was to be the next day—Friday, at three sharp. Fifteen minutes ahead of that time Lucinda skated over to Eighth Avenue to make sure Tony had been left in charge of the stand, as so ordered. He was there, looking less anxious and more excited. At three sharp a youngish policeman, big, brawny, with a stout chin, appeared and greeted the two.

"I'm Jerry Hanlon. I expect the lad is Tony," and looking down at Lucinda he winked an eye. "And this would be the young lady who bribes an honest patrolman and wants to see justice done. I'm pleased to meet you, Miss." He held out a big, brawny hand and shook Lucinda almost off the pavement.

He crossed the street to a tobacco shop and took his stand inside the door, with an eye to the street. Lucinda was to skate up and down the block, as if there were nothing on her mind. When the boys appeared she was to wave her hand to Jerry Hanlon as a signal, and get fast out of the way.

School out, boys and girls began flooding the streets. Lucinda, too tense to skate, took her stand on the corner whither they were headed and watched for the fattish boy who was ringleader of this particular racket. She spotted him when he was half down the further block. She skated back and stood where Jerry Hanlon could see her. Her heart was pumping fiercely. Suppose the boys didn't do it. Suppose nothing happened! Could she ever persuade Jerry Hanlon to come back for a second time? He was supposed to be on the school corner when it emptied every afternoon. She turned to watch the end of the street; there were maneuverings going on. Five boys were lining themselves up in Indian file, hands on shoulders. They started down the street like a released torpedo, after making sure that Tony was tending the stand.

Lucinda took a long breath and waved as if all the Campbells were coming over the border. Jerry Hanlon slipped out of the tobacco shop and stood back of the wooden Indian. The boys were three-quarters towards their goal when he came into motion. He stepped off the curb into the middle of the street as the torpedo struck. Over went the stand—over went every orange and apple on it. A shower of gold and red and russet filled the street. The boys, fruit, and Jerry Hanlon were messed up together. One boy got an upper cut that laid him flat; one got a kick in the shins that sent him sprawling; two, Jerry Hanlon grabbed by an ear each. Lucinda butted, head-on, into the last like a rambunctious goat. He went down hard before the onslaught, Lucinda straddling on top of him. She sat there while Jerry Hanlon put the fear of God and the law in all five, impartially.

He called to Tony, had him take out his book from his pocket, and write down the names, where the boys lived, what their fathers did. He told them, jerking the two boys he held by the ears, glowering at them all, that if they so much as swiped one orange again or any boy started monkey-shining 'round the stand, he'd have them all up in the precinct court as quick as a cat could wink her eye.

The five went their separate ways; if a steam roller had gone over them they could not have looked more crushed. Bystanders hooted them out of sight while they helped Tony, Lucinda, and Jerry Hanlon to recover the fruit. Much was ruined, but wasn't it worth it? Lucinda stayed to wipe clean what could be put back on the stand. "Are we chortling?" she asked Tony. "Are we beamish? Were they slithy toves and did we go for them snicker-snack!"

Miss Peters, coming home early that afternoon, found written on the pad:

I am skating 'round to Tony's stand. Something's going to happen. If it happens right I shall be coming home with banners waving. O frabjous day!

HOUGHTON shook himself out of his daydream.

"It's a deadly and sinister weapon. I don't think I'll ever let anyone have it. It's a ball that bounces higher than the height from which you drop it. Come, I'll show it to you."

Peter Graves scratched his head and looked curiously at Houghton. He got up and followed the inventor back into the small concrete chamber.

"Is this the invention with which you could completely wipe out Houndstooth?"

"Did I say that? Well, I might not be able to wipe all of it out with one, but I could certainly cause a tremendous amount of damage. There are nice hard concrete roads through Houndstooth. They suit my invention well. It would work best in modern towns and cities—it's just about useless in the country."

Peter Graves

BY

WILLIAM PÈNE DU BOIS

Illustrated by

William Pène du Bois

"This sounds quite a bit like a riddle," said Peter.

They had entered the concrete chamber and Houghton was loosening the two great iron vises which so tightly gripped the big aluminum-colored ball in the corner of the room. He removed it, fondled it as though measuring its weight, shook it, held it near the floor, held it near the ceiling. He then handed it to Peter, "It feels and looks rather innocent, doesn't it?"

Peter's heart was pounding fast. He felt that he'd been handed a bomb with a sizzling fuse. He found that the ball weighed little but nevertheless he gripped it furiously. He had

41

a feeling that if he let it drop to the floor it would mean the end of everything. He studied it closely a moment, then nervously looked at Houghton Furlong.

"Try dropping it, but watch it, it's tricky. Be sure you catch it."

Peter dropped it from the height of his waist, then instinctively bent his knees and leaned over to catch it close to the ground. The ball hit the concrete, making a surprisingly clear metallic ting sound. It instantly zoomed upward, slipping between his hands and rising to the height of his shoulders had he been standing straight. He leaped and grabbed it in a clumsy and desperate lunge. Sweat was dripping from his forehead. He again squeezed it tightly, this time tucking it firmly under his shirt and under one arm.

"As you see," said Houghton, "it bounces higher than the height from which you drop it. That's what makes it so dangerous." He held out his hands. Peter cautiously slipped the ball out from under his shirt and handed it to him. Houghton replaced it in its double vise and secured it tightly. "Its core is a small ball of Furloy like those strapped to the. floor here. The core has an antigravity force of twenty-five pounds. This core is covered by twenty-eight pounds of duraluminum. The duraluminum is attracted to the ground by gravity but at the contact with the ground, the Furloy becomes activated, multiplying the normal bounce and making the ball bounce higher than the height from which it is dropped. Do you know why it is a dangerous weapon?"

"Vaguely," said Peter.

Houghton paused for a moment. He was staring at the remarkable ball. "Let's just for the fun of it, imagine that we really did want to wipe out Houndstooth. Where should we start?"

42

"Let's start with the high school," said Peter Graves.

"All right, the high school. This doesn't necessarily mean that the high school would go first, but it's a good starting point in which to gather a crowd. In the afternoon when all of the children were piling out and heading for home, I could innocently bounce my ball from the height of about one foot or less on the concrete pavement in front of the school. The ball would start bouncing, each time higher than the time before, each time harder than the time before, each time ringing forth with a louder clear metallic sound. The children would gather around and watch the ball, bobbing their heads up and down as if hypnotized by it. Soon the ball would be bouncing as high as the school house. The children would still be watching it but might back away and enlarge the circle. A darker spot might form in the pavement caused by this constant pounding. Before long the ball would come crashing down from a height of a half a mile or more and violently crack the pavement. The children would be snapped sharply out of their hypnosis and would start running away in all directions, screaming and yelling. On its next bounce, the ball would come tearing down from an even greater height, hit the cracked spot in the pavement and careen off, possibly knocking a huge chunk of masonry off the school house. By now, the children would be home, spreading everywhere a wide assortment of wild rumors. The supernatural quality of the terrible ball might cause a panic. Some would think that the city was being bombarded by a white meteor which hits, destroys, bounces off, and hits again. A white streak of duraluminum would come crashing down from ever-increasing heights, breaking water mains, causing fires, crashing through roofs into buildings where it would bounce with increasing violence until it had crushed and bashed its way out again.

43

There would be no signs of airplanes, not a suspicion of an enemy attack, just this strange pounding bombardment suggesting a weird and sinister assault from another planet." Houghton wiped his brow. "That's more or less the general idea. Of course I could shorten the destruction process proportionally if I started out with twenty or thirty balls all bouncing at once."

"WHEW!" exclaimed Peter. "It's terrible, and it's such a simple idea—a bouncing ball!"

"Please believe me most completely. I haven't the slightest intention of giving this invention to anybody, even less the intention of ever using its destructive powers myself. I hate all instruments of destruction. I keep it locked up carefully in this concrete vault so that even robbers or prowlers couldn't unknowingly lay their hands on it or accidentally start it bouncing. You, by the way, are the first outsider to see or feel this terrible invention."

"Why don't you destroy it completely?"

"Ah," said Houghton, "that's an entirely different story. Right now I'm experimenting on what might be a wonderful use for its peculiar energy. Watch this." He took the ball out of the double vise, held it about an inch from the floor and let bounce. The ball hit his hand and bounced back to the floor, hit his hand again and bounced back, faster and faster. Houghton seemed to try not to move his hand at all but the ball was pushing it higher and higher with increasing force. "See that," he shouted. "Maybe this energy could be controlled. A piston made of this combination of metal and Furloy might conceivably be bounced in a cylinder—a nice little engine would result that would run without fuel." The ball had now pushed Houghton's hand up to the height of his waist. The accelerating

44

rhythm and the clear metallic sounds of the ball hitting the concrete floor fascinated Peter. "May I feel it?" he said, sticking out his hand. "No!" shouted Houghton, "it's hitting too hard!" The ball slapped Peter's hand and bounced off crookedly. Peter shrieked and lunged for it, but missed it completely. The ball bounced from the ceiling to a corner and then crazily and rapidly started bouncing diagonally back and forth across the room. They both dove and sprawled and leaped and grabbed and plunged—the ball was going too fast. It smashed through their fingers, it caromed violently off their arms and legs, its speed had in an instant become uncontrollable. There was a sharp crack and a brief flash as it shattered the naked electric bulb and plunged the room into darkness. Houghton grabbed Peter by the arm and dragged him quickly through the great iron door. He pushed the door closed and pulled Peter out into the yard. Peter was shaking all over and crying. "It was an accident," said Houghton, "an accident, an accident! It's not your fault, it was an accident!"

"Shall I ring the alarm?" Peter stammered out.

"No, just stand right here!" They were a hundred yards or so from the house, under a big tree. "The ball is too dangerous. It might hurt some of those dozens of people who answer my calls for help. Let's just hope that it will pound its way through the roof fast, with a minimum amount of damage, and bury itself in some soft earth somewhere!"

The Horrible House of Houghton was shaking violently as if it were in the throes of a frightful attack of indigestion, or were having some sort of horrible trembling fit. The ball was rapidly bashing its way out of the concrete chamber. The noise was tremendous. You could no longer distinguish separate bounces, there was just a ghastly metallic thrashing sound

45

which seemed to get louder and louder. The whole house started to quiver crazily and windows were splintering on all sides. Shingles were shaking loose and sliding off the roof, shutters dropped off, a succession of short circuits started fires blazing on all floors. The plumbing was shaken and rattled into a maze of spitting pipes. The thrashing suddenly ceased as the ball bashed its way out of the vault. A few separate bounces could again be heard as it banged around upstairs, then it ripped its way through the roof and streaked to freedom in the sunset light. Houghton dashed after it. "WE'VE GOT TO GET IT AND DESTROY IT!" he shouted. The ball hit the concrete road and made a prodigious bounce off into the fields. There it careened from field to field like a stone skipping on water, finally coming to a stop a good quarter of a mile away. Houghton grabbed it and stuffed it under his coat. It was battered, scarred, and flattened completely out of shape. They took it back to what was left of the house. The Horrible House of Houghton had been shaken and burned until it had completely collapsed. What was left of the roof seemed to have snuffed out most of the fire, the broken plumbing had flooded out the rest. There were many little fountains playing in the wreckage. Houghton managed to turn off the water supply, then went into the garage which was fortunately untouched, being a good fifty yards from the house. He put the ball in the vise, took a metal saw and hacked off a big chunk of duraluminum. The ball was now in the control of the antigravity force of Furloy. Houghton took it outside and let go of it, and watched the dreadful product of his invention streak away from the earth, never to be seen again on this planet.

47

THE wolves were bad that winter of 1859 in Iowa. The snow was deep and they were hungry. At night they hunted in packs and we could hear them howling from down toward the timber more than two miles away. Sometimes they came closer to the house. Then Bounce would growl and whine to get out. Father would say, "Quiet, Bounce; that pack would make short work of you! Quiet! You stay safe inside."

The timber wolves carried off two of neighbor Allen's half-grown pigs, and the prairie wolves got most of Mrs. Allen's chickens. In pioneer days, this was a great loss because all that folks had was what they brought west in their covered wagons. We were glad that Father had made our sheds with tight doors and that he had thatched the wild grass heavily on the roofs. The sheds were small and the stock was crowded, but every animal was safe, even though there were wolf tracks in the snow outside.

Wolf! Wolf!

BY

FANNIE R. BUCHANAN

Illustrated by

Wladislaw Finne

Toward spring the nightly howling stopped. Father thought the pack had moved to the south where they were finding more prey. The snow melted and we saw no more tracks. We were so busy with our eight little pigs, our twin baby lambs, and Blossom's new calf that Mother let us do our lessons at night so we could help Father all day. Now that we could let the stock out again, we were pulling down the side walls of the crowded sheds to make them larger. Mother was planning to have twice as many chickens for next winter. The big gander and the three gray geese were happy to be outside. Every day they wandered down into the meadow.

48

One morning before daylight, Bounce set up a great growling and whined to get out. Father opened the door and followed him with the gun. He found everything quiet and he said Bounce had just been having a bad dream. But when we went to feed the chickens, Joey's pet hen was gone. That night Father made a bed for Bounce in a corner of the open chicken roost. Along toward daybreak he wakened us by barking and yelping wildly. Again Father got up and went out. Bounce came up from the meadow crying and wanted to follow Father into the house. Then we all got up. Mother lighted the lantern and we went out to the pens. One of the twin lambs was gone!

Mother said, "No fox could have carried away a lamb."

Father said, "This is the work of a timber wolf, and a big one."

To comfort Joey and me, Mother hunted up an old bear trap and oiled the spring. Father set it by the gate and left the bars down. He fastened the trap by a chain to the post. In the night when Bounce began whining and barking, we could hear the chain of the trap clanking.

Father took his gun saying, "I guess we've got the thief this time!" We soon heard a shot and then no more noise. When Father came in he said, "We caught a big one, all right. I think that fellow could have carried off Blossom as well as her calf!"

Next morning Joey and I measured the big gray wolf. He was sixty-nine inches from the tip of his wicked nose to the tip of his tail. What big cruel teeth he had! What powerful jaws!

"There's a bounty on the scalp," Father told us, "and that pelt is worth a good price. If you boys want to skin him, maybe Mother will divide with you," and he winked at Mother. Mother touched the toe of her shoe against the great shaggy leg. "You may have the whole of it if you promise never to go wolf hunting down in the timber alone."

"We won't," we promised. "We won't need to. The bear trap got the thief!" But that evening, when the geese came up from the meadow, the youngest goose was not with them.

Father was patting Bounce and he said, "There must be another wolf about, possibly the mate of the one we caught, but Bounce is no match for wolves. He must sleep in the house. I'll stand guard tonight, and then we must work fast and close up the sheds. We'll set the trap at the gate again, but I think the wolf will smell me and keep her distance."

That night we didn't sleep well. Mother kept going to the window, and she made hot coffee for Father when he came in to get warm at midnight.

It was neighbor Doonan who wakened us about four o'clock. He lived five miles beyond the timber, and had come for help. His wife was taken very sick and he wanted Mother to stay with her and their baby while he rode the twenty miles on into town to fetch the doctor.

Father offered to ride Mr. Doonan's horse for the Doctor and let Mr. Doonan take Mother over in our wagon. Father said he would stop by Allen's on the way and send young Jim to stay with Joey and me while Mother was away. We boys were up and wide awake. We had pulled our clothes on, hoping to be taken along, but they told us to go back to sleep till Jim came. They shut Bounce in the kitchen to take care of us. Mr. Doonan was very anxious. He harnessed the horses in a hurry, and by the time Father galloped away toward town Mother was climbing into the wagon.

It was bright moonlight and we watched them drive away. Then we tumbled back onto the bed just as we were, shoes and all.

I was just beginning to get sleepy when Bounce began to growl. I ran to the window and there, right at the gate was a

50

big timber wolf. I could see her quite plainly, for the moon was still high in the west and in the east the sky was growing light. She looked even larger than the one we had trapped. Her eyes were like balls of fire. I guess she had heard Bounce growl, for her lips were drawn back in a snarl which showed her sharp teeth. What if she were after the other twin lamb!

"Quiet, Bounce, quiet," I whispered, and made him lie down while I hid behind Mother's muslin curtains to watch.

Just then Joey woke up. "Quick, Joey," I whispered. "Here's another wolf. Watch where she goes while I get the gun." Father always kept the loaded gun on a rack above the door. But I had to carry the fireside bench over before I could reach high enough to get it down.

"Hurry, Tommy, hurry," Joey whispered. "She's going over to the chicken roost." Pretty quick the chickens started making a fuss, and then Joey saw the old wolf run toward the pasture with the big black rooster in her mouth.

"Make Bounce stay in," I ordered Joey. "He might get shot." I felt very safe with Father's gun in my hands. Joey made Bounce lie under the bed, and we sneaked out, closing the door quietly. The wind was blowing right toward us and that carried our scent away from the wolf. We didn't make a bit of noise, and she didn't know we were following. We saw her go around the straw stack, down toward the timber side of the field.

"I bet her den is in that stack," Joey said. "We'll hide in the straw till she comes out," I whispered. "Keep on this side with the wind and she won't smell us." When we got to the stack, we crouched down to wait. I was hunched on one knee with the gun across the other knee. Suddenly we heard a squawking noise, and then around the stack the big black rooster came staggering.

The next instant, around came the wolf after him. That minute the gun went off in my hands. It kicked me flat on my back in the straw and knocked the breath out of me. It was all so quick I didn't know what had happened till Joey was pushing the straw out of my face and yelling, "You got her! You hit her! You killed the old wolf!"

Neighbor Jim, on his way to stay with us, was cutting across to our place when he heard the shot. He started running fast. As he got nearer the house, he heard Bounce barking as if he had treed a buffalo and tearing around the kitchen like a cyclone mixing with a blizzard. When he opened the door,

Bounce tore off down the meadow like a prairie fire. Jim was after him still on the dead run.

Suddenly he met the black rooster, looking as if it had been put through the grist mill, then he stumbled over the shotgun and ran into the dead wolf, but not a boy was in sight!

All at once, out of a hole crawled Joey, holding a clawing, scratching wolf whelp in his bare hands. Close behind Joey, I came, my face and hands covered with blood, but holding on to another whelp. And after me came Bounce, holding a third cub by the scruff of the neck.

"Go in and get one," I shouted. "There's a whole litter

53

of cubs in there!" But Jim grabbed Joey and me and shook us till our shirts ripped open. "You idiots! You dumb idiots! To crawl right into a wolf den!" He reached for the gun, but we raced off to the house to shut the cubs up. We wanted to keep them for pets.

Jim called us idiots, but he didn't know what numbskulls we were until he found out we had shut the cubs in the cave among Mother's crocks of milk and pans of fresh eggs!

We had to pull the straw stack to pieces to get the rest of the litter. There were seven more cubs, and we were most of the morning catching them. We forgot we had had no breakfast. By noon we were as hungry as wolves ourselves and as scratched as though we had been crawling through a bramble patch.

Every time we caught a cub we would race off to the cave to shut it up. Jim helped us carry the last one in, wrapped in his coat to keep its claws padded. It was then he found the milk crocks upset and the eggs scrambled. He said we couldn't leave them there!

We had a hard time finding another place. At last Joey had an idea. The washtub! But how could we keep them in it? In those days, spare boards were as scarce as fences and there wasn't a loose board on the place. At last we carried out the three benches from the house and turned them upside down over the top of the tub.

By the time Father got back that night we boys had decided that wolves do not make good pets. Father said we had better make pelts of them instead. He said we had earned the bounty that was paid for scalps and a holiday besides. Then he patted my head and said there might even be bounty enough to buy a boy-sized rifle, though I had done very well with a man-sized gun.

54

Growltiger's Last Stand

BY T. S. ELIOT

Illustrated by

Feodor Rojankovsky

GROWLTIGER was a Bravo Cat,
who lived upon a barge;
In fact he was the roughest cat
that ever roamed at large.
From Gravesend up to Oxford
he pursued his evil aims,
Rejoicing in his title of
"The Terror of the Thames."

His manners and appearance did not calculate to please;
His coat was torn and seedy, he was baggy at the knees;
One ear was somewhat missing, no need to tell you why,
And he scowled upon a hostile world from one forbidding eye.

The cottagers of Rotherhithe
knew something of his fame,
At Hammersmith and Putney
people shuddered at his name.
They would fortify the hen-house,
lock up the silly goose
When the rumor ran around the
shore: *Growltiger's on the loose!*

Woe to the weak canary, that fluttered from its cage;
Woe to the pampered Pekinese, that faced Growltiger's rage.
Woe to the bristly Bandicoot, that lurks on foreign ships,
And woe to any Cat with whom Growltiger came to grips!

But most to Cats of foreign race his hatred had been vowed;
To Cats of foreign name and race no quarter was allowed.
The Persian and the Siamese regarded him with fear—
Because it was a Siamese had mauled his missing ear.

55

Now on a peaceful summer night, all nature seemed at play,
The tender moon was shining bright, the barge at Molesey lay.
All in the balmy moonlight it lay rocking on the tide—
And Growltiger was disposed to show his sentimental side.

His bucko mate, *Grumbuskin,* long since had disappeared,
For to the Bell at Hampton he had gone to wet his beard;
And his bosun, *Tumblebrutus,* he too had stol'n away—
In the yard behind the Lion he was prowling for his prey.

In the forepeak of the vessel Growltiger sat alone,
Concentrating his attention on the Lady *Griddlebone.*
And his raffish crew were sleeping
      in their barrels and their bunks—
As the Siamese came creeping in their sampans and their junks.

Growltiger had no eye or ear for aught but Griddlebone,
And the Lady seemed enraptured by his manly baritone,
Disposed to relaxation, and awaiting no surprise—
But the moonlight shone reflected
      from a thousand bright blue eyes.

And closer still and closer the sampans circled round,
And yet from all the enemy there was not heard a sound.
The lovers sang their last duet, in danger of their lives—
For the foe was armed with toasting forks
      and cruel carving knives.

Then *Gilbert* gave the signal to his fierce Mongolian horde;
With a frightful burst of fireworks
      the Chinks they swarmed aboard.

56

Abandoning their sampans, and their pullaways and junks,
They battened down the hatches
        on the crew within their bunks.

Then Griddlebone she gave a screech,
        for she was badly skeered;
I am sorry to admit it, but she quickly disappeared.
She probably escaped with ease,
        I'm sure she was not drowned—
But a serried ring of flashing steel Growltiger did surround.

The ruthless foe pressed forward, in stubborn rank on rank;
Growltiger to his vast surprise was forced to walk the plank.
He who a hundred victims had driven to that drop,
At the end of all his crimes was forced to go ker-flip, ker-flop.

Oh there was joy in Wapping
        when the news flew through the land;
At Maidenhead and Henley there was dancing on the strand.
Rats were roasted whole at Brentford, and at Victoria Dock,
And a day of celebration was commanded at Bangkok.

THERE was only one duty that Agba, the mute stable boy, disliked, and he disliked it with such an intensity that the blood pounded hotly through him all the while he did it. It was the cleaning of Hobgoblin's stall.

Hobgoblin was a big, and—to Agba's way of thinking—a coarsely made stallion. He was as unlike Sham as a bull is unlike a stag. Yet Hobgoblin was king of Gog Magog, and his stall a palace. The walls were padded thickly with the fuzz of cattails covered over with leather, so that Hobgoblin would not mar the sleekness of his hide nor the perfection of his tail. The floor was laid with chalk and abundantly strewn with straw which Agba had to change three times a day. A manger of wood was not good enough for Hobgoblin. His was of marble. As for his blankets, they were emblazoned with the Earl of Godolphin's own crest. Even his fly-sheets bore the crest.

The Lady Roxana Picks Her Mate

BY

MARGUERITE HENRY

Illustrated by

Wesley Dennis

"Hobgoblin's th-th-the Earl's star o' hope, Hobgoblin is," Titus Twikerham told Agba one rainy day when they were both in his stall. "Flowing in this-here stallion's veins is the p-p-purplest blood in the k-k-kingdom."

The groom stopped to wipe out the corner of Hobgoblin's eye with a clean pocket handkerchief, then went on. "The Earl—he's g-got his heart set on Hobgoblin. Through this-here

58

stallion he's got hopes to b-breed the best line o' horses not only in the kingdom, but in the world."

Agba preferred to listen to the drumming of the rain, but the groom's voice rose above it.

"Right this m-minute, whilst we're standin' here, the Earl is lookin' for a mare worthy of Hobgoblin. Now," he said, rapping his knuckles on Agba's head, "now ye understand why Hobgoblin's stall is finer th-th-than yer runt's. Hobgoblin's King of Gog Magog, he is!"

After that, whenever Agba pitched the old straw out of Hobgoblin's stall and laid in the new, his lips were set in a firm line. He hated Hobgoblin. Hated the bigness of him. Hated his powerful legs and hindquarters. Hated the fat sleekness of him. But most of all he hated Hobgoblin's eye. It had no brilliance at all. Only a sleepy look, except when the animal was aroused. Then it showed a white ring.

"Here is where Sham should be," Agba thought with every thrust of his fork. "Purple blood, indeed! Sham's ancestors came from the stables of the Prophet himself!"

One day, soon after the groom had explained Hobgoblin's importance, Gog Magog seethed with excitement. The Earl of Godolphin made frequent visits to Hobgoblin's stall. Usually his gait was dignified and his bearing stately, but this day his steps were quick and his words clipped short.

As for Titus Twickerham, he was so nervous that he could not control his stammering.

"Y-y-y-you, Ag-g-g-ba. Y-you lay a fresh l-l-litter of st-st-straw in the new m-m-mare's stall. And w-w-wash out the mang-g-g-ger. Then p-p-put in a measure of wheat b-b-bran. The mare, Lady Roxana, arrives t-t-t-today."

The excited pitch of Mr. Twickerham's voice when he said

"Lady Roxana" made Agba bite his lips. It was the very tone he used in speaking of Hobgoblin. *Lady Roxana! Hobgoblin! Hobgoblin! Lady Roxana!* The names rankled in the boy's mind. He hated them both. Without even seeing Roxana, he knew she would be fat and sway-backed and ugly.

As Agba prepared the mare's stall, he saw the Earl and a dozen noblemen come down to the paddock. They walked about, talking in hushed, expectant voices, twirling their riding rods, taking pinches of snuff, sneezing lightly.

Suddenly a cry went up from the grooms. " 'Ere she comes! 'Ere she comes!"

Agba flew out of the stall. He made field glasses of his fists. He strained his eyes down the lane. But the late afternoon sun blinded him. At first he saw nothing at all. Only the hawthorne trees and the yews, standing dark and still.

Then all at once he could make out a blur of motion. It cleared. It became a shiny red van drawn by two dapple-grays.

60

The grays were clattering over the bridge now and up the hill between the yews and hawthornes. They were nearing the stables. The driver, an enormous man in red livery, was drawing rein. As the horses jammed to a stop, a lackey hopped down from his perch beside the driver and went around to the back of the van. He let down the tail gate. Then, bowing from the waist, he handed a leading string to the Earl's head groom.

"Lady Roxana, daughter of The Bald Galloway!" His voice boomed out as if he were announcing a princess at a ball.

The noblemen and all the horseboys waited tensely. Titus Twikerham looked to the Earl of Godolphin with questioning eyebrows. The Earl nodded. And so, bristling with importance, the spidery figure of the groom led Lady Roxana down the ramp and into the paddock. Slowly, gently, as if he were unveiling a statue, he lifted her hood and threw off her scarlet blanket.

An awed silence fell over the little company. Then, as though the wall of a dike had given way, there was a torrent of noise. Jeweled hands broke into spontaneous applause. Every voice shouted in admiration.

The Earl of Godolphin laughed aloud. Here, at last, was the answer to his dream!

Except for her tail, which was a smoky plume, Roxana was the shininess of white marble in the sun. And she wore no housings at all, only a halter made of silken rope, and across the browband were tiny rosettes of blue satin.

Roxana pawed the springy turf. She seemed glad that the jolting, jarring ride was over. A high whinny escaped her.

Suddenly there was an answering whinny, so shrill and joyous it sent shivers up and down Agba's spine.

"Aha!" spoke up one of the noblemen. "Hobgoblin is already welcoming his mate."

61

A smile played about Agba's lips. The whinny of welcome had come from Sham, *not* from Hobgoblin.

For a full minute Roxana alerted. Her head went up; her tail went up; her ears pricked. The noblemen gasped. If Roxana had been beautiful before, she was a living statue now.

Agba's heart melted. He had intended to hate Roxana, but all the hate was washed away.

"What symmetry!" exclaimed the Duke of Bridgewater.

"She is built like a fawn!" cried Lord Villiers.

"Aye. Exquisitely made," said the Earl of Marmaduke.

Agba scarcely heard their remarks. Way down at the end of the stables he saw Sham's head thrust out. He watched

Roxana toss her mane at him, like a girl tossing her curls. He heard her whinny, this time softer, fuller than the last.

Now there were two answers. The deep, grunting neigh of Hobgoblin and the ecstatic bugling of Sham.

"Twickerham," the Earl spoke tensely, "Hobgoblin shall meet his mate. Have him brought out."

Again the paddock was bathed in stillness. It was so quiet that Agba could hear a leaf drifting lazily to earth. A goldfinch flew overhead in yellow arcs, spinning a thin thread of song.

Titus Twickerham's words rang in Agba's ears. *A mare worthy of Hobgoblin.* That overfed monster! Agba could stand the unfairness no longer. He ran to Sham's stall. He threw wide the door. Out streaked a tongue of golden fire. It was Sham, trumpeting to the skies, Sham tasting his freedom with a wild leap. He overtook Hobgoblin being led out of his stall. He whirled around and challenged the king of Gog Magog. Hobgoblin jerked his head into the air, breaking the catch of his lead rope. Then they charged, the noisy thudding of their bodies lost in savage screams.

The grooms were benumbed, stupefied. For seconds they were unable to move. Then they all began running at once, getting in each other's way, throwing bucketfuls of water at the furious stallions. It was useless—like trying to smother a forest fire with hearth brooms. The air crackled and ripped with the sound of flailing hooves and snorts and shrieks.

Sham was little and quick. His legs were steel rods. He danced on them, making fierce thrusts. Hobgoblin was like a great war horse beside Sham. Now he swung his lumbering body around and gave a tremendous kick with all the power of his hindquarters.

Agba saw Sham drop down on the ground to miss the blow. In a second he was up again, spinning around to face Hobgoblin, beating at him with his flinty hooves. He saw Sham open wide his mouth and use his strong young teeth, not to bite, but to hammer with. The blows seemed no heavier than hailstones to Hobgoblin. Yet they maddened him into a wild rage. He lunged, baring his teeth, ready to sink them into Sham's neck.

With a mighty cry, Sham tossed his head upward, catching Hobgoblin under the jaw, actually lifting him up on his hind feet. The little horse rained blow after blow on Hobgoblin, forcing him farther and farther up on his hind legs until finally he fell over backward, thrashing and kicking.

Agba beat his fists together. The great Hobgoblin was down! The massive, heaving, hulking body was grunting in pain and defeat.

A ringing cry of victory burst from Sham. With a rush he sought Lady Roxana. He leaped about her, prancing lightly as if his legs were set on springs. He arched his magnificent neck. He plumed his tail. His eyes were bold, his body wet and shining. Sham, the fleet of foot, the pride of the Sultan's stables, was on parade before the beautiful Roxana.

Suddenly they were together, touching each other with their noses, talking in excited little nickers. Then, manes and tails in flowing motion, they streaked to the far end of the paddock. It seemed plain to Agba that both Sham and Roxana wanted to be far away from the distasteful, groaning Hobgoblin.

Agba wanted to sing for joy. He longed to talk, to laugh, to cry. His hands flew to his throat helplessly. But it was Roxana whose voice substituted for his own. It was her whinny, high and joyful, that said all he wanted to say.

RED sniffed long and deeply at the track, and raised his head to look at Danny. He sat down, tail flat on the ground behind him, staring down the slope. Danny watched. Red never had been a trailing dog, and would not now become one. But if he could catch the body scent of Old Majesty, and was urged to the attack, he would chase the big bear and finally bring it to bay. Danny climbed back to the summit of the mountain and sat down. The wind was almost straight out of the west, blowing gently but steadily. Clouds scudded across the sky, and the feathered tips of the pine trees bent. For a long while Danny stared steadily into the valley, and looked from it to Red.

Old Majesty was not there now or Red would smell him and indicate his presence. But there was no sign that he had been alarmed and knew that a pursuer was on his trail. Danny looked back down to the spring where he had found the track. He could follow the trail if he wanted to, and eventually work it out, but he must wage a battle of

Big Red Tracks Old Majesty

BY JIM KJELGAARD

Illustrated by Bob Kuhn

wits as well as one of scientific woodcraft. Fresh as it was, it would still take a long while to puzzle out that trail on the hard, rocky ground. Danny looked again down the slope, at the vast number of decaying logs that lay undisturbed. All of them were full of grubs, and if Old Majesty wanted to rest a few days he would not stray far from this place. Probably he was resting now, and not far away. But exactly where was he and what was the best way to go about finding him?

66

Danny rose, and with Red padding beside him travelled straight up the top of the mountain. He crossed the valley at its head, crossed the next mountain to the one beyond, and swung down it. He came off its sloping nose into a forested valley, and struck due east. But all the while he had been both studying the ground beneath him and watching Red. The big setter had stalked away three or four times to hunt partridges that he had scented in the thickets. But not once had his nose gone to the ground, and Danny had seen no bear track leading away. Old Majesty, then, was somewhere within the circle he had made.

Danny walked due east, crossing the noses of the mountains whose heads he had walked around and returned to the foot of the slope where the grub-ridden logs lay. He walked around it, up the valley that separated it from the next hill, and again sat down to ponder. He ate bread smeared with bacon grease, gave Red some, and sat down with his back against a boulder. Twilight came, and erratic bats swooped up and down the little stream before him. But pitch darkness had descended on the wilderness before Danny started up the mountain again.

He left his pack beside the stream, carrying only a three-cell flashlight and his rifle as he climbed. The wind still blew steadily from the west. A whippoorwill shrieked, and Red halted to peer toward the sound. Danny waited for the big dog to catch up with him. He was still a hundred feet below the mountain's crest when he stooped to crawl.

The back of his neck tingled, and little shivers ran up and down his spine. Old Majesty, just twice in his whole terrible career, had been seen in daylight by men who carried rifles. Ross had missed his shot, and Danny had dared not shoot for fear that a wounded bear might injure Red. But, though the big bear had been hunted many times by day, as far as Danny knew this was the first time anyone had ever thought of stalking him by night. He reached the summit of the mountain, and felt in the darkness for Red. His fingers found and clenched the big dog's fur.

Almost imperceptibly he felt Red stiffen, and Danny laid the rifle across his knees while his other hand stole forth to clamp about the big setter's muzzle. He thrilled with pride. Again his guess had been the right one. Old Majesty had not wandered away, but after eating his fill of grubs had merely gone to sleep in some secluded thicket. Now he was back. From down the slope came the ripping sound of a log being torn apart. Then an eerie silence.

It was broken by the buzz of an insect in a nearby tree, and Danny snapped his head erect. A light wind blew out of the valley. Red maintained his tense stance. The wind eddied around, blowing from all directions, and Red shrank close to the earth. A clammy hand brushed Danny's spine. He let go of the dog's muzzle to pick up his rifle. He clutched it very tightly, wrapping his fingers about the breech with one hand on the trigger. Something was happening out there in the darkness, something that only Red could interpret, and in that moment Danny knew that he was afraid.

Red turned his head, and held it poised while he remained rooted in his tracks. Slowly he swung his body about, facing up the ridge now instead of into the valley. Inch by inch he continued to turn, facing down the other side of the razor-backed ridge, and swinging until he had made a complete circle and was staring into the valley again. Then, Danny understood. He bit his lip so hard that he felt the taste of blood in his mouth, and let go of Red's ruff to reach into his pocket for the flashlight.

They were hunting Old Majesty, but there in the black night the great bear was also hunting them. He had come back to feed on the grubs in the dead logs, scented Danny and Red, and rather than run again had elected to try conclusions in the darkness, the time that he favored most and that was most favorable to him. Danny swallowed hard as the complete realization of that was driven home to him, but he grasped it perfectly. Old Majesty was no ordinary bear, but bigger, wiser, fiercer, and more intelligent than any other bear that Danny had ever known. Beyond a doubt he remembered Red, and that Red had once brought him to bay. Even though he might now fear the dog, he still knew that he would have to fight it out sooner or later, and was selecting that fight to his own advantage.

In the darkness he had walked clear around them, nerving himself to the attack and trying to choose the best method for it. Now he was just a little way down the hill, looking them over, reading them with his nose and listening for their next move. Danny drew back the hammer of his rifle, and in the night its metallic little click was startlingly loud. He held it in his right hand, clutching the flashlight with his left, and spoke softly.

"Stay here, Red. Stay with me."

Down the slope pebbles rattled, and there was the scraping of a claw on a rock. Danny thought hard, trying in his mind to reconstruct an exact picture of the mountain side as he had seen it earlier that morning. The nearest big rock, he thought, was about sixty yards from where they stood now and Old Majesty must have walked on it. Half-tempted to flash the light and shoot, he hesitated. The bear might come nearer, present a fairer shot. If he did not, if instead of attacking he chose to run, Danny could always urge Red forward to follow him. Somewhere in the lost wilderness Red would once again bring Old Majesty to bay.

Red was once more facing up the ridge, and had taken two stiff-legged steps forward. Danny poised the flashlight and rifle. Red did not turn his head again, so the bear was standing still. Danny snapped the light on. Its white beam travelled into the night to fall like a silver cage about something huge and black, something that stood scarcely twenty yards up the spine of the ridge. The wind blowing out of the valley eddied around it, curled the long hair that hung from its belly.

Danny raised the gun, supported it on the hand in which he gripped the light, and aimed in its uncertain glow. This, he thought, was not real or right. It was something that you did only in a dream, and awoke to find it a blurred memory. But the cold trigger about which his finger curled was real enough, as was the crack of the rifle and the little tongue of red flame that licked into the darkness. He heard the sodden little "splot" as the bullet struck and buried itself in flesh. Red's battle roar rang through the night, and at almost exactly the same second the big dog and Old Majesty launched themselves at each other.

Danny shot again and again, desperately working the lever of his gun and pumping bullet after bullet into the on-coming black mass. A feeling of hopelessness almost over-whelmed him. The bear kept coming. It was as though Old Majesty was a monstrous thing, an animated mass of some-thing that had no more life than a stone or a rock, and upon which bullets had no effect. Wide-eyed, Danny saw it within thirty, then twenty feet of him, and in that moment he knew that he would have died if it had not been for Red.

The big setter met the charging bear, and closed with him. Old Majesty's paw flashed, raked down the dog's chest, and Red reeled away to roll over and over on the ground. His

attention diverted from Danny, Old Majesty lunged after the dog.

Danny shook his head. He seemed still to be in a dream, in the throes of something terrible from which sane awakening only could release him. Feverishly he found himself ripping the box of cartridges apart, pumping more bullets into the rifle's magazine. His legs seemed to belong to someone else as he ran forward through the night, held the muzzle of his gun within two feet of Old Majesty's ear, and pulled the trigger. The big bear jerked convulsively, quivered, and settled down to stretch his great length on the earth.

For a moment Danny stood pale and trembling, the gun dangling by his side and the flashlight painting the unreal scene before him. He saw Red, whose coat was now stained with crimson, rise on three legs and prepare to renew the battle. He lunged at the bear, but stopped and turned toward Danny, his jaws very wide open, panting hard. Danny faltered, the rifle clattered to the ground, and tears rolled unashamed from his eyes. Red was everything Danny had thought him and very much more. Beautiful, courageous, strong—and noble. He would fight to the death if need be, but would not molest or disgrace a fallen enemy. Danny snapped back to reality.

"Red!"

The cry was wrenched from him. He ran forward to kneel beside the wounded dog. His hand strayed to Red's left chest and leg. Blood trickled through his fingers as he felt torn flesh and muscles. Even as he turned the light on, he knew that Red would never win another prize in a dog show. His left front leg was ripped half away. Danny picked the dog up, and carried him down the mountain to where he had left the pack. He knelt beside him, dusted the gaping wounds with sulfa

72

powder, and wrapped a clean white bandage around them. Danny took off his jacket, made of it a soft bed for the big setter, and built a fire.

Morning came slowly. The sun strove to break through the mists that blanketed the valley, and the little stream ran quarrelsomely on. Red lay stiffly on the coat, but raised his head to grin and wagged his tail in the dawn's dim light. Danny unwrapped the bloodsoaked bandage and looked at the wound. There was no infection. But it would be a long time before Red was able to travel. Danny rigged his fishline and caught trout in the little stream. In the middle of the afternoon he climbed back up the mountain and looked at the still form of Old Majesty. Danny shuddered. Even now, if it were not for that giant, quiet thing, last night would be like a dream. But let the bear lie where it was, let it remain, a fallen king, in the wilderness it had once ruled.

Day followed day as they camped by the little stream. Red got up from his bed to walk stiffly about, and Danny watched with his heart in his eyes. Red's wounds were healing well, but an ugly scar showed and he would never again have much use of his left front leg. Danny gathered the dog to him, and hugged Red very tightly.

On the eighth day, with Red limping behind him, he started down the valley toward home. They camped that night in another little valley, under the shadow of Stoney Lonesome's laurel thickets. With Red's fine head pillowed on his lap, Danny sat before the leaping little fire he had built and stared into the darkness. Somehow he seemed to have changed. The old Danny Pickett had gone forth on the outlaw bear's trail, but a new one was returning. And the new one was a Danny Pickett able to do what he never could have done before.

BUD got up at four-thirty and dressed, in the bleak dark of that Washington's Birthday morning. The cold and the excitement made him shake all over like a leaf as he went stumbling out into the barn. But he climbed the mow and dug into the hay savagely with the fork to pull himself together. And when he came down Tug was there to give his hand a warm, reassuring lick.

The white terrier was all but well now. Only a few healing scars remained from his encounter with the gypsy dogs, and his limp was entirely gone.

Bud hustled through the work in time to give Cedar a last brushing down, then fed and watered him with care and went in to breakfast. For Aunt Sarah's sake he made a valiant effort to eat, but he was keyed too high that morning to enjoy the taste of food. Uncle John came out with him to help harness, and by eight

Cedar of Red Horse Hill

BY STEPHEN W. MEADER

Illustrated by Lee Townsend

o'clock they were ready to start. Bud waved good-by to Aunt Sarah and drove the colt out of the dooryard to the musical jingle of bells. Tug went too, sitting erect between their feet.

All down the snowy miles to Riverdale Bud had to check Cedar's pace, soothing him constantly by voice and hand, for the colt felt like skylarking.

"This jog to town is a good thing fer him," Uncle John said. "It'll take some o' the devilment out of him, an' maybe he'll be ready fer business at race time."

At the outskirts of the town they overtook the Hunters' sleigh, in which Cal and his father were riding, and accom-

74

panied them to the speedway. There was still nearly an hour before the first heat was scheduled to begin, and Bud blanketed the colt and walked him slowly up and down while the others were getting their tickets for the grandstand. Uncle John reported his injury to the race committee and made the necessary arrangements for having Bud drive in his place.

The holiday had brought out a far larger crowd than had been present the afternoon before. Not only had many come afoot, but there were rows of cutters ranged along the sides of the track, with an occasional automobile among them. The sky was overcast and the air sharply cold.

"Looks as if it might snow later," said Uncle John, casting a weatherwise eye aloft. He had come back for a last look at Cedar before the race.

A gong began to clang at the judges' stand. "Ten minutes," said Uncle John. "Warm him up a bit back here, then take him up over the course so it won't be strange to him. Good-by, lad."

Bud took Cedar's blanket off and let him stretch his legs a trifle on the road back of the stand. When he seemed well limbered up the boy swung his horse to the foot of the speedway and jogged him up past the grandstand. Then along the line of jingling sleighs and pungs he guided Cedar toward the starting-point. There were laughter and a few jeers as they passed—the strong young horse, with his winter coat as smooth as Bud could brush it, but looking a bit rough and uncouth about the legs; the scarred old cutter, its moth-eaten cushions well dusted and its steel runners polished till they gleamed; and sitting very straight under an ancient buffalo robe, the serious-faced boy with his eyes to the front.

Eight horses besides Cedar were moving up to the start. Most of them were local trotters. They had beautiful, clipped legs, and right at their tails—on them, in fact—sat their drivers, in sulky sleighs that were no more than light skeletons of braced steel, with ridiculous little shells of seats above.

As they swung into position Bud looked off down the mile straightaway with a pounding heart. He felt himself in a sort of daze, his arms heavy, helpless. Then almost before he knew it the starting gun had sounded. Ahead of him flew the other eight, close-bunched.

A laugh went up as the boy gritted his teeth and urged the sorrel colt after them. Hot tears of anger filled his eyes. But the swift rhythm of Cedar's haunches under the taut reins brought back his confidence and even a thrill of pride. He steeled himself for the job ahead.

And now from the crowds that lined the snow path came scattering cheers as they went by, for some of the men from the upper end of the county and some of Bud's schoolmates recognized them. Slowly, very slowly, it seemed to the boy, they were coming up—overhauling first one rival and then another, till, as the wire drew close, there were six behind them.

Cedar finished in third place. Bud swung him around to pass the grandstand on the return journey. He could not bring himself to look up. He was red with shame. But there were many good horsemen along the track who had seen the colt's fine spurt and who threw Bud a word of encouragement as he went back for the second heat.

Well, there should be no leaving at the post this time! Bud gathered the reins, and the sorrel picked up speed as he neared the start. Over the line he went like a shot, right abreast of the leaders. Halfway down the track Bud looked sidewise. The winner of the first heat, a game little chestnut gelding named Billy D., was holding even with the boy's sleigh seat, trotting with all that was in him. The rest were trailing behind. Bud thrilled to see the red colt then. As his grip on the reins tightened, Cedar responded, speeding faster and faster, with the wind in his mane, over the hard-packed snow he loved. And he crossed the finish line with a good three lengths to spare.

There was a yell from the crowd as the time went up. Bud looked at the board and nearly choked with surprise. Two-eight, it said. Surely there was a mistake. In a minute they would find it out and change the "0" to a "1". But no, the crowd was still cheering. "Cedar! Cedar!" cried the voices in the stand, hailing a new popular favorite. And flushed this time with pride, Bud grinned up at the throng, trying to find Uncle John and Cal and Tug.

The colt was over his first nervousness now, and Bud let him take plenty of time in going back for the final test. When they reached the start the boy got out of the sleigh and stooped to rub down Cedar's steaming legs with a dry piece of sacking. A man spoke, so close to his shoulder that it startled him.

"Give 'im the whip, this last heat," he said in a low voice. "They're goin' after yuh. That colt's got better time in 'im, yet, an' you'd better use it. Don't look around, but drive like the devil, all the way!" And the man was gone before Bud could open his mouth to reply. The single glimpse he got of him had shown a sallow, thin fellow with a black mustache, wearing a great coonskin coat.

Already the horses were back on the track. Bud was thinking quickly, disturbed by the uncalled-for advice of the stranger. It was true enough that he must do his best to win this last heat, but why had the man been so anxious to tell him so? Was he betting on Cedar? Uncle John's words came back to Bud as distinctly as if he were hearing them spoken: "Don't let anybody tell you how to do. Drive your own race." And the boy resolved that, green as he was in such matters, he would use his own judgment and disregard all outside counsel. Still worrying a little, he swung the big red colt into place above the start.

Down they came, all together, like a cloud before the wind, as the flag dropped.

Cedar was rocking along, smoothly as ever, almost in the center of the group. Suddenly Bud saw two horses moving up, one on each flank, and though less than a quarter of the course was finished their drivers were plying the whip savagely. As the sleighs drew even with Cedar's head both men pulled inward a barely perceptible distance. The colt's flying forefeet were very near to striking their runners.

In another instant he might have broken, for he was disconcerted and tossed back his head. But Bud pulled him far off to the left and spoke to him once or twice as Uncle John would do. The young pacer held his stride and a second later was going again like the wind, outside and nearly abreast of the others.

Beyond the half mile they had passed all but the little chestnut, Billy D. He fought them hard all the way down, but Cedar's mighty strength was too great a handicap. Bud was slacking off on the reins at the finish, and the colt drifted easily under the wire, a length to the good.

The spectators came pouring out of the stand as Bud guided Cedar off the track. A crowd of curious men and boys surrounded them, staring open-mouthed at the young stallion while Bud wiped down his legs and blanketed him. After a moment Uncle John shouldered through the onlookers, followed by Tug and the Hunters. No words were needed to express the farmer's joy. It glowed in his square, brown face.

"That was drivin', boy!" he said, and gripped Bud's hand. Then he looked around at the crowd. "Here, let's git the colt out o' this an' give him a chance to rest," he added.

78

In the lee of a pine thicket near the upper end of the speedway they found a sheltered place to tie the horses and eat their lunch. When Cedar was cool enough they gave him a light feed and a little drink.

"What was it happened up there near the start in the last heat?" asked Uncle John as they consumed Aunt Sarah's sandwiches and pie.

"Two of the drivers tried to box me," said Bud, and he went on to tell how Cedar had escaped from the trap. "There was another funny thing happened," the boy remarked. "Just before the last heat a man came and warned me to drive for all I was worth and lay into the colt with the whip. Do you suppose he really meant to help me? I didn't like his looks, so I didn't pay much attention to him."

$1000 to the WINNER
FREE FOR ALL MEETING
FOR THE
SNOW-RACING
CHAMPIONSHIP
OF NEW ENGLAND

RIVERDALE SPEEDWAY
FEB-21-22

"He might've wanted Cedar to win," said Uncle John, "but it sounds to me as if he's been trying to use the colt up—kill his speed fer this afternoon. Who was the feller?"

Bud described the stranger, but neither Uncle John nor Myron Hunter could remember having seen him.

The next two hours were hard for the youthful jockey. No one talked much. They all took turns at leading the blanketed pacer up and down to keep his legs from stiffening. Now that the first flush of winning the elimination race had passed, Bud had moments of bitter doubt. He thought of the crudeness of their preparations for the final and compared them mentally with what was going on in the big, steamheated box stalls at the hotel stable, where grooms and trainers were even then putting the last fine touches on Chocorua and Saco Boy.

He thought of Cedar—a raw young colt, driven down that forenoon over ten miles of country road, raced in three hard heats in the morning, and handled clumsily by an amateur driver. What chance had he to win against those famous pets of the racing-game, fresh from a night's rest and maneuvered by wise and tricky hands?

Then he looked up at the big red horse stepping proudly along at his side, saw the courage that glowed in his eye and the strength of his arched neck—and shame filled the boy's heart. Cedar, at least, had no yellow streak.

Two o'clock came, and the young pacer was put back between the shafts of the cutter. Uncle John pulled the last buckle tight with his left hand and gave the colt's cheek a lingering pat. "I guess it's time to go down to the judges' stand," he said. "They'll likely make the three hosses parade past 'fore the first heat."

They led Cedar down the track, still in his blanket, as far as the upper end of the grandstand. There the wraps were taken off and Bud took his place once more in the sleigh while the others climbed to their seats in the pavilion.

There was a great throng gathered at the track that cold, gray afternoon. The Governor had come over from Concord, and by his side in the decorated box loomed the gigantic figure of a famous New Hampshire Congressman who never missed a good harness race if he could help it.

Driving up past the crowds to the judges' stand, Bud realized with dismay that he and Cedar were a part of the spectacle that these thousands had come to watch. Luckily his stage-fright did not pass through the reins into the horse. He was as gay as ever, and even danced a little as the band played.

Close by, their blanketed forms the center of deep knots of men, were the colt's two opponents. Bud watched them as their coverings were stripped off. Saco Boy stood forth magnificent —a great black stallion with fire in his eyes and mighty mus- cles leaping in his neck and shoulders. He was more massive and even taller than Cedar, but, Bud felt, no better propor- tioned.

Then his glance shifted to Chocorua. Instantly the old hatred he had felt when he first saw her returned. It seemed as if no horse had a right to such slim, long racing shanks. She was built like a greyhound, and the similarity was made more striking by her chest and legs. Her head was long and narrow and wicked. With her ears back she was like a reptile—venom- ous.

As Bud looked past her his eye was caught by a coonskin coat and a thin, dark-mustached face above it. It was the stran- ger of the morning, standing close by the mare's head and engaged in an earnest conversation with two men. One was a hard-faced, smallish man in black furs—Andy Blake, the mare's driver. The other was Sam Felton himself. The fatjowled magnate's eye met Bud's and flashed with recognition. Was it Cal who had said that the Feltons never forgot a grudge? There was something of vindictive triumph in that glance that the boy did not like. And the mystery that had puzzled him was cleared up at last. Instead of a friend, the man who had given him the tip was an enemy—one of Chocorua's backers. No wonder he had urged Bud to drive the colt to a needless whipping finish in the morning race. Perhaps it was he who had engineered the attempt to box Cedar, as well. The boy thanked his stars he had followed Uncle John's advice.

From the judges' booth sounded the sharp, impatient banging of the gong. "Ten minutes!" came the call, and Bud gathered the reins once more for action.

Bud took Cedar on a little warm-up spin along the track, then came back with the others to the judges' stand. There was another laugh at the rude racing turnout from Red Horse Hill, for many people in the crowd had not been present that morning. Andy Blake, mounted close behind the tall hind-quarters of his mare, grinned spitefully at Bud's reddening face. But old Billy Randall, who held the reins over Saco Boy, gave the lad a friendly nod.

"Sorry 'bout John gittin' hurt," he said, "but you drove a good race this mornin'. That's a great youngster you've got there."

From the judges' stand the horses' and drivers' names were read out and the conditions of the race announced. Three heats were to be driven and the championship decided on points if no horse won twice. As the announcer put down his megaphone a babel of sound rose from the stands—cheers and shouts of encouragement. The three drivers turned their horses' heads and jogged slowly up the track toward the start.

Bud had an entirely different feeling from the one with which he had entered the morning race. He was alert and tense

82

now, determined to fight. They swung around at the head of the snow path and got under way. Nearing the start the big, black trotter flashed out ahead, fiercely impetuous. He left the line a good four lengths beyond the others, and Bud expected to hear the jangling of the recall bell. Instead came the report of the gun, and the starter's flag fell. In spite of an outcry from the crowd and the wild gesticulations of Andy Blake the heat was on.

A great excitement entered Bud's veins. His grip on the reins tightened, and he shouted to Cedar through the whipping wind. The colt was pacing swift and sure as in the forenoon, one pointed ear cocked back for Bud's voice, the other forward. Chocorua's evil head, close by their sleigh-seat at first, dropped back and back till Bud could see her no longer, and the colt drew up little by little on the great trotting stallion.

It was such a finish as horsemen dream of. Scarcely half a length apart down the last quarter fought the sorrel and the black. There was so little to choose that many called it a dead heat. But with the sting of Randall's whip on his shining side, Saco Boy flung himself under the wire a nose ahead.

"Two-five and a quarter!" bawled the timekeeper. And as Bud came out of the spell of the race he realized that thousands of voices had been calling on Cedar to win.

Again the long mile back to the starting-point, and then a little breathing-spell as they got ready for the second heat. Blake, sullen and resentful, had saved his mare after the uneven start. She stood there poised on her slim legs, hardly breathing as yet, while the black stallion puffed and pawed and flung white spume flecks back over his ebony neck. Cedar was quieter, but the exertions of the day had begun to tell on him. His deep sides rose and fell with the effort he had made. Bud soothed him with pet names and rubbed him unceasingly as they stood waiting.

It had begun to snow when the starter called them out—long, slanting darts of white hurled across the track by the keen north wind.

They brought their horses to the right-about and came down to the post again. The tall roan mare leaped to the front this time, with Randall and Bud driving close at her heels. Blake was not lagging now. From the start he drove her—drove her with hard hand and hard voice, the whip ever poised above her lean back. And still, as she fled away, came Cedar after her, eager as a hawk, his swift feet thudding on the firm-packed snow. Off to the right the great black horse held the pace for a while, then burst into a thunderous gallop, and they left him and sped on.

It was a terrific gait the mare was making. And she held it to the end, for Blake began using the whip at the three-quarter post and brought her in under a flying lash. Gallantly Cedar followed, but at the finish there was still a length that his weary legs could not make up.

Bud had to shut his jaw hard, for he wanted to cry as he stood by Cedar's side after that second heat. There was a faint, constant trembling in the steel muscles under the colt's damp hide and his coat was bright no longer, but dark with sweat. Rubbing and working at those beautiful legs as if his life depended on it, the boy talked to him breathlessly, pleading with him, begging forgiveness for the one last trial that Cedar must endure. Twice he had given his best and lost. The race and the purse were gone, of course—utterly beyond their reach, but Bud knew they must keep on and see it through.

When he looked up for a moment men were jumping in the air in excitement, shouting and pointing toward the judges' pavilion. On the board were figures which at first Bud read without believing. They said: "2.04."

84

Then at his elbow he saw Billy Randall standing. The old trainer's voice was queer and husky as he spoke.

"I wanted to look at that colt o' yours, lad," he was saying. "I guess we're through—Saco Boy an' I. Once he breaks in a race he's done for the day. But you've got the greatest snow horse in New England there under that blanket—"

"Ye're durn right!" interrupted a voice behind them, and Bud turned quickly to see Long Bill Amos. "The finest pacer I ever see!" continued the teamster. "An' if you don't beat that roan she-devil—now—" He choked. "Look at her! By gosh, I didn't come all the way from Boston to see this colt get trimmed."

Bud looked at Chocorua. There she stood, ears back and head hung low, her eyes rolling wickedly at the grooms who toiled over her legs. She was fresh no longer.

Randall nodded at Bill in full agreement.

"Now look here, boy," said the veteran driver to Bud. "It would ruin some horses to give 'em the punishment that Cedar's takin' today. But I know him. Know his blood. Know his trainin'. He'll stand it. You beat the mare an' you've *won*!"

"Wh-what?" Bud gasped.

"Sure!" put in Amos. "It'll be decided on points. Take a look at that board, front o' the judges' stand."

Bud's eye followed his pointing finger, and a gust of hope swept through him. The board on the pavilion read:

	First Heat	Second Heat	Third Heat
Saco Boy	1	3	—
Chocorua	3	1	—
Cedar	2	2	—

85

To put a figure "1" after Cedar's name in the third heat would give him a first and two seconds, while the best either of the others could make would be a first, a second, and a third.

With Long Bill helping him, Bud bent down and redoubled his efforts on the colt's legs. As he worked he whispered to the brave young horse over and over, that this time he *must*, and he felt Cedar's soft lips fumbling playfully at his ear.

The stand was in an uproar when the red colt and the roan mare went back for the final heat. But through the shouting Bud heard a deep, familiar bark and looked up to see the white terrier between Uncle John and Cal. The farmer was bent forward, his face gray and strained, and Cal was giving vent to shrill yells of encouragement. Bud waved a stiff mitten and went on as if in a dream.

Driven whirls of snow were cutting their faces as the jockeys turned above the start once more. Men along the track were huddled close together for warmth and thrashing their arms to shake off the numbness. It was blowing hard, and Bud knew the temperature must be near zero.

There were only two of them left to race, for Saco Boy had been withdrawn. Bud looked down the track through the white storm that hid the far-off grandstand and the town. The wind had swung to the northeast now, and into it they must go. The boy gathered the reins. Cedar's red haunches quivered into action. For the last time they crossed the starting-line.

How they got down to the half-mile post Bud never knew. The air was full of white, and snow particles bit at his eyelids, half blinding him. He was calling the colt's name again and again and leaning forward, always watching the roan mare's head where she raced alongside.

86

The smoothness was gone out of Cedar's gait. Every tired muscle of him was in revolt, and he was racked with a mighty effort at every stride. Yet on and on he held and never slackened. Into the final hundred yards they came at last, with the lean gray head still on their flank. And now the sorrel labored hard, his sides all streaked with frozen sweat, his head and neck stretched out. But he paced on with weary legs.

Cut by the whip, the mare came up desperately, inch by inch. Bud knew that no whip could better the valiant fight the red pacer was making. "Cedar—Cedar, boy!" he cried, and to the anguish of his voice some last reserve of the colt's great heart responded, for his nose was still beyond Chocorua's when they lunged under the line of the wire.

A S far back as he could remember, Ray Rand had loved the woods; and about the time he was ten years old he had decided to spend his life in them. This determination did not waver as time advanced; but from his early dreams of being a hermit or a trapper, he turned to an earnest, whole-hearted desire to enter the forestry service, not as a second-rate man, but as a college graduate with an M.F. (Master of Forestry) after his name.

It takes money to go to college, especially to a high-class forestry college, and there was very, very little money in the Rand family. Ray was seventeen when he graduated from high school, a time when a boy's life must necessarily take a turn, for he either goes to college then or he never goes, as a rule. Sometimes circumstances force the decision, but more often it depends on the boy himself.

When Ray graduated he had less than ten dollars of his own, but he had an abundance of clean, solid grit. Searching the papers for a summer's job, he found an announcement by the chief for-

Knob Mountain Tower

BY MERRITT

P. ALLEN

Illustrated by

Raymond Lufkin

ester of the Adirondack Mountain region that a man was wanted to watch for forest fires from the Knob Mountain lookout-station. The salary was one hundred dollars a month and camp. It sounded good, and eventually Ray appeared in the chief forester's office.

"What can I do for you?" the broad-shouldered, keen-eyed official asked.

"I am applying for the Knob Mountain job."

"Know what it is like?"

"No, sir; but I think I can watch for fires."

"It is a man-sized job, son. The work isn't much, but it is the solitude that gets you, unless you like it. I seldom get a man to stay the season through. It is seven miles straight back in the woods. There are no camps near, and you are not allowed to leave your post night or day. There is a telephone, but you don't use it for pleasure, since it only runs to this office. Twice a month we send a man up with supplies, and I drop in occasionally; you will probably see no other persons until you come out in the fall."

"I like the woods," Ray said. "I shouldn't be lonesome."

The chief looked doubtful. "Why not get a pal to go with you?" he suggested. "You could make a camping-trip out of it and have considerable fun, alternate the work and divide the wages."

Ray shook his head. "I need all the money," he said.

The chief's face became thoughtful, for he had once been a boy in need of money.

"What's the idea?" he asked kindly.

Ray told him.

The chief smiled. "Want to enter the service, eh? Well, that puts a different face on the matter. I guess, after all, there is no reason why you shouldn't have the job."

Within a week, Ray was established on Knob Mountain with two weeks' provisions, a few books, a clock, a camera, and a light rifle of his own, besides the professional equipment provided by the service. His camp was the watch-tower itself. It was of steel, round, and rose twenty feet above the rocks of the mountain peak. The ground floor was a tiny kitchen, the next a sleeping-room, and the third and top, the observation-post. Such a view! On clear days Ray could see through the

89

binoculars hundreds and thousands of acres of land and water, deep forest for the most part, except for occasional small valley clearings and lakes, and on the east, the long, glistening expanse of Lake Champlain. When the sun was just right, the spires of Montreal glistened a hundred and more miles to the north; and at night, lights, none nearer than seven miles, twinkled here and there below.

Over this mighty tract it was Ray's duty to watch and, should smoke appear, to locate it as best he could on his maps and telephone the news to the chief's office. There was plenty of rain that season, and he had but two small fires to report.

The chief called up frequently, partly to keep in touch with the boy to whom he had taken a fancy, and partly in an attempt to catch him away from his post. But he never did; for though Ray longed to steal away for a ramble in the woods, he always kept within sound of the telephone-bell as he had promised to do. A man came up with fresh supplies once a fortnight, and the chief dropped in unannounced three or four times; but aside from them, Ray saw no one except at a distance through the glasses.

On a sleepy afternoon in August, the chief was on the wire. "I am going to be away for a few days," he said, among other things. "If anything happens, ask for Mr. Adams who will be in charge here."

"Yes, sir," Ray answered. And after more talk, he asked as usual, "Any news?"

"No. Oh, yes! the Lake Placid bank was robbed last night of a hundred thousand in cash. The police think the thieves got away through Malone. That's all. Good-by."

Lake Placid, the famous summer resort, was not so very

far away, about fifteen miles through the woods to the south-west, but hidden from the Knob tower by an interposing mountain. The robbery was of no consequence to Ray, but for some reason it was so much in his thoughts after that, that at first he believed it to be a dream when he was awakened in the night by a light and opened his eyes to see three men in his room, one with a drawn revolver.

"Get up," the man commanded, "and find us some grub."

"Who are you?" Ray asked, knowing it was no dream.

"Never mind that."

Ray looked about quickly.

"We've got your rifle," the man said. "No use making a fuss. Get up!"

Ray got up, dressed, and went downstairs between two of the men. Without a word, he set out some provisions, and the

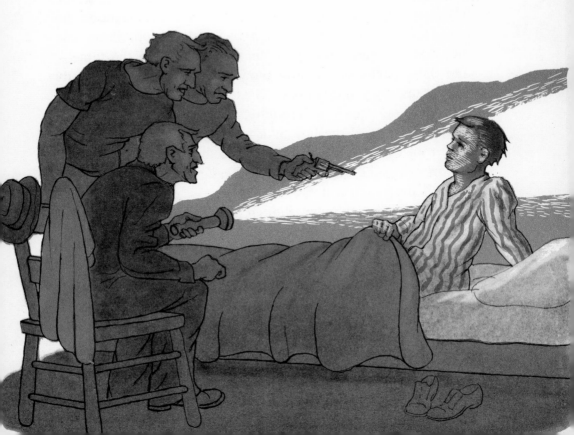

men ate hungrily, one of them standing guard at the door and all of them casting frequent glances at three canvas packs on the floor. When they finished, dawn was breaking, and he could see their faces better—cruel, hard faces.

"Climb!" the leader said suddenly, pointing up the stairs with his revolver. "Go clean to the top and stay there, or I'll shoot you down like a hedgehog." And there was no doubt but that he meant it.

Ray went up the stairs obediently, for there was nothing else to do; he stood no show against three armed men.

"He can't signal from there, can he?" one asked anxiously.

"No," another answered. "Nothing there but the 'phone. I know these places."

Ray went up through his bedroom to the observation-post, and, looking through the window, saw, as he expected to, the severed telephone-wires dangling from their rock-propped pole a hundred feet away. He went back to the head of the stairs. The two flights were in line, so that from where he stood, he could look directly down on the table on the ground floor. The men were dumping the three canvas packs upon the table— and those packs were full of money. Gold, silver, but mostly banknotes, lay in a great pile. The leader glanced up suddenly, saw Ray, and, quick as lightning, snatched his gun and fired. The bullet missed the boy by a few inches, glanced from the steel roof over his head, and crashed through a window. Not a word was said, and none was necessary. Ray tumbled back out of range and sat down.

He had seen enough, though, to tell him that those men were the bank-robbers who, instead of going through Malone, had fled straight into the woods. While the police were searching every car on the highways and railways, the bandits were counting their loot on the mountain-top. Only one person be-

92

sides themselves knew this, and that one was cooped up in the top of a steel tower, helpless.

There was no possible way of getting down, for the outside of the tower was smooth, and to jump the twenty feet to the rocks below would mean a broken leg if nothing more. There was nothing to do but wait; so he waited. If only some one would happen along! He took up his post by the window, and about noon could scarcely believe his eyes when up the trail came the man who brought his supplies.

Regardless of the circumstances, Ray leaned as far out as he dared and shouted wildly: "The men who robbed the Lake Placid bank are downstairs. They will shoot. Run!"

The man stopped in his tracks, then came on again; and out of the tower door calmly walked the leader to meet him. They were in league!

Ray sank back in dismay. His last hope was gone. There was not one chance in a thousand that another person would come that way. How long would the bandits stay in the tower? What would they do with him? They dare not let him go. Would they kill him? They looked capable of it. Whatever they did, it would not be pleasant.

Ray could hear them talking, and, dropping flat on the floor, put his ear as near the head of the stairs as he dared and listened. The supply man was relating how the search was progressing, which was the very reason for which he had been planted in the village below. The fact that they were supposed to have gone west or north pleased the men immensely, and in louder and more confident tones they began outlining their plans. At dark they would go down into separate valleys, and the next day, passing as trampers, would go to the nearest railroad points and get away by train. The supply man would go back as usual, but would soon receive a telegram saying that

93

his brother was dead in New York, after which, of course, he might be expected to depart hurriedly. "And the boy?" some one asked. They would tie him up and leave him, they decided. It might mean his death by starvation, but they couldn't help it. Ray shivered.

After a while the supply man left the others and came up the two flights of stairs.

"Make out a list of the things you want brought up next time," he said. "I'm going down about three o'clock."

He made no attempt to explain his friendship with the bandits. Ray wondered if the man thought him fool enough to be unable to put two and two together. At any rate, he decided to be as taciturn as the next one and merely agreed to have the list ready.

The man went downstairs again, and shortly after, Ray heard the tower door shut and the key turn on the outside. Looking down from his window he saw the supply man and two others spreading blankets and coats on the rocks in the shade of the tower. They were tired after their night's work and lay down heavily. Evidently the leader preferred a softer couch, for Ray heard him coming up the first flight of stairs; then the cot in the tiny bedroom creaked, and soon all was still below.

The boy sat down to think, and decided that rather than be tied in the tower to die by inches, perhaps he would jump to the rocks, when the time came, and take his chances, slim as they were. As he laid his plans the only sound was the ticking of his alarm-clock on a shelf beside him. It was a very small clock, which he had bought because it could be easily packed up the mountains, thicker, but not much more in diameter, than a watch. It had a modest tick, for a clock, but when it was aroused, it *would* ring!

94

Ray's thoughts turned idly to this clock; and of a sudden he had an idea. He pondered it for a full two minutes, then, looking down again and making sure that the men outside the tower were sound asleep, he stole to the stairs and peered into his bedroom. The bandit leader was sleeping furiously. The boy went back for the clock and holding it carefully in his hands, began descending the stairs very, very cautiously. His heart was in his throat, for he knew that if he awoke the man, he might be shot. He reached the floor, and, not daring to pause, so precious was every fraction of a second, crept past the cot on his tiptoes and so on down to the ground floor.

The three packs full of money were on the table and he had a great desire to open them, but he knew that time was more precious than money, and went about his work. Moving silently as a ghost, he took down a good-sized tin can partly full of dried hulled corn, emptied two thirds of the corn out on the table, leveled off the remainder inside the can, and on this corn placed an empty cocoa can. Taking a pencil and a leaf from his note book, he wrote:

The three men who robbed the Lake Placid bank are in the Knob tower with the money. They will leave at dark, separately, for railroad stations. The man who brings me supplies is in with them and will get away tonight if you don't nab him. Telephone wires are cut and I am a prisoner in the tower.

Ray Rand

This note he placed in the small can inside the larger one, then, taking up the little clock, he wound it and set the alarm at half-past five. Smiling a little, he placed the clock upon the note, put the cover on the cocoa can, then proceeded to bury it completely with the corn from the table. He felt the weight of the large can in his hands, held it close to his ear in an attempt to detect the clock's ticking, then set it back on the shelf, confident that on one could guess that it contained anything but the article advertised on its outside. Three minutes later he was safely back upstairs.

"Got that list ready?" the supply man called up from the kitchen an hour later.

Ray dropped it down to the man, who eyed it sharply to see that it contained no hidden message, then put it in his pocket.

"I wish that you would take back that package of hulled corn and tell the merchant you got it of that I ordered pop-corn," Ray said to him.

"I ain't going to fuss with that," the man growled.

96

RAYMOND
LUFKIN

"Take it along," the leader commanded. "It will make things look more natural."

"Well, where is it?"

Ray directed him to the shelf and held his breath while he took down the can and thrust it into his pack-basket. But the man suspected nothing and soon started away.

It was already dark in the valleys when the bandit chief ordered Ray to come down. As the boy stepped into the kitchen he was seized, and in two minutes was bound hand and foot and laid on the floor.

"You're a gritty chap," the leader said, standing over him in the darkness. "I hate to leave you this way, but we must get

97

away and don't want you telling what you know too soon. If things go right, I may be able to send you help in two or three days. I will leave a dish of water and some food on the floor and perhaps you can get enough of it to keep you going."

Two or three days or a week to remain bound, with only a little food and water picked off the floor, dog fashion! He might never be found until it was too late. He wished then that he had jumped to the rocks as he had planned.

"We'll be moving," the bandit said to the others. "You know where to go from here."

Silently they picked up their precious packs and stepped out into the darkness. Then came the sound of many feet, blows, a couple of shots, and presently a big voice boomed:

"Got 'em tied up, boys? Anybody hurt? Good! Now where's Rand?"

"Here!" Ray shouted, "inside!"

Two electric torches flashed through the doorway. A man wearing a sheriff's badge entered and cut Ray's bonds.

"There's your friends," he said, pointing outside, where the robbers were nicely handcuffed and guarded by a dozen men. "We got the other one down in the village. Found your note, you see. And say! that was a mighty bright idea fixing the alarm-clock as you did. I happened to be in the store when the fellow brought in that hulled corn. The clerk set it back on the shelf, and a few minutes later—*rippity bang!* We couldn't think what was up till we dug into the corn and found the little clock going like a cyclone. And there was the note under it! Best thing I ever heard of. Say, I guess you'll come in for a fat slice of the reward."

Ray did come in for his share of it, and later, after the chief had heard the story, he received a scholarship to a forestry school that is second to none. He is there now.

THE word massacre filled the white settlers with terror.

"The Indians are coming! The Indians are coming!" Without waiting to hear more, people packed what belongings they could carry and started the long journey back East. Others armed themselves as best they could for the attack and gathered together in groups, knowing that there was strength in numbers. Sometimes, leaving the women and children at home, the men went out to attack the Indians, preferring to strike first rather than be scalped in their beds later. Fear spread like a disease, nourished on rumors and race hatred. For many years now the whites had lived at peace with the Indians of western Wisconsin, but so great was this disease of fear that even a tavern rumor could spread it like an epidemic throughout the country.

Massacree!

BY CAROL RYRIE BRINK

Illustrated by Kate Seredy

After one such rumor people began arriving at the Woodlawn farm from all directions. They came bringing what food and bedding they could carry. They did not know how soon they would dare return to their homes, nor whether they would find anything but a heap of charred sticks when they did return. Of course, school was not to be thought of, and, in spite of the general fear, the children were delighted with the unexpected holiday.

With shouts of joy the young Woodlawns greeted Maggie and Silas Bunn, Jane and Sam Flusher, and Lida Silbernagle. Katie and her mother came, too. Katie's eyes were round with alarm, and she kept close in the shadow of her mother's hoop skirt. The other children played I-spy around the barn and farmyard, their pleasure keenly edged by the nearness of danger.

Mrs. Woodlawn was in her element. She loved a gathering of people, and one of her great griefs in Wisconsin was that she saw so few outside her own family. Now she had all the neighbors here, and could herself serve them beans such as none but she, outside of Boston, knew how to bake, and slices of turkey which had their proper due of praise at last. Happy in the necessity of the moment, she did not let her mind dwell on the danger from the Indians.

Caddie helped, too, but after she had broken a dish and spilled applesauce over the kitchen floor, her mother told her that she had better run and play; and Caddie ran.

The day wore slowly on, and nothing unusual happened. The children tired of their games and sat together in the barn, huddled in the hay for warmth, talking together in low voices.

The night came, gray and quiet, slipping uneventfully into darkness. The February air had a hint of spring in it. Would the promise of spring ever be fulfilled for them? Or would the Indians come?

After dark, sentries were stationed about the farmhouse to keep watch during the night, and the women and children made their beds on the floor of the parlor after the bedrooms were filled. No one undressed that night, and fires were kept burning in the kitchen and dining room for the men to warm themselves by when they changed their sentry duty. Windows were shuttered and lanterns covered or shaded when carried outside. A deep silence settled over the farm. They did not wish to draw the Indians' attention by needless noise or light.

But the night passed as the day had passed and nothing fearful happened. The children awoke stiff and aching and rubbed the sleep out of their eyes, surprised to find themselves lying in such queer places.

But the second day was worse than the first. People were restless and undecided. Should they go home or should they stay on? The food supplies they had brought with them were giving out. They could not let the Woodlawns exhaust all their supplies in feeding them. Yet the redskins might only be awaiting the moment when they should scatter again to their homes to begin the attack. It was a gray, dark day, not designed to lift anybody's spirits. A fine mist, almost but not quite like rain, hung in the air and curtained all horizons in obscurity.

The women and the little children, crowded into the farmhouse, were restless and tired of confinement. The men paced back and forth in the farmyard, or stopped in groups beneath the four pine trees that sheltered the front of the house, and which Father had named for Clara, Tom, Caddie, and Warren. The men polished and cleaned and oiled their guns, smoked their pipes, and spat into the mud which their boots had churned in the tidy dooryard. Everyone felt that the strain of waiting had become almost unbearable.

In the afternoon a few of the men went to get more supplies. The others watched them go, fearful and yet somehow relieved to see any stir of life along the road.

"Caddie," said Mrs. Woodlawn, "go fetch me a basket of turnips from the cellar, please." Caddie slipped on her coat, took up the basket, and went outside where the cellar door sloped back against the ground at the side of the house. She had to brush by a group of men to get into the cellar. They were talking earnestly together, their faces dark with anger and excitement.

"It is plagued irksome to wait," one of them was saying as Caddie brushed past.

She went into the cellar and filled her basket. "Yes, it's irksome to wait," she said to herself, "but I don't know what they mean to do about it. They'd be sorry enough if the Indians came."

But what they meant to do about it was suddenly plain to her as she came up the stairs again with the turnips.

"The thing to do is to attack the Indians first," one man was saying. Caddie stopped still in her tracks, listening unashamed.

"Yes," said a second man. "Before they come for us, let us strike hard. I know where John and his Indians are camped up the river. Let's wipe them out. The country would be better without them, and then we could sleep peacefully in our beds at night."

"But the rumor came from farther west. Killing John's tribe would not destroy the danger," objected a third man.

"It would be a beginning. If we kill or drive these Indians out, it will be a warning to the others that we deal hard with redskins here."

Caddie set her basket down upon the stair. It suddenly seemed too heavy for her to hold. Massacre! Were the whites to massacre the Indians then? A sick feeling swept across her heart. Surely this was worse than the other. As if her thought had occurred to the first speaker, but in a more agreeable light, he said: "Let them say the men of Dunnville massacree the Indians, instead of waiting to be massacreed!"

"Woodlawn will be against it," said the more cautious third man.

"Woodlawn puts too much faith in the Indians. If we can get enough men to our way of thinking, we need not consult

Woodlawn. I don't believe in caution when our lives are in danger. Wipe out the Indians, is what I say. Don't wait for them to come and scalp us. Are you with me?"

White and trembling, Caddie slipped past them. The men paid no attention to the little girl who had left her basket of turnips standing on the cellar steps. They went on talking angrily among themselves, enjoying the sound of their boastful words. Caddie went to the barn and into the stalls. There she hesitated a moment. Pete was faster than Betsy, but he was not so trustworthy. When he didn't want to go, he would run under a shed or low branch and scrape off his rider. Nothing must delay her today. Caddie slipped a bridle over Betsy's head. She was trembling all over. There was something she must do now, and she was afraid. She must warn John and his Indians. She was certain in her heart that they meant the whites no harm, and the whites were going to kill them. Good John, who had given her the little calico and buckskin doll with its coarse horsehair braids!

Oh, for Tom and Warren now! But they were gone with the men for supplies. Oh, for Father, who was always so wise and brave! But she could not wait for him to come back to tell him what he would never believe about his neighbors, unless he had heard it himself.

Caddie flung herself on Betsy's back and dug heels into her flanks. She was away across the field and into the dripping wood. The gray mist was turning into fine rain. There was still snow in the wood and there would still be ice on the river.

There was no proper sunset that day, only a sudden, lemon-colored rift in clouds in the west. Then the clouds closed together again and darkness began to fall. The ride was long, but at last it was over.

Blue with cold, Caddie rode into the clearing where the

Indians had built their winter huts. Dogs ran at her, barking, and there was a warm smell of smoke in the air. A fire was blazing in the center of the clearing. Dark figures moved about it. Were they in war paint and feathers? Caddie's heart pounded as she drew Betsy to a stop. But, no, surely they were only old women bending over cooking pots. The running figures were children, coming now to swarm about her. There was no war paint! No feathers! Surely she and Father had been right! Tears began to trickle down Caddie's cold cheeks. Now the men were coming out of the bark huts. More and more Indians kept coming toward her. But they were not angry, only full of wonder.

"John," said Caddie, in a strange little voice, which she hardly recognized as hers. "Where is John? I must see John."

"John," repeated the Indians, recognizing the name the white men had given to one of their braves. They spoke with strange sounds among themselves, then one of them went running. Caddie sat her horse, half-dazed, and cold to the bone.

Indian John's tall figure came toward her from one of the huts. His step was unhurried and his eyes were unsurprised.

"You lost, Missee Red Hair?" he inquired.

"No, no," said Caddie, "I am not lost, John. But I must tell you. Some white men are coming to kill you. You and your people must go away. You must not fight. You must go away. I have told you."

"You cold," said John. He lifted Caddie off her horse and led her to the fire.

"No understan'," said John, shaking his head in perplexity. "Speak too quick, Missee Red Hair."

Caddie tried again, speaking more slowly. "I came to tell you. Some bad men wish to kill you and your people. You

104

must go away, John. My father is your friend. I came to warn you."

"Red Beard, he send?" asked John.

"No, my father did not send me," said Caddie. "No one knows that I have come. You must take your people and go away."

"You hungry?" John asked her and mutely Caddie nodded her head. Tears were running again and her teeth were chattering. John spoke to the squaws, standing motionless about the fire. Instantly they moved to do his bidding. One spread a buffalo skin for her to sit on. Another ladled something hot and tasty into a cup without a handle, a cup which had doubtless come from some settler's cabin. Caddie grasped the hot cup between her cold hands and drank. A little trickle of warmth seemed to go all over her body. She stretched her hands to the fire. Her tears stopped running and her teeth stopped chattering.

"You tell John 'gain," said John, squatting beside her in the firelight.

Caddie began again slowly. She told how the whites had heard that the Indians were coming to kill. She told how her father and she had not believed. She told how some of the people had become restless and planned to attack the Indians first. She begged John to go away with his tribe while there was still time. When she had finished John grunted and continued to sit on, looking into the fire. She did not know whether he had yet understood her. All about the fire were row on row of dark faces, looking at her steadily with wonder but no understanding. John knew more English than any of them, and yet, it seemed, he did not understand. Patiently she began to explain again.

But now John shook his head. He rose and stood tall in

106

the firelight above the little white girl. "You come," he said.

Caddie rose uncertainly. She saw that it was quite dark now outside the ring of firelight, and a fine, sharp sleet was hissing down into the fire. John spoke in his own tongue to the Indians. What he was telling them she could not say, but their faces did not change. One ran to lead Betsy to the fire and another brought a spotted Indian pony that had been tethered at the edge of the clearing.

"Now we go," said the Indian.

"I will go back alone," said Caddie, speaking distinctly. "You and your people must make ready to travel westward."

"Red Hair has spoken," said John. "John's people go tomorrow." He lifted her onto her horse's back, and himself sprang onto the pony. Caddie was frightened again, frightened of the dark and cold, and uncertain of what John meant to do.

"I can go alone, John," she said.

"John go too," said the Indian.

He turned his pony into the faint woods trail by which

she had come. Betsy, her head drooping under a slack rein, followed the spotted pony among the dark trees. Farther and farther behind, they left the warm, bright glow of fire. Looking back, Caddie saw it twinkling like a bright star. It was something warm and friendly in a world of darkness and sleet and sudden, icy branches. From the bright star of the Indian fire, Caddie's mind leaped forward to the bright warmth of home. They would have missed her by now.

She bent forward against Betsy's neck, hiding her face from the sharp needles of sleet. It seemed a very long way back. But at last the branches no longer caught at her skirts. Caddie raised her head and saw that they had come out on the open river bank. She urged Betsy forward beside the Indian pony.

"John, you must go back now. I can find my way home. They would kill you if they saw you."

John only grunted. He set his moccasined heels into the pony's flanks, and led the way onto the ice. Betsy shook herself with a kind of shiver all through her body, as if she were saying, "No! no! no!" But Caddie's stiff fingers pulled the rein tight and made her go. The wind came down the bare sweep of the river with tremendous force, cutting and lashing them with the sleet. Betsy slipped and went to her knees, but she was up again at once and on her way across the ice. Caddie had lost the feeling of her own discomfort in fear for John. If a white man saw him riding toward the farm tonight, he would probably shoot without a moment's warning. Did John understand that? Was it courage or ignorance that kept John's figure so straight, riding erect in the blowing weather?

"John!" she cried. But the wind carried her voice away. "John!" But he did not turn his head.

Up the bank, through the woods, to the edge of the clearing they rode, Indian file. Then the Indian pony stopped.

Caddie drew Betsy in beside him. "Thank you!" she panted. "Thank you, John, for bringing me home. Go, now. Go quickly." Her frightened eyes swept the farmstead. It was not dark and silent as it had been the night before. Lanterns were flashing here and there, people were moving about, voices were calling.

"They're starting out after the Indians!" thought Caddie. "Father hasn't been able to stop them. They're going to massacre."

She laid her cold hand on the spotted pony's neck. "John!" she cried. "John, you must go quickly now!"

"John go," said the Indian, turning his horse.

But before the Indian could turn back into the woods, a man had sprung out of the darkness and caught his bridle rein.

"Stop! Who are you? Where are you going?" The words snapped out like the cracking of a whip, but Caddie knew the voice.

"Father!" she cried. "Father! It's me. It's Caddie!"

"You, Caddie? Thank God!" His voice was full of warm relief. "Hey, Robert, bring the lantern. We've found her. Caddie! My little girl!"

Suddenly Father was holding her close in his arms, his beard prickling her cheek.

"Oh, Father," cried Caddie, remembering again her mission and the last uncomfortable hours, "Father, don't let them kill John! Don't let them do anything bad to the Indians. The Indians are our friends, Father, truly they are. I've been to the camp and seen them. They mean us no harm."

"You went to the Indian camp, Caroline?"

"Yes, Father."

"That was a dangerous thing to do, my child."

"Yes, Father, but some of the men meant to go and kill them. I heard them say so. They said they wouldn't tell you they were going, and you weren't there. Oh, Father, what else could I do?"

He was silent for a moment, and Caddie stood beside him, shivering, and oppressed by the weight of his disapproval. Father's brows were knit in thought, John's dark face impassive and remote.

Caddie could bear the silence no longer. "Father, the Indians are our friends," she repeated.

"Is this true, John?" asked Father.

"Yes, true, Red Beard," answered John gravely.

"My people fear yours, John. Many times I have told them that you are our friends. They do not always believe."

"My people foolish sometime, too," said John. "Not now. They no kill white. Red Beard my friend."

"He brought me home, Father," said Caddie. "You must not let them kill him."

"No, no, Caddie. There shall be no killing tonight, nor any more, I hope, forever."

Over her head the white man and the red man clasped hands.

"I keep the peace, John," said Father. "The white men shall be your brothers."

"Red Beard has spoken. John's people keep the peace."

For a moment they stood silent, their hands clasped in the clasp of friendship, their heads held high like two proud chieftains. Then John turned to his pony. He gathered the slack reins, sprang on the pony's back and rode away into the darkness.

DONALD slipped out of the firelit circle so quietly that none of the laughing men noticed his going. He went to Henri's canoe, rolled himself in his own beaverskin robe, and lay down beneath the canoe with his face toward the river. Above his bed, Beacon Rock towered nine hundred feet high, like a giant sentinel keeping unceasing watch over the broad River of the West. This was better. It was quiet here. He could think his own thoughts, and, perhaps, find answers for the questions in his mind. There were many questions clamoring for answers now that the excitement of the long journey was nearly at an end —questions that he had been able to ignore before, but that cried out now, demanding recognition.

There was this matter of education, for instance. Why must he go away to school? There were schools in the Red River settlement where he had been learning to read and write English, along with French. Why could he not stay there? He didn't know why he must go to Fort Vancouver, but Big Mac had planned that he go. He had planned it when Donald was a very small boy. The plan had something to do with a letter which Big Mac kept locked in a small metal box. Donald had seen him take out that letter and sit for a long time, just looking at it, and he had noticed that his father's face had changed at this time. It had changed to the face of a stranger, hard and cold.

White Cloud's face had changed, too, when she had seen Big Mac looking so, with the letter in his hand, and she had

Young Mac of Fort Vancouver

BY MARY JANE CARR

Illustrated by Richard Holberg

111

slipped out of the house and off into the woods. Donald had wanted to go with her, but she had whispered: "No, no! Stay here with him." Bairn, his big husky dog, had crept after White Cloud, though, stealing along like a shadow through the woods. Big Mac had called Donald to him then, and said:

"You are going to prove that they are wrong, someday, son! Do you understand?"

Donald had answered, "Yes, sir!" But he had not understood—and he didn't understand now. He only said that he understood to make his father happy. Big Mac had put the letter back in the box then, and after a while White Cloud and Bairn were back, and the dark time was over. Big Mac had put money in that box, too. When Donald had asked White Cloud about the letter she had given a strange answer: "You will understand someday, but not now, Petit Amisk." That was her name for him, "Petit Amisk," a combination of French and Cree, which meant Little Beaver. When he had asked about the money, she had answered: "That is to help you grow wise." And he had never inquired further. He did not like to see that sad look in White Cloud's eyes. He understood the sad look and the money now. The money was to send him away to school—away from White Cloud.

Henri had never been away to school, and still there was never a better guide or bowman than he. In all the Hudson's Bay service, no one was in greater demand for difficult and swiftly run passages than Henri. Governor Simpson himself, who required the greatest accuracy and skill in his bowmen, always chose Henri for the head of his canoe when he could get him. The Iroquois Indians, who were the world's finest canoe men, acknowledged Henri their equal on the water.

Then there was White Cloud. She had never been away to school, but surely there was no one wiser than she in the White

112

Man's world, the world to which his father seemed to want him to belong. She knew the language of the Woods and Water Persons, a language that was not taught in books. She made her own songs, too—words and music. And she knew even the secrets of the stars. She was kind and beautiful. Henri's children, Pierre and little Nanette, loved her as much as they loved their own mother. Anyone would love White Cloud. Even Bairn liked to lie at her feet when she sang her songs in French and Cree. She spoke both languages, because she was of both bloods.

Donald wondered now if Bairn missed him much. The dog had been his own for seven years. He recalled clearly the winter night that Bairn came. They had heard something scratching at the door. White Cloud had opened the door and, in a rush of freezing air, a starving female husky, lost or run away from some trapper's sled team, had staggered across the threshold with a puppy held between her jaws. A skinny puppy, all eyes and ribs. The mother's feet were cut and frozer. by long travel on sharp ice, and she was weak from hunger, but she would not eat. She was too far gone—poor brave one! She dropped the puppy before the fire and lay down with a long, shuddering sigh. She never moved again. But the puppy gobbled the food they gave him, and begged for more. Donald named him what his father had called him when he was a little fellow—Bairn, which meant child, in Scotch. His father's name for White Cloud was Bonnie. It meant in Scotch what *chérie* meant in French.

The boy brought himself back to the present with an effort. Tomorrow the York Factory Express would reach Fort Vancouver. The men would dress for their arrival at the fort. He would dress up, too. He would put on his deerskin trousers and shirt and tie a sash around his waist—the scarlet sash that

White Cloud had embroidered for him. He would put on his high-laced painted moccasins, and slip the sharp-bladed hunting knife that had been his father's, in his belt. He would deck Henri's canoe with dyed plumes and ermine tails, and he would hang the insignia of York Factory—a large "Y.F."—on the prow of the canoe, just below the flag bearing the motto of the Hudson's Bay Company, *"Pro Pelle Cutem"*—"Skin for Skin." He would lead the boatmen in song as they swept down the river toward the fort landing. He would sing louder than he had ever sung. He would jump on shore before the canoe touched land, clearing the water with one strong leap. They would all think—the people of the post—Dr. McLoughlin, too: "He is a true son of the North, this Young Mac!"

And only he would know better. He would know that down in his heart where only he could see, he was not truly brave. He was afraid of this strange sky with no friendly bright-bannered aurora in it; of this land that was green even in the winter time, that was never buried for wonderful months of skiing and sleighing, under mountains of snow; of this lonely world, with no White Cloud, no Henri, no little Nanette, no Pierre, no Bairn. He could never earn the Northman feather.

Donald put his head under the beaverskin robe. The soft fur brushed his cheek like a gentle hand. He whispered an ancient Cree supplication, part of his own medicine song which White Cloud had made for him: "Brother Beaver, give me your brave heart!" But the ache in his throat did not lessen. He kept his head under the robe. In the shadow of the canoe, he was hidden from sight of the men, but it was best to take no chances. He would have died if they had seen the tears on his cheeks—the shameful tears of a pork eater. And finally, while the *voyageurs'* fire burned low, and the round white moon climbed high above the towering rocks that lined the opposite

114

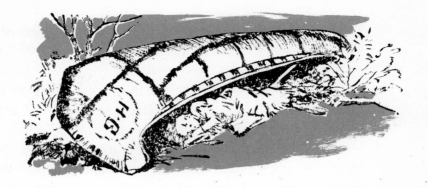

shore, and spilled her silver down on the broad bosom of the
Columbia, Donald MacDermott fell asleep.

Donald was awakened by a low snarl which he recognized
even before he was fully aroused, as the snarl of a timber wolf,
dreaded by all wilderness travelers. His hand closed quickly on
his gun which lay on the ground beside him. He lifted his head
cautiously and peered out. He listened, scarcely breathing.
Had he only dreamed that threatening snarl? It had seemed to
come from near at hand, but now there was not a sound to be
heard, other than the out-of-door sounds familiar along water-
ways at night—the rustle of wind in the branches, the soft lap
of waves against the shore. The camp lay quiet and peaceful in
the moonlight. The bed of coals that had been the campfire
drew his eyes. Those heaps on the ground near the fire were
the cooks, Baptiste Lucerne and André Tremaine, sprawled
under their blankets, their feet to the warmth. In chill weather
the men all slept close to the fires, but this night air was pleasant and the *voyageurs* lay scattered around the camp, some in
the open and some under shelter of their upturned canoes.
George Nelson's deerskin tent showed clear and white against
a background of young evergreens. The boy was surprised to
see that no one was on guard duty. Did they believe this country so safe, then?

115

Donald's eyes sought for the sleeping place of Henri. He was relieved to see his friend lying only a few yards away, rolled in his Hudson's Bay blanket. Henri never slept under a canoe unless it was storming. He didn't want walls of any kind around him when he was "on the march." It was a habit of self-protection he had formed in dangerous Indian country long ago. No matter how sharp a man's eyes might be, Henri said, they couldn't see through wood, and an upturned canoe was too handy a screen for a red man, bent on mischief. Too, Henri slept with his ears wide open. He would have been aroused the first thing if any intruder, human or animal, had been prowling around the camp. That snarl must have been only part of a dream.

Donald's tense hand relaxed its hold on the rifle, and he was about to settle back into the warmth of the beaver-skin robe, when a movement at the foot of his bed jerked him once more into startled attention. In the half-shadow cast by the upturned canoe, his eyes made out the form of a large animal. It was a timber wolf, crouched as if ready to spring. The boy felt a chill, like a cold hand, run along his spine. He hesitated for just a second while the chill shook him; then he snatched his rifle and rose on his elbow, but before he could fire, the animal tottered in a queer manner, and then fell on its side at the foot of the bed. Amazed, Donald lowered his rifle, and stared. The fallen animal didn't move. It appeared to be dead, although no shot had been fired! Cautiously, the incredulous boy drew himself to a sitting position and gently prodded the quiet figure with the barrel of his rifle. There was no response. Then a smothered laugh from in back of the canoe brought swift suspicion. The animal *was* dead! Its lifeless body had been propped up there as a joke on him! Donald leaped over the prostrate wolf, and peered behind the canoe. Sure enough,

116

there was Jacques Colbert and Baptiste Lucerne, kneeling on the ground and shaking with smothered laughter.

"Shhh!" whispered Jacques, his finger on his lip. "Make no noise to wake that wolf, Young Mac! She is one big bad devil-wolf, *non*?"

"Ho, little brother!" gasped Baptiste. "What are you doing out with your gun at midnight? Not hunting, surely?"

Suddenly the whole camp seemed to break into laughter. The boy turned to see figures rising from the ground all over the camp, and he knew that the men had been only pretending sleep and waiting to see how the joke on him had turned out.

At first a wave of anger swept over Donald, but it passed as quickly as it had come. He was conscious of a little glow of pride. They had all seen that he was not a coward! To be aroused from a sound sleep to find a snarling wolf at one's bedside—that was enough to frighten any man, surely! He had felt the touch of the cold hand of fear, to be sure, but he had thrown it off. Let them have their fun! They had seen, and they knew that he was no coward! If he had covered his head and called for help—! But not one of them could say that he had shown fear. Resting the butt of his rifle on the ground, the boy folded his arms across his chest, put one foot on the stiff carcass, and faced the laughing camp with an air of triumph.

"Behold!" he cried, in French. "Behold a real hunter!"

The men fell silent to listen.

"You call yourselves hunters!" Donald called out. "You boast of your fine shots! Many times I have heard you brag of how you felled a bear with only one shot! One shot, bah! You have to *shoot* to kill! But Young Mac has only to raise his gun, and the wild animals fall dead from fright! You have just seen it happen!"

Henri's powerful shoulders shook with laughter. Good

enough! Young Mac was swaggering now, in true *voyageur* fashion!

A roar of cheers went up from the men. The boy had turned the tables on them, very neatly, and they were not only willing, but delighted, to acknowledge his victory. Young Mac was truly one of them—a full-fledged *voyageur*. He would have a tall tale of his own to tell now! They clapped one another on the back, and shouted: "Ha! So you thought that you were a hunter, eh? But you have to *shoot* to kill! Bah!"

Henri LeGrand finally silenced their cheers with an upheld hand. The guide went toward Donald, and the men drew near and formed a half circle around the two. The boy's eyes widened, and his heart began to beat quickly, for he saw that Henri held in his hand a plaid ribbon to which a red feather was attached. The men of the brigade were perfectly quiet now, watching their guide and Young Mac.

"Tomorrow," said Henri, "Young Mac's first voyage comes to an end at Fort Vancouver. A long, hard journey, it was, and he complained not once. He took his place at the paddle with the best of you. On the long portage he carried his heavy pack like a man. He ate the greasy rubaboo without a grumble, and when there was nothing in the pots for supper, he pulled his belt tighter, and said not a word, though all his growing bones cried out for food. He sat tight when the canoes shot rapids, and sang to keep up our spirits. Not even at the *Dalles des Morts* (Canyon of the Dead) where the tall white crosses tell of boatmen who died in the boiling water, did he falter. Did any of you see him falter?"

"*Non! Non!*"

"Now you have just seen him frighten a timber wolf to death. Is he not one of us? Is Young Mac not a Northman?"

118

"Oui! Oui!" the *voyageurs* shouted: "Yes! Yes! Behold Young Mac, the Northman!"

"You have learned the creed of the *voyageur*," Henri said to Donald. "The creed that has made the sons of the fur trade able to look death in the face without flinching; to know fear, as all men must know fear, but not to be conquered by fear. To be able to think clearly and quickly. To keep a high heart. It is voted that you have earned the right to wear the feather of a Northman." Henri lifted his arms to place the band on Donald's head, a ribbon with the plaid of Big Mac's clan and a red feather. "So tall the boy has grown!" the man thought. It seemed to him only yesterday that he had swung this lad up to ride on his shoulder along with his own Pierre. "Now then! It is done!" He pressed the headpiece in place. "Have you not something to say, Young Mac?"

"Merci!" said Donald almost in a whisper. He felt that he could not speak above the pounding of his heart.

"Oho!" laughed Henri. "Say more, Young Mac, and say it in English! That is the tongue they use at Fort Vancouver! You are a King George man now!"

Donald turned toward the watching men and saluted them gravely. He spoke in the language that he had not used for a long time, not since Big Mac had spoken it with him: "Thank you! I—I am very proud that you call me one of you. Thank you all. I am sorry that I cannot go on with you—but I shall keep forever the red feather to remind me that I am a Northman. And—some day we will go on another voyage—together."

The night air rang with the applause of the brigade men. In the midst of their cheering, Jacques and Baptiste scurried up a tree, as agilely as squirrels.

119

"But, you two! Where are you going?" Henri shouted after them.

"We go to cut a lobstick!" Baptiste shouted back, and Jacques' voice called, as branches showered from the tree: "Yes! We mark forever the spot where Young Mac, a *real* hunter, saved his brothers from the fierce devil-wolf!" *Voyageur*-fashion, the story was growing tall!

"A lobstick for Young Mac, of course!" the men agreed, several of them leaping to join the two at work in the tree, and before long a tree was shorn of its branches with the exception of a tuft at the very top, a sign to all who would come that way that some event, important in *voyageur* history, had happened on this spot.

Long after the silence of sleep had settled down on the camp, Young Mac lay awake. He had something precious to keep forever now—the Northman feather, a talisman of courage. Yes, and this night he had gained something more, something that would enable him to wear the badge of honor with pride, an understanding that had come to him with Henri's words—

"To know fear, as all men must know fear; but not to be conquered by fear."

He understood now that it was not unmanly to feel fear and to be lonely. It was unmanly to let fear and loneliness conquer one. The great men of the fur trade, the strongest ones, perhaps all had known fear and been very sick at heart sometimes, in the wild, isolated countries where they had to spend months—years—of their lives.

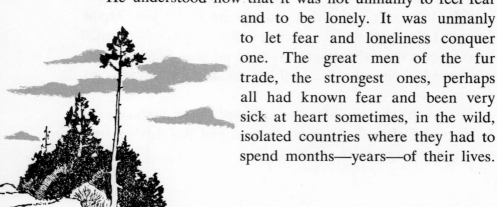

George Simpson, who was governor-in-chief of all the far-flung Hudson's Bay territories, and who was known as a man of iron, who ruled other men with a rod of iron, perhaps even he had known times when he wanted to run away from all the hardships. This Dr. John McLoughlin of Fort Vancouver, whom they called the King of the Columbia, because the thousands of Indians there feared and obeyed him, maybe he, too, was frightened at times, and felt that it would be easier to weep than to laugh. His own father . . . suddenly, with a clearness that startled him, there came to Donald a memory out of his childhood: he had run in out of the snow where he and Pierre had been playing with Bairn. They had been trying to teach Bairn to draw a sled, when Bairn was still a puppy and didn't want to be taught such serious business. He had run into the house for a piece of harness, and had been sur-prised to see his father sitting there with his face in his hands. He had asked: "Are you asleep?" And his father had looked up with a strange smile and had said something strange:

"Not asleep! I was just remembering. . . ."

The words had small meaning for Donald then, and he forgot them right away. Now when they came back across the years, he understood. His father, far from his home, had been lonely, remembering.

The boy put up his hand and touched the precious head-piece which hung above him, suspended from the canoe. He marked the date well in his mind—October 18, 1832. He would not forget this day when the men of the York Factory Express had voted that he had earned the right to wear the Northman feather. He knew now that he could meet whatever lay ahead with a courageous heart. Tomorrow—Fort Van-couver—let them come!

THE days went by, and the summer adventurers drew nearer and nearer to the mountains. The weather was hot and fine and the air of merriment with which the expedition had begun only deepened with the passing hours. The Governor was a man who could do serious business gaily. They would find out what sort of land lay beyond the mountains which the French were beginning to claim, but they would make a frolic of the adventure if they could. The long line of horses and mules moved leisurely enough. The gentlemen stopped to hunt deer and elk; they sang as they ate and drank beneath the trees. Sometimes they slept at the houses of planters; sometimes in their own tents. Roger grew into the beginnings of manhood, sharing the days with his father and the other men, and Mr. Reid rode with flapping elbows and knees, scarcely noticing his horse so intent was he on the birds that rose about the cornfields standing in full tassel, the snake fences, the hawks wheeling in the blue sky,

The Golden Horseshoe

BY ELIZABETH

COATSWORTH

Illustrated by

Robert Lawson

and the forests of beech and oak, pine, walnut, and sassafras, hung with curtains and festoons of vines, and intersected by narrow game trails.

With every day the character of the country was changing, growing more rolling. Here, Mr. Reid noted, the forest was master, and the century-old truce between the woodland and the field which he had found at Stafford Green was here not yet begun. Instead of mansions, he saw cabins of logs stripped of

122

their bark built in clearings where the stumps still stood ragged in the midst of the corn or served as barbaric fences for the thin cattle, their roots interlacing into a crude barrier. Here man was on sufferance. It was the wilderness that laid down the terms under which he might be allowed to live, a small mean creature, at its fringes. The courage of the men and women whom he saw in the clearings gave Mr. Reid a new admiration for the spirit of mankind; but it was of the wilderness he dreamed— the wilderness that stretched over hill and valley as far as his thought could pierce, still savage and untamed.

Two companies of rangers had joined the Governor, and in the evening Mr. Reid loved to sit by their fires and listen to their stories of adventure in the forests, planning new verses for his ode from the tales they told him.

He also came to sit with the Indians, who liked him but the Raccoon was always quiet and aloof in his presence. The Scotchman seemed unable to break down the boy's shyness, though sometimes he caught the child staring at him with a friendly look, and once or twice he thought, curiously enough, that he caught a gleam of amusement in the boy's eyes.

Raccoon now could walk all day and swing into camp untired. He slept on the bare ground and drank water from his hands and ate sparingly of what he was given. Now he could speak in the Indian language, though with a haltingness that the whites never suspected.

Crouched over the fire, with the darkness like a blanket about his shoulders as he had always dreamed, he talked with his companions, who—now that he had proved himself—were no longer harsh.

"Scarred Wolf, tell me the story of the first Opechancanough, our ancestor," he begged.

Scarred Wolf enjoyed talking to new ears.

"He was a great fighter," he said, "bold as an elk in the fall and cunning as a weasel. He was Powhatan's brother and hated the English. In those days he led twenty-four hundred warriors. It was he who was the hand and mind behind the massacre of the whites that took place many, many moons ago, when he hoped to sweep the last of the pale-faces into the sea from which they came. His dream failed, though he grew to be an old man, so old that he could no longer follow the war trail; but even then he had himself carried on a litter by young braves and still led the fighting."

Raccoon stared off into the faintly stirring shadows. His blood was warrior's blood on both sides, and the first Opechancanough on his litter seemed as real and near as the Admiral Stafford in his flagship who had fought the Spanish.

In these days the Raccoon was learning to live very close to the earth. He heard sounds that he had never heard before. Everything he saw and smelled meant something to him. By the behavior of the birds and squirrels, by the turn of the leaves, by the smallest breaking of a twig, he learned to read what was taking place unseen about him; though even then Scarred Wolf laughed at his ignorance.

"You have been wasting your life indoors and studying out of books made from paper," said the Indian. "That is dead wisdom. Are not the sky, and these trees, better teachers than Mr. Reid? It was from this red earth you were born, and your dust some day will blow on these winds. There is a spirit here that moves in the shadows, and cries out with the voice of the swans, and walks among the trees, and strikes with the arrows of lightning. Empty your heart of pride, and watch, for not a grass-blade moves without a reason and that reason is important for you to learn."

At last there came a day when Scarred Wolf pointed silently from a hilltop and Raccoon had his first sight of the blue ridge of the mountains cutting the sky line. To a child raised in the flat tidewater country it appeared very wonderful to see the land tilted thus against the clouds. The rivers had reached their falls now and narrowed to fresh-water streams in which the tides no longer ran; the road had narrowed, too, to a trail; and instead of coaches with Negro outriders they now met occasional packmen, with their lines of packhorses, trafficking on the wilderness trail, taking in cloth, sugar, rum, tools, and medicines to the scattered cabins, and bringing out the precious beaver skins—tall morose-looking men in coon-skin caps, with guns slung at their saddle-bows and eyes almost as learned in forest lore as Scarred Wolf's own. Governor Spotswood was as courteous to a woodsman as to a great land-owner, and more than once he stopped the pack-trains and invited the packmen to dine with him, giving them such food and drink as they had never tasted before, spread on damask cloths and served on fine china.

It was during one of these trail-side repasts that the rivalry between Rambler and Grenadier was brought to a head. The Governor had been questioning Sam Hutton, a well-known wilderness man, about what he knew of the country beyond the mountains, and after luncheon he had examined some of the fine beaver pelts with which the packhorses were loaded, and in turn showed Sam Hutton the horses of his own expedition.

The packman ran an experienced eye over the animals.

"Nice young horse, that strawberry," he remarked, jerking a thumb at Rambler. The Governor smiled.

"He belongs to young Stafford," he answered. "I should imagine that he is the best horse we have."

"Then you would be mistaken, sir," said his secretary

125

quickly. "He's a good enough horse for one Virginia-bred, I admit, but my Grenadier would show him his place at any distance."

"It's possible, sir," said the Governor with an air of displeasure at the interruption, "but I myself have not such a preference for all things English."

Sam Hutton brought his big hands together in a clap.

"A race, gentlemen!" he exclaimed. "What better chance for a race? I'll bet on the Virginia colt, beaver skins against tobacco at Mr. Byrd's trading house at the falls."

"I'll take you," said Mr. Bridge with an ugly smile.

"If there's to be a race, it must be tomorrow when the horses are rested," said the Governor. "And remember, Mr. Hutton, the laws about betting. We'll pitch camp here, and Mr. Hutton, you and your men must be our guests. Are you willing, Colonel Antony, that your son should race the colt?"

"Roger must answer for himself, sir," said Colonel Antony. "But I know he has long been an admirer of Mr. Bridge's Grenadier, so I believe he will be glad to show him some sport."

Roger bowed eagerly.

In a few minutes it was known throughout the camp that there was to be a race next day, and a hundred wagers were laid, openly among the gentlemen, and secretly among the rangers and Negroes. Even the Indians were interested, and the Raccoon was greatly excited by the news. A quarter-mile through a natural clearing was staked out in preparation, and everyone was airing his knowledge of horseflesh.

After supper the Raccoon felt a strong impulse to look at the two horses, but he was anxious that neither Roger nor young Caesar should see him, so he stood in the shadow of the trees watching the animals in the dusk. Suddenly his attention was caught by voices. A man's voice, which he recognized as Mr. Bridge's, was saying in low urgent tones:

"You will do as I tell you, George, or you'll have cause to regret it. There's no danger to you. Early in the morning before the grooms are up, take two or three strong horsehairs—"

Then the figures moved away, and Raccoon could see the

English secretary leaning towards his Negro groom, urging and explaining something; but what that something was, the Indian boy could not hear, though he followed quietly among the trees trying to come again within earshot.

When the others were all asleep, the Raccoon lay long pondering. Had the secretary only been talking of some charm to help his horse, some harmless superstition? But if so, why did George hold back? No, the Raccoon thought, there must be a danger to Rambler. He could not discuss it with Scarred Wolf, who knew much about deer but little about horses. And at last he fell into a deep sleep still uncertain what Mr. Bridge had meant by his curious words.

It was broad daylight when the Raccoon woke. The Indians had gone so silently that no crackling twig had wakened him. He heard a hunting horn blow and a sound of cheering and knew that it was a signal for the beginning of the race. There was something wrong, he remembered, but he had not been able to guess it; and then, as he sprang up from the ground, the explanation came to him as clearly as though a voice had spoken, and he ran off towards the crowd in the clearing, running with all the swiftness he had learned in these last days.

The crowd was gathered—gentlemen, packmen, rangers, Negroes—looking small against the background of savage and indifferent trees behind them. The horses were already in place, but the Governor was talking with the riders. As the Raccoon ran, he saw Grenadier advance to another position a little farther along the course and knew that the black was being given a handicap because he carried the heavier rider. Raccoon's breath was coming in gasps. He saw Joseph Bentley raise a pistol towards the sky, and at that moment he burst panting through the crowd and threw himself on his knees, on

128

the ground, his quick brown fingers searching above Rambler's nearest hoof, while a volley of surprised exclamations sounded over his head.

"What's this? What's this?" cried Mr. Bentley in a sputter, lowering his pistol uncertainly.

"Give the lad a moment," said the Governor. "Let's see what he is doing."

Rambler, usually impatient of strangers, stood still as the Indian boy crouched beside him.

"What's the trouble?" asked Roger, leaning down from the saddle.

Mr. Bridge rode back scowling.

"Is this delay necessary, sir?" he asked the Governor. "Let someone give that boy a hiding for interrupting his betters."

"Let him alone," said the Governor, who was watching the Indian boy with great interest.

Just as the Raccoon thought that he must be mistaken, his fingers, steady in spite of his nervousness, felt something infinitely narrow and strong fastened tightly above Rambler's left hind hock. Drawing his knife, he severed it, and rose to his feet holding three or four horsehairs that had been knotted above the hoof.

"Ha!" said the Governor. "I have heard of that trick for barely laming a horse. Boy, what do you know of this?"

Raccoon shook his head and tried to escape through the crowd. His one desire now was to get away from the eyes that were looking at him—Roger's and Colonel Antony's, Mr. Reid's and young Caesar's.

But as he turned, the lash of a riding crop came stinging across his face and another blow fell on his shoulder. Mr. Bridge had ridden up to him, and, shouting angrily, "You put it there, yourself, you Indian dog!" was raining blows upon him. It was Mr. Reid who sprang from the crowd and caught the secretary's wrist in his big clumsy hand.

"For shame, sir!" he cried in a passion. "The boy speaks no English. He cannot defend himself."

130

Roger had jumped from Rambler and was running forward white with anger, when the Governor's cool tones cut through the storm.

"Gentlemen, gentlemen!" he said smoothly. "Stop where you are. Mr. Reid, release Mr. Bridge's wrist. He will not strike the boy again. Sir, I am accustomed to being obeyed when I speak.

"Now, gentlemen, we have witnessed the detection of a foul act such as no man of honor would be guilty of. We know that heavy bets were made on this race and must suppose this to be the work of some servant who was deeply interested. We all owe this Indian boy a debt of gratitude, but none more than Mr. Bridge who has been spared the embarrassment of being winner in an unfair race. Mr. Bridge and Roger Stafford, I desire you to shake each other's hands and the race will then be run."

Roger's face flushed and he hesitated as Mr. Bridge, still in the shadow, held out his hand, his teeth showing in a yellow smile.

"Gentlemen!" said the Governor again, and one felt the force that usually lay hidden under his friendliness and merriment.

Unwillingly, Roger put his hand in the other man's, bowed to the Governor, and swung into the saddle in silence. He had not glanced at his father for advice.

"Egad," thought the Colonel, well pleased, "my son is growing into a man, it seems."

Roger sat in his saddle looking straight ahead of him as Mr. Bridge rode past him to the starting point. The pistol spoke and the two horses started forward almost with one bound. For a hundred yards Grenadier held the lead, but Rambler was running as he had never run before.

"Egad," said the Colonel out loud, "it's as though he were as angry as Roger."

The boy's spirit seemed to have passed into the horse—his stride was almost an onslaught, and as he tore by Grenadier he reached sideways towards the other horse with open mouth and only Roger's quick jerk at the rein swept him past his rival and on to the finishing line. There was great applause among all the gathering.

"Virginia forever!" exclaimed the Governor, smiling.

But Roger listened to the congratulations all about him with an absent-minded look. His eyes glanced here and there, but did not find what they were seeking.

"Excuse me, sir," he said to the Governor. "I have an errand I must do."

"I guess what the young man's errand is," said Sam Hutton. "A pretty race, Governor Spotswood, and we wilderness men are mighty obliged to you for letting us see the English horse beaten. Not that fine things don't come out of England, like yourself, sir, and none finer, if you'll excuse the liberty, sir."

The Governor smiled and turned to Mr. Bridge who had ridden up. His eyes hardened at seeing Grenadier's sides bloodied by the spurs. The secretary was still riding with a heavy hand on the curb.

"Do not blame your horse, Mr. Bridge," said the Governor, still politely. "He is not accustomed yet to the land. If you will come to my tent, sir, at noon, I have important dispatches I will ask you to carry for me to the Burgesses. And as we are nearing the end of our expedition, it will be wiser if you will await our return at the Capital."

"I shall be only too glad, sir," said Mr. Bridge. "It will

be a stride nearer London. And I am expecting word of a legacy which will make it necessary for me to return to my estates. To tell you the truth, sir, I shall not be sorry to leave this wilderness—" he made a gesture with his hands— "and—" he paused, smiled insolently, and added "its varied inhabitants."

"Leave 'em as fast as you like," said Sam Hutton cheerfully, turning his back full on the secretary, and through a contemptuous silence Mr. Bridge rode away from the summer adventure.

But meantime, Roger had thrown his reins to young Caesar and, after a word or two of instructions to the Negro as to the care of the horse and a pat on Rambler's arching neck, he was off towards the edge of the clearing.

He found the Raccoon sitting quietly, stitching sinew through a newly cut pair of moccasins, a red welt across his cheek. The other Indians were there also. Roger put his hand on the younger boy's shoulder.

"He doesn't speak my tongue," he said to Scarred Wolf, "but tell him my heart is grateful to him. I wish that I might take on me the blows that he received. Tell him I hope that some day I may be his friend when he needs one, as he this day has been mine."

Roger hesitated. He had a purse with a jingle of gold coins in it; but, looking into the eyes of the Indian boy, he had another impulse. There was a fine knife at his belt in a silver sheath, newly come from London on the Merryweather—a thing of which he was very fond and whose loss he would feel. He unbuckled it from his belt and laid it in Raccoon's hands.

"Tell him I give him my knife and hope that good fortune goes with it," he said. "Let it remind him of this day and of the debt I owe him."

ANOTHER day a tall sallow man hailed the storeboat near a log cabin in the midst of a deep Virginia forest. "Hello, the boat! Have you got a blade for a crosscut saw?"

Father and Pappy made a landing and looked curiously about them. The cabin was new and the windows were without panes. The settler had succeeded in clearing only a hundred feet or less of timber, and the stumps were still standing.

"But it's rich bottom land, once you get down to it," he said. "And there's plenty of game for anybody's rifle."

"Any turkeys around here?" Pappy asked. "I'd like to set my teeth in a juicy drumstick right now."

"Yes, there's turkeys. My brother shot two last week."

Steve and David looked at each other. "Father," Steve said, "we'd like to go ashore for a while. May I take my rifle and the dogs?"

"Them's pointer dogs," the settler remarked. "They make good hunters if you can keep them from yawping."

Hello, the Boat!

BY PHYLLIS CRAWFORD

Illustrated by

Alexander Dobkin

"May we go, Father?"

Father turned to the woodsman. "Any panthers in these parts?"

"Nary a painter this side of the hurricane tract up toward Chillicothe."

"All right, boys. Do you think you're going to find a turkey?"

"Maybe."

134

The settler shook his head doubtfully. "You mought, and again you moughtn't. The turkey is a right timorsome bird, and you have to have the knack of creeping up on him. My brother can, but I can't, though I hear them a-gobbling in the woods now and again."

"Well, a walk won't hurt you boys," said Father. "Keep near the river and head downstream, and we'll pick you up when you get tired."

The two boys started off cheerfully, with Steve's long heavy rifle, the small curved powder horn, and the square leather pouch containing his bullets, flint and tinder. At a stern word from the older boy, the dogs kept quietly to his heels.

They crossed the little clearing and plunged into the woods. The sunlight flickered through the branches overhead and cast patterns on the moss and dried leaves beneath.

David squinted up at the blue sky.

"Oh, my!" he said. "It makes me dizzy. I never saw such tall trees. What kind are they?"

"Oaks, elms, red maples, I guess. I'll wager it's dark in these woods when all the leaves are out."

A fat squirrel scampered out on a low branch and scolded angrily. Patch sprang forward with a deep growl.

"Quiet!" Steve ordered. The dog slunk back and whimpered.

"We don't want anything but turkeys, do we, Steve?"

"No, no little game for us."

They walked along in silence for some time, steering around the giant trees that had fallen and taking care not to step on any twigs that might crackle. Except for the occasional song of a wood thrush or the chattering of squirrels, there was hardly a sound.

David glanced about him. "We're miles away from every-

135

thing," he said in a low tone. "Suppose we got lost!"

"I was thinking about that," said Steve. "Hush! Look at Brownie and Patch!"

The dogs had halted and were standing motionless with their tails in a straight line, noses pointed toward a scraggly thicket off to the left.

"A turkey!" Steve whispered.

He deftly loaded the rifle and crept toward the thicket. As he drew near, there was a noise like a snort. He raised his gun, ready to strike the flint.

"It's a bear!" David said in a piercing whisper. "Let's run!"

Steve shook his head and took another step. Then he lowered the gun and began to laugh.

"Sooey!" he shouted.

A great sandy-colored hog tore out of the thicket and scurried off, grunting and squealing. The dogs gave chase with loud barks that rang through the forest.

Steve dropped his rifle and laughed until he rolled on the ground among the brown leaves. David threw himself on the ground and kicked up his heels.

"Turkeys! Bears!" said Steve, with a whoop. Wait till Pappy hears about this."

"And Father and Susan," David giggled, "and Mother."

Steve wiped his eyes on his blue calico sleeve and began to laugh all over again. Finally he sat up.

"Well," he said, "if there ever was a turkey around here, I guess we scared him all the way to Tennessee."

The boys got up and brushed the leaves out of their hair and off their clothes.

"Here, Brownie! Here, Patch! Now maybe we've lost the dogs." Steve whistled and whistled.

136

After a minute he said, "Dave, you whistle a while. I'm all out of breath."

David took it up, and whistled until he was gasping for breath. At length the dogs loped into sight among the big tree trunks. They ran up wagging their tails and leaped at the boys, licking their faces until they cried out.

137

Steve pushed the dogs away and wiped his face. "Well, I hope the boat waits for us. Let's get a little piece on our way."

He picked up the rifle and the powder horn, and looked in his pouch.

"Tarnation!" he exclaimed. "The tinderbox must have fallen out of the pouch. Help me hunt, Dave."

They scuffed among the leaves, but the dogs made the search harder by digging until the leaves flew.

"Get out of the way, Brownie," David said. "You'll get your nose kicked. Oh, there it is, Steve!"

Both boys and dogs made a dive for the shiny tinderbox, and David rescued it from Patch's jaws before the dog could dash off with it.

"Now which way do we go, Steve?"

The older boy scratched his tousled red head. "I'm all turned around. This way, I guess."

They set off again. In every direction they could see nothing but trees, and there were no paths. A twig dropped on Steve's head. He looked up and saw a red squirrel scampering from branch to branch ahead of him.

"I don't like to kill him," he said, "but as long as we can't have turkey, fried squirrel is pretty good. I'm mighty tired of fish and salt meat."

He took painstaking aim, fired, and the squirrel dropped. "Fetch it, Brownie!"

The dog brought him the squirrel, and he handed it to David, who swung it by the tail at his belt. Steve reloaded the gun carefully and they walked on.

Another squirrel and another fell as the crack of the rifle disturbed the quiet of the forest.

"Let me try, Steve," David begged.

He could hardly hold the long rifle steady, but he pointed

138

it at the next squirrel, and fired. The kickback of the gun sent him sprawling.

"You hit him!" Steve said excitedly. "But he's still alive. Quick! We can't leave him like that."

He hastily cleaned and reloaded the rifle, and as his shot rang out, the squirrel fell. Brownie ran to fetch it.

David got up and dusted himself off. "I could have killed him right off if the gun hadn't hit back at me," he said.

Steve tossed the limp squirrel to him. "You'd better practice some more before you try shooting live critters, Dave," he said quietly. "Tain't fair to shoot just for the pleasure, and leave them to starve because they can't step lively any more."

David kicked at a moss-covered rock and hung his head.

"I'm getting awful tired," he mumbled. "Don't you think we've got enough for supper now?"

"I reckon so."

They quickened their pace and strode along without speaking. Finally David stopped and looked around again.

"Steve, there's nothing but trees anywhere," he faltered.

"Looks like it," Steve agreed. "Come on. We must make haste."

"Maybe we're lost!"

"I guess so. Pretty soon it will get dark. It gets dark sooner in the woods than it does on the river. And we'll be all alone in the dark with the wildcats and hoot-owls all around us."

"Steve! Quit it!"

Steve's eyes began to twinkle, but David did not notice.

"Maybe a panther swam across the river from Ohio, and is waiting on a limb up in that big oak tree yonder. We'll build a fire to keep warm, and that'll keep the wildcats and panthers and wolves away for a while. They'll sit round in a ring with their eyes shining at us. As soon as we go to

139

sleep, the fire will go out, and they'll rush in and GRAB US!"

David turned a white face to him. "Does it really happen like that? Or are you trying to scare me?"

"Don't you think that would be exciting?"

"Steve, I wish you'd quit. Let's get out of here."

"Wait a minute." Steve walked around a tree, studying its gnarled trunk. "Here's the mossy side. That means this is north. Now the river ought to be somewhere to the northwest. Let's head straight for that patch of sunlight yonder and keep on in a straight line from there."

They broke into a jog trot and hurdled the logs that got in their way. David clutched at the squirrels fastened under his belt and began to puff. Brownie and Patch raced ahead, wheeled and came back, then ran off again. In a few moments they were out of sight.

At the sound of their distant barking, Steve shouted, "They've found the boat!"

They tore along until they began to sniff the faint odor of fish and decayed vegetation that indicated the river was near. Finally they emerged among the willows at the water's edge, but there was no storeboat. A neat little two-masted barge was disappearing around a bend with a flash of oars. They could still hear the patroon's voice crying, "Pull! pull! pull!"

A flatboat floated past. At one end was a haystack, around which five cows were feeding. In the doorway of the cabin, a woman in spectacles sat in a rocking chair and knitted. Her knitting needles flashed in the late afternoon sunlight. Two men and three boys were sitting at the stern, trailing fishlines in the wake of the craft.

Steve and David hallooed from the bank, and received an answering shout from the boys on board. Brownie and Patch

140

made several threatening dashes into the water and barked frantically.

And still no storeboat. When the flatboat had passed, there was not even a leaf on the surface of the river. Two crows flew overhead, cawing raucously.

David swallowed hard. "What'll we do, Steve?"

Steve squared his shoulders. "We'll be all right. Don't worry. We've got the dogs and rifle for protection. Besides, maybe the boat stopped on the Ohio side to sell something.

He began to whistle, but it was not a tune. Then he stopped and cocked his head.

"Listen!" he said, and a smile spread over his freckled face. "Isn't that Katy?"

More and more distinctly they heard the sound of a fiddle.

"There she comes round the bend!" cried David excitedly.

Steve cupped his hands. "Hello, the boat!

"Hello, the mighty Nimrods!"

The boys waited impatiently to see Father and Pappy run the storeboat ashore at their feet. Instead, Father kept his course in the middle of the river.

"Father!" Steve wailed.

Father waved and grinned broadly. Pappy, sitting cross-legged on the roof, switched to a doleful tune. The storeboat nosed around the next bend, out of sight.

"I guess we walk," Steve said. "Come on."

He whistled to the dogs and they trudged along, keeping close to the bank. Sometimes they had to seize the willow branches to keep from slithering into the river.

"They can't go very far before we catch up with them," Steve said. "We can walk faster than they can float. The current's only two or three miles an hour. Pappy said so."

"We ought to have swum after the boat when it passed," David said.

"We may have to, at that." Steve grinned ruefully.

But when they swung around the sharp bend, the boat was waiting, made fast to a willow tree on the bank.

The rest of the family greeted them with loud cheers and a great blast on the horn. Warm and breathless, the boys climbed on board, and the dogs leaped to the deck beside them.

"Where's my turkey?" Pappy demanded. "Them ain't no turkeys dangling from Davie's belt."

Between giggles the boys told the story of the big sandy hog.

"So that," Steve concluded, "is why we thought we'd better take what we could find, which was squirrels. But after that trick you played on us, Dave and I are going to eat them all ourselves."

"Every scrap!" said David.

142

"I wonder who's going to cook them," said Mother, as if talking to herself.

"Well, you can have some, Mother," Steve conceded.

"That's good," said Mother. "But I always give your father part of my supper."

Father spoke up. "And I always share with Pappy."

"I always give everything away to the girls," Pappy drawled. "I wouldn't leave Miss Susie out."

"So I guess that fixes us all, doesn't it?" said Mother serenely.

"Why didn't you stop for us, Father?" Steve asked.

"I thought you wanted to walk," said Father in mild surprise. "Besides, there's a cabin over yonder. Your mother wants to see if she can buy a couple of loaves of bread. She says she can't bake bread in her bake-oven."

"Hello, the boat!" A tall gaunt man was thrusting his way through the bushes.

"Howdy, stranger," Father returned.

"Have you got any sugar aboard the boat?"

"Plenty. Will you step into the store?"

Down below, the man looked around and nodded approvingly. "That's a fine chance of dry goods, storemaster."

"The best. Can I make a bargain with you? I don't ordinarily sell groceries, but I think we can spare some sugar from our own barrel. And then you might buy some of our store goods. They're dog cheap, considering what you get for your money."

"That's a recommendation," said the farmer. "But I'd be mighty obliged if you'd just sell me some sugar. My old woman's making apple butter. Seems the rot's getting into the apples in my root-cellar, and she's run out of sugar trying to use them up."

Mother came down the little ladder. "Can you tell me what day your wife does her baking?" she asked.

"Wednesday, I reckon."

"Would she be able to spare two loaves of bread? How much do you think she'd take for them?"

The man pointed to the shelves. "For a piece of calico like that," he said, "I reckon she'd swap you the whole batch and eat corn pone for a week."

"It's a bargain," said Father. "Let's fetch the madam."

After a long consultation with the farmer's plump wife, a trade was made, and the storeboat set off again, the richer by three loaves of fresh bread, a barrel of flour, a peck of dried apples, and a kettleful of apple butter.

"I hope she'll like those calicoes when she gets them made up," said Mother doubtfully. "They weren't what I'd pick for her. But she does make good bread."

144

THE log walls of Boonesborough were twelve feet high. According to Benjamin Franklin it took two axmen six minutes to fell a fourteen-inch-thick pine, which made three sixteen-foot palisades. These were sharpened to a point at one end and set close against each other in a four-foot trench. Inside, a firing-board six feet from the ground ran around the entire stockade. The Boonesborough fort was a rectangle of log walls, or palisade, one hundred seventy by two hundred fifty feet, with four corner-towers and two heavy log gates. Thirty cabins within the stockade were built into the outside wall. It was separated from the surrounding forest by a stump-dotted clearing. When the riflemen inside were at their firing posts, no enemy could cross this no-man's-land alive. Only cannon could demolish their wilderness citadel.

Boonesborough

BY JAMES DAUGHERTY

Illustrated by James Daugherty

They never knew these days whether the laurel bushes hid a dozen or hundreds of the prowling Indian varmints watching for a chance to make a deadly shot.

One day the lookout saw several redskins crawling out into the open. In the excitement Boone and his men made a dash for them across the clearing only to find too late that they had been caught in an ambush. Boone went down with a bullet in his ankle and a huge savage swinging a hatchet down at his defenseless skull, but a point-blank shot from Simon Kenton's rifle dropped the Indian in his tracks. In the running fight to reach the stockade Kenton managed to carry the disabled Boone to safety. Simon Kenton was a young wildcat with nine lives for the Indians to catch and tie to the back of a frightened

145

horse for a mad ride among the tearing branches.

Then again two hundred Shawnees surrounded the clearing and poured lead into the stockade for two days. The fifty riflemen at the portholes clipped every redskin that showed an inch from cover, while the women molded bullets and loaded hot rifle barrels. Boonesborough was having its baptism of fire and remembering about the dark and bloody ground, hard to hold. When several parties of armed settlers came in like little armies with supplies of salt and powder, the watching Indians retreated, taking news of mighty advancing troops of long-knives to the Chillicothe villages. The defenders welcomed the newcomers with boisterous joy.

A midsummer Sunday afternoon was a still, quiet time for Daniel's daughter, Jemima Boone, and Fanny and Betsy Calloway (crammed with the Lamentations of Jeremiah and the wrath of God from the Sunday morning Bible reading) to slip down the winding lazy Kentucky River in a canoe. The long afternoon drowsed on to milking time, and there were no signs of Fanny and Betsy and Jemima. "Where are the girls?" ran from cabin to cabin. The river searchers came in with bad news—they had found the empty canoe and the girls' tracks and those of five Indians on the river bank. A swift council of the best trackers figured out the rescue plan. It was a pretty sure guess that the Indians would make for their tribal village on Licking River, and the hunters knew the lay of the land.

Boone, John Floyd, and the Calloway boys started at dawn on the trail. The girls had slyly, and even under the cat-eyes of their captors, left plain signs—a broken branch or piece of ribbon. Every hour the traces grew fresher as the savages, believing they were out of reach of pursuit, became less careful and finally camped in seeming safety. It was a terrible moment for the pursuers when they crept in close. They knew that at the least suspicious sound the savages would instantly toma-hawk the captives. The hunters fired together. Two Indians dropped in their tracks, and the others dived into the forest.

The awful tension and suspense had snapped like a thread. There was wild joy when the happy party came out into the Boonesborough clearing. Everyone told the story with all the details, over and over. Three weeks later Samuel Henderson and his sweetheart Elizabeth Calloway came to Justice Boone who solemnly performed the ceremony of the first marriage in Kentucky. Later Flanders Calloway married Daniel's beloved daughter Jemima, and Fanny Calloway married young John Holder, who was to make a great name as an Indian fighter.

The life of a pioneer family was a comic-tragic drama of struggle and violence. Each one had many stories. The lives of these movers on the Wilderness Road and forest settlers were a rough and violent saga full of lights and shadows, sweet and bitter as the wild persimmon, rough and tough as the shag-barked hickories, fierce and tender as the tall waving corn of the valleys.

Boone's story was the story of a whole people. It had all their griefs and tragedies and restless longings and rich half-fulfilled dreams, all their ranging freedom and mortal bondages. It rang with the roaring laughter and boisterous fun; it was dark with the unfathomable silent anguishes by new-made graves; it was full of lost hopes and dreams of grandeur. Through it rushed the winds and the voices of the valley, the vast Ohio valley. Through the story runs the clamor of distant voices, of the generations springing up from the bottom lands, the fat corn lands, saying: "We are the nation of the valley, the tall corn-fed, hog-fed sons of the West. We make our own destiny and we like it. We make our own glories and shames and we've just begun. Our songs and our dreams are made of the new moon over the dry corn shocks, of the wind in the maple groves, of the silver-weathered rails in the fence along a prairie road."

148

A pattern of fur-clad hunters and long-eared hounds and pack horses carrying iron salt-kettles, trailing among the black leafless trees, made a silhouette on the blue-white snow that lay deep over the winter world of Kentucky. They were going to French Lick to boil thousands of gallons of water at the salt springs in order that desperate Boonesborough might have the salt that kept the meat from putrefying so Boonesborough could eat and live.

In the dead of winter the salt-camp at French Lick felt safe from the Indians, whose custom was to take the war path only in the spring or summer. But one gray evening in February as Boone was coming back to camp after a long day's hunt, he was completely surprised by an ambush of four Indian warriors. He tried to run for it but in the deep snow it was useless. The Old Fox of Kentucky was caught again. They were the very Shawnees from whom he had escaped years ago on the Finley expedition. It was a tough heart-breaking moment but he had been there more than once before and had come through. Now it was a quick shift of tactics from physical action to a game of wits and bluff.

The Indians were a large war party under Chief Black Fish headed for a surprise attack on Boonesborough. Suddenly to have caught the great chief of the white men so excited them that Boone was able shrewdly to persuade them to change their plan. The silent white hunter must have turned eloquent and impressive as he stood in the midst of the savage council that was to give the tomahawk vote of life or death for the unsuspecting salt camp. Fantastic as it sounds, nevertheless the war party agreed to leave Boonesborough till the spring, when Boone promised he would arrange a peaceable moving of the settlers farther north where they might live as adopted Shawnees. For the present the Indians would return to Chillicothe with the unscalped salt-boilers as their prisoners. All this was argued out in talk and translated back and forth by a Negro named Pompey.

Though Boone had saved the fort on the Kentucky and the salt-camp from bloody butchery by his courage and wits alone, some of the men were bitter and resentful against him as they marched half-starved and frozen into the winter encampment of the Shawnees at Chillicothe. After a while Black Fish led a party with the white captives to Detroit to exhibit them and perhaps sell them to General Hamilton.

Detroit in 1776 was a British fort and trading post perched on the open waterway of the Great Lakes. The rich fur trade of a vast area of wild North America passed through there on the way to make fortunes in far-off King George's England. Now there was a revolution in the colonies. It would be bad for the fur business. Inside the fort the redcoated British soldiers went through their daily drill. They dreamed in their barracks of English lanes and ale houses and rosy English sweethearts.

Outside the fort the red tribes came and went at will. They traded and treated with the English soldiers and traders after their touchy quick-changing fashion. White trappers, wild and savage as the Indians, drifted in with their fur packs to swap for ammunition and to liquor up. A trader coming in with a keg of French brandy would leave town with great bales of fine furs, and a wild drunken orgy of whooping and fighting would follow. The Indians brought in from the border raids white captives, men, women, and children, as well as scalps. For these General Hamilton, the British commander, paid fixed prices in money, Indian finery, and war paint. The black faces of African Negroes mingled in the fantastic pageant.

150

Around these wilderness outposts surged a drama of fierce passions and violent deeds.

It was a grand show-off when Black Fish's party stalked out of the forest with the great Daniel and ten of his men as captives. The whole town thrilled to see the legendary hero of the border in the flesh. Boone was as persuasive with the British as with the Indians. He showed his commission as a captain in His British Majesty's army and told of his fictitious plan to capture Boonesborough in the spring. Hamilton was delighted with him. But when it came to selling his prisoners, Black Fish insisted that Boone was his personal property and he was not for sale, even though the general raised the price to the fabulous sum of one hundred pounds.

Boone took a long look at Detroit as he rode back into the forest with the returning Indians. It might be the last time he would see white faces.

The naked Indian children stared in wonder at Daniel Boone, and the lean wolf dogs snarled and snapped, not liking his strange white smell as he sat squinting at the fire in the smoky huts of Chillicothe. He was thinking his white man's thoughts as he watched the tall idle warriors and the bronze squaws grinding corn, scraping the skins, kneading the buffalo robes to make them soft. He had done very well pretending he was an Indian, pretending he was happy and satisfied, and pleasing the great chieftain Moluntha with his clever hunting. He looked wistfully at the fat Indian ponies, thinking of a dash for freedom when the right moment came. They had washed away his white blood in the river, pulled out half his hair, and painted him with strange symbols that meant he was the adopted son of the chief Black Fish. He knew by heart the strange rhythms of the mysterious ceremonial songs and

151

dances. He was quick to share in the red laughter or laments.

One evening he came back tired from tedious labor at the salt licks to find the braves in war paint dancing to the pounding drums and shrill war chants. Sitting in his familiar place, he watched the wild frenzies rise and sway around the flickering campfires. There were five hundred warriors preparing for a surprise attack on Boonesborough. He knew how few were the defenders and that the fort was in bad repair. The whole settlement would be utterly unprepared. His hour had come and he was ready. Before dawn he slipped out like a shadow and was gone. Now again he was the hunted fox of the wilderness with the red dogs in close pursuit.

"On the 16th I departed before sunrise in the most secret manner and arrived at Boonesborough on the 20th, after a journey of one hundred and sixty miles, during which I had but one meal." Brief autobiography. How did he know the way all the four days and nights with the Shawnee pack one jump behind?

He was not so young as he used to be but tough and long-winded. When he came at last to the Ohio at full spring flood, he remembered he could not swim. It was the desperate tight spot he had known so often, but the angel of the wilderness showed him a leaky canoe stranded on a sand bar and he made a swift down-stream crossing on the yellow waters to the Kentucky shore that he knew like the back of his hand. Familiar landmarks cheered him. He shot a buffalo and cooked his first meal in four days. He was in sight of Boonesborough. He had kept his rendezvous with destiny.

It was a strange figure that came across the clearing into Boonesborough and said he was Daniel Boone. For weeks they had said Daniel Boone was a goner for sure this time.

Even Rebecca's faith had failed and she had returned with the family to the settlements. Boone was sorry, yet glad, too, for she was safe. His brother Israel and Jemima, his beloved daughter who had married Dick Calloway, were there to give him a warm welcome. But it was no wonder Rebecca had gone. Many a husband and father had never come back across the clearing.

The news of the coming Indian raid roused the settlers to action. The neglected log walls were repaired and everything made ready for an attack, the swift short Indian attack with which the borderers were familiar. But weeks passed and no Indians were seen. Then another escaped white man brought in news that Boone's flight had delayed the Indians. Boone then took a raiding expedition across the Ohio and burned an Indian village, getting back just a few hours ahead of the great war party of over four hundred Indians with some forty French Canadians under the direction of their officer De Quindre.

There were about fifty men and boys, besides the women and children, behind the log stockade when the Indians surrounded the clearing of Boonesborough. Instead of the usual sudden attack, an Indian came out of the woods with a white flag and by calling back and forth arranged for a parley. Every hour of delay meant a nearer hope of reinforcement coming in from Harrodsburg. Three of the defenders met Black Fish, Moluntha, and Catahecassa near the fort for a powwow. There was talk of friendship and peaceful surrender. The chief promised that the whites would be taken safely on horses to Detroit if they surrendered peaceably. There need be no bloodshed if the Americans would agree to abandon the fort.

Boone said he would explain to his people and in two days give an answer. He was glad to find that the Indians had heard from a white captive that there were several hundred defenders in the fort. The Indians believed their offer of safety was sure to be accepted.

Inside the fort the chances were talked over and argued and weighed after the democratic way of the backwoods. The odds were ten to one and worse against defense, and not a man, woman, or child would be spared if—But the tough cantankerous spirit of the frontier urged: "Go ahead or bust." They would not have been where they were if they had not been stubborn survivors of a rough, tough, restless race who lived and died in their own independent way by the rifle, the ax, the Bible, and the plow. So they sent back the eagle's answer: "No surrender," the answer of the sassy two-year-old baby democracy, the answer of Man the Unconquerable to the hosts of darkness—"No surrender."

The iron-faced chiefs and the ornery Frenchman De Quindre took the answer grimly back to their council, while the settlers got in their cows, corn, and water from the spring without interference from the Indians. The next move was an Indian trick which was perfectly transparent to Boone, but he took the chances of playing it to win time.

The Indians proposed a grand council of nine on each side to sign a treaty of peace, after which they would depart, they said, like lambs. The council sat under the sycamore trees within rifle shot of the fort. At a wave of the hat from the delegates the riflemen in the fort were to open fire and cover the nine men's dash back when trouble started.

All day they sat in the shade and smoked, talked, and ate while a fancy treaty of peace, including a sworn allegiance to the British Crown, was agreed on, to be signed tomorrow at the same place. In the night an ambush of Indians was set around the treaty tree. The next day when the nine appeared

154

from the fort, Black Fish met them with eighteen powerful young braves. After the signing came the two-to-one handshaking. Two Indians grabbed for each white man and a mob jumped from the laurel to finish the job. Then the nine Kentucky wildcats let loose with teeth and claws, and the fur flew. Shooting began and the nine raced for the fort. They had won the first round.

Next day there was a great hubbub in the forest, bugles blowing and orders for retreat bawled out, and the pack horses were seen crossing the river at the ford. But the old border fox in the fort was not fooled. The gates of Boonesborough remained shut and the Indian trick failed. The real danger was an Indian rush on the gates under a heavy fire from all sides. This was what kept the riflemen waiting and watching at the portholes day and night.

But to charge across the clearing under the fire of Kentucky rifles was so contrary to the Indian way of fighting that all of De Quindre's urging for a mass attack was useless. Instead, the savages remained under cover of the woods, firing continuously. Day and night under the heavy encircling fire of the enemy, the riflemen stuck to their posts, blazing away whenever an inch of Indian hide was exposed to view. The women passed out the scant rations and scarce water, loaded guns when the firing was fast, molded bullets, comforted the children, and prayed the prayers of the pioneer faith. Each slow day under the burning sun was an eternity; each night they thanked the God of their Fathers that some protecting angel had kept the gates.

From high up in a distant tree a sniper began sending bullets inside the fort and Jemima Boone was hit. Boone drew a bead at two hundred yards on the sniper as he was reloading, and put a bullet through his head. The figure that pitched

155

from the high tree was black Pompey. Colonel Calloway, of the old school, became irritated at Boone's cautious tactics and contrived an impressive wooden cannon. The roar and smoke of her first shot scared the Indians for about a mile out of range, but when the smoke cleared from her second blast she had burst wide open and was permanently disabled. But she was the wonder of the wilderness as long as she lasted.

More serious was the tunnel which the enemy was driving toward the fort. It carried to the defenders the sinister fear of exploding mines that would breach the wooden walls. Day by day they could hear the digging come nearer. It wore on their strained nerves like the gnawing of a rat in the night.

Hour by hour a week dragged on. In the inky blackness of the seventh night a bright flame suddenly shot across the clearing in a long arc and dropped on a cabin roof. It was the dreadful flaming arrow. Now they were dropping fast on the pine roofs of the cabins. Worse yet, the savages had crept across the clearing in the darkness and started fagot fires against the log palisade on all sides. The spreading glow lit up the clearing as the hungry little flames ran along the shingles. Against the glow the frantic silhouettes of the defenders trying to beat out the flames drew stinging gun fire from the enemy. Suddenly a figure leaped up on a burning roof and in a fury of flame and bullets beat out the fire. When he had finished he calmly jumped down to safety. But the fires along the stockade were taking hold and the last remaining buckets full of precious water would be of no avail. The riflemen were standing at their posts holding their fire, waiting for the final mass attack, and women stood clutching their children. To Boone it seemed the last card had been played and lost. As the red light flickered over his set face, suddenly he felt a drop of water strike the back of his hand, and as he looked up heavy drops struck his face. In a few minutes the God-sent rain streamed down in drenching sheets. The burning stockade hissed, steamed, glowed; and the fire went out. Something beyond human power had saved Boonesborough by the skin of its teeth.

Still the firing from the forest kept up incessantly. No one knew how near the tunnel was, but it seemed almost under their feet. The September pouring rain had soaked everyone to the bone. They would soon be passing around the last ration of food. Hope held desperately to ever slimmer chances. No Indian attack on a fort had ever been known to keep up so long.

Utter darkness of a night of lashing rain set in on the ninth day of the siege. In the fierce movement of the storm it seemed as though the savage demons of all the wild valley had come down for vengeance. It was a blind night when a man could not see the end of his rifle barrel. Nothing now could stop the mass rush of the savages across the clearing. The riflemen stood grimly at their posts in the pouring rain and waited. In the darkness time stopped. They shifted and growled, trying to keep their powder dry, and muttered to each other. At long last the night lifted. Out of the shapeless grayness the world was taking form. The morning came with no firing from the enemy, and the lookouts reported no signs of Indians in the forest. It looked like another false retreat. A scout or two came back with the news that the Indians were on the march this time for sure.

Then two white men crossed the clearing shouting and waving. One was Simon Kenton who had not been able to get through the lines. It was true that the Indians had gone. The white medicine was too strong. The spirits of the forest were beaten and the white gods prevailed. A surge of wild joy was in the hearts of Boonesborough when the log gates swung open and let out the starved cattle. There was whooping and firing to welcome eighty backwoodsmen from Harrodsburg, riding in too late for a rescue but in time for the celebration.

158

As I was a-walking
     one morning for pleasure,
  I spied a cow-puncher a-riding along;
His hat was throwed back
     and his spurs was a-jingling,
  And he approached me, a-singing this song:

Whoopee ti yi yo, git along, little dogies,
  It's your misfortune, and none of my own.
Whoopee ti yi yo, git along, little dogies,
  For you know Wyoming will be your new home.

Early in springtime
    we round up the dogies,
Mark 'em and brand 'em
    and bob off their tails;
Round up the horses,
    load up the chuck wagon,
Then throw the dogies
    upon the old trail.

Whoopee Ti Yi Yo

AMERICAN COWBOY BALLAD

Illustrated by Hans A. Mueller

It's whooping and yelling and driving the dogies;
  Oh, how I wish you would all go on!
It's whooping and punching and go on, little dogies
  For you know Wyoming will be your new home.

Oh, you'll be soup for Uncle Sam's Injuns,—
  It's "beef, heap beef," I hear them cry.
Git along, git along, git along, little dogies,
  You're going to be beef steers by and by.

Whoopee ti yi yo, git along, little dogies,
  It's your misfortune, and none of my own.
Whoopee ti yi yo, git along, little dogies,
  For you know Wyoming will be your new home.

SOMETHING was making Younger Brother restless. At night he dreamed of strange experiences and new places. He dreamed of floating down a river on a raft of logs. The river grew so wide he couldn't see its other side. The water was blue, the color of turquoise. Younger Brother could feel himself gliding smoothly on the water until he hit something and awoke. Every night he had that dream of gliding in watery space until he hit something that awoke him. He never knew what it was that he hit. In the daytime he tried to reason it out and he grew restless.

He wanted to glide in the daytime and find the thing that awoke him. He knew he glided toward the west. It must be the wide water of the west that he saw in his dream. He had always wanted to go to the wide water. Perhaps if he did he could find the Turquoise Woman.

Westward Bound

BY

LAURA ADAMS ARMER

Illustrated by

Lorence F. Bjorklund

He came to think more and more about the Turquoise Woman of the western sea. Ever since he had dressed the juniper stick for the girl to carry in the dance, he had dreamed of the turquoise water at night, and thought of the Turquoise Woman in the daytime.

He was terribly restless. Mother's weaving was beautiful on his pony; so was Father's bridle, but he knew the Turquoise Woman was calling him to the west. Every morning he drove the sheep toward the west. Maybe if he went far enough he could find the wide water.

He grew to hate the sheep because he must take them back toward the east every afternoon.

One morning, after awaking from his gliding dream, he told Mother he would not take the sheep out that day as he must be about other business.

"Son, are you crazy? The sheep must be herded," said Mother.

"Then you must herd them, for today I travel west on my pony."

Mother looked at him and did not say a word. What she had been dreading had come to pass. Her younger son was leaving her.

She packed dried meat and corn cakes in a flour sack and tied them on his pony's saddle. She rolled a sheepskin in a blanket and tied that on.

Younger Brother put his bow and arrows in front of the saddle and was ready to leave. He shook hands with his father, merely saying:

"I ride to the west."

He put his arms around his mother, who clung to him for a moment, then said:

"When you are hungry, the mutton will be ready."

He mounted his pony and was off without once looking back at the hogan. When out of sight and hearing he sang wildly as he rode,

> *The Sun Bearer travels a trail to the west,*
> *The Moon Bearer travels a trail to the west,*
> *Westward the stars move. Westward move I.*

The rocky cliffs answered back, *"Westward move I."*

The pony neighed as he scented a coyote howling on a hill. A hawk screeched as it flew toward the west. Above the crooked rocks Yellow Beak circled in the blue. The boy stopped his pony and called to him,

"My trail goes to the west."

He skirted the crooked rocks and rode far beyond. By the time the Sun Bearer had reached the zenith the boy had passed the Waterless Mountain. He never looked back. The west was calling.

When he stopped to rest on top of a cedar ridge, he tied the pony to a tree and lay flat on his back. Dim in the distance he could see the blue peak of the western mountain. In the valley ahead he could trace the wash by a rolling line of dust blowing along its course.

"That means a sandstorm," he said to the pony. "We had better move quickly to shelter."

As he rode toward the valley, which must be crossed, the storm increased. The sand blew higher in the air until it obscured the sun. The pony struggled on against the wind. The boy knew that shelter must be found. He couldn't keep his eyes open. His ears and hair were full of the fine dust. He dismounted. It was impossible for the pony to struggle further against the fury of the storm.

Younger Brother unrolled his blanket, put it over his head, and stood close to the pony as if to shelter him. The sand was blowing so thick it was like a fog enveloping them. The boy knew there was nothing to do but wait.

He could not see ten feet ahead of him. Loose tumbleweeds flew past him. Sometimes they were hurled into the air, out of sight. Sand piled up against the sagebrush and in some cases covered the lower shrubs. Clouds of dust enveloped the boy and the pony, each standing with bowed head and closed eyes, helpless before elemental fury.

Darker and darker grew the atmosphere; colder and colder, the wind. Younger Brother thought of his mother's warm hogan with the sheepskins around the fire, but he said to himself, "I must travel to the west."

162

While he stood there fighting the thought of the cozy family group, he was startled by a cry—a long shrill cry of despair. He could see nothing.

The cry was human. Out of the wilderness it came, adding terror to the storm. Younger Brother did not move. The pony trembled. The cry came nearer.

Younger Brother opened his eyes for a second. He could see nothing but whirling sand and tumbleweed. He shut his eyes again and leaned close against the trembling pony.

Another cry pierced the air. It sounded nearer, much nearer. When Younger Brother opened his eyes again he could distinguish a form moving toward him.

He, too, trembled and clutched the pony's bridle to hold him. The pony reared in an effort to escape the phantom-like form in the dust. The boy's impulse was to mount and ride away but something kept him rooted to the spot.

Before he knew what was happening, the phantom figure fell at his feet. The cry was silenced. Younger Brother looked down on the limp figure of a white boy. He was dressed in khaki and wore high laced boots. His hat was missing and his blond hair curled in a tangled mass about his forehead.

Younger Brother leaned over him. The white boy looked up at the Navaho, with eyes as blue as Hasteen Tso's. He spoke the only Navaho word he knew, "Toh."

Younger Brother untied a canteen of water from the saddle and the white boy lifted it to his lips. The *toh* revived him. Together the two boys sat by the pony with Younger Brother's blanket about them. The wind was abating.

By sunset the dust no longer flew and the boys could see the western mountain dark against a vermilion sky. Younger Brother rolled his blanket, mounted his pony and motioned the white boy to sit behind him.

Together they rode toward the western mountain.

Mile after mile of gray sagebrush stretched toward the purpling mountain, the only distinctive landmark in sight.

The white boy was straining his eyes in search of a lone cottonwood where he had left his roadster early in the afternoon.

Younger Brother kept a lookout for smoke from some hogan, as he had no desire to sleep out on the desert.

The pony was the first to find a camp, for he scented water and galloped gladly toward it. Younger Brother let him have the rein and soon, around a little rise of ground, they came upon a spring. The white boy shouted with joy, as he recognized the lone cottonwood by the spring; and there was his roadster, the cause of all his trouble. It had run out of gasoline, five miles from a trading post. The boy had started to walk to

164

the post for help, when he was overtaken by the sandstorm and lost.

He motioned to Younger Brother to dismount and the two boys proceeded to set up a tent that was stored in the back of the car. The white boy took out his pots and pans while Younger Brother made a campfire of sagebrush. Soon the smell of coffee brewing and bacon frying made the boys realize how hungry they were.

"Gee, this is the real thing," said the white boy, as he opened a can of sardines and put two of them on a cracker.

"Have some?" he asked the Navaho. Younger Brother shook his head, "No."

When the big yellow canned peaches were passed, they were not refused. They are not taboo for Navahos, but fish is. My! They tasted good! Younger Brother watched every move of his new friend. He was a big boy about fifteen and though strong and muscular, seemed tired out after his fight with the wind. That was because he had become frightened and lost his head.

After supper Younger Brother watered the pony, removed the saddle, and took the blanket and sheepskin into the tent. Then he hobbled the pony so that he couldn't wander too far away.

He gave a parting look at the western mountain all purple against the darkening sky, then went inside the tent and lay down on his sheepskin. He kept all his clothes on. He was much interested in watching the white boy unlace his boots, take off his khaki clothes and put on his white pajama suit, which looked just like the clothes the old Navaho men wore all the time in the summer, only this suit was much whiter.

He watched the boy brush his short blond hair and they

both laughed at the sand that shook out of it. Then he untied the woolen string wound around the coil of his own hair and let the long black mass hang over his shoulders. He had no brush so he just ran his fingers through his hair and managed to get a lot of sand out.

The white boy watched him coil and tie his hair again. To him it seemed funny that any boy should have long hair like a girl's but he was learning many new and different things as he traveled.

The boys slept soundly all night and in the morning the white boy tried to make Younger Brother understand what he wanted to do. He pointed to the auto and he pointed down the road, said "toh" and shook his head for "no."

The Navaho boy thought he wanted water and started toward the spring with a bucket. The white boy gesticulated, "No."

Then Younger Brother had an inspiration. He said excitedly:

"Jedi-be-toh. Jedi-be-toh."

Suddenly the white boy recalled that the Navahos call gasoline *"jedi-be-toh."* He was delighted that they understood each other. He realized that *jedi* meant the sound of the engine. *Toh* meant "water" and *be* meant "its," so there was the Navaho word for gasoline—"automobile its water."

He was so delighted he shook Younger Brother's hand and pointing down the road and to the pony said, *"jedi-be-toh."* After a while he succeeded in making himself understood and the two started out again, riding the pony.

At the post the trader interpreted for the boys. He asked Younger Brother where he had come from.

"From the Waterless Mountain," said the boy.

"Why are you with the Pelicano?"

166

"The Pelicano boy was lost in the black wind. I put him on my pony. Tell the Pelicano my pony needs hay."

Half a dozen Navahos were standing around and leaning against the counter. They had never seen Younger Brother before. They thought he was a smart boy to get hay for his pony.

The trader told the white boy it was up to him to pay for hay as well as for gasoline.

"Sure thing. I expect to, but how am I to get back with this gas?"

"Where are you heading for?" asked the trader.

"Grand Canyon. I expect to meet my folks there."

"I'll ask the kid what he will do for you."

Younger Brother said he was riding west and if the Pelicano wanted him to he would go with him. Of course they could not pack much gasoline on the pony, but enough to get the car to the post, where the tank was filled and everything set for a western trail.

The white boy led the way in his roadster and Younger Brother followed his tracks.

As he rode alone again he noticed clouds piling in the sky. The land was strange and new to him but the sky he could always read. He said to his pony, "The voice of the thunder will be heard in the land today."

It wasn't long before drops of rain spattered in the dust and on the sagebrush. It smelled so good, so fresh, just as it smelled at home near the Waterless Mountain.

The little pony jogged along, glad of the clouds which made shade for his going. He still followed the track of the roadster.

In the distance thunder was rolling and banging. By the time Younger Brother reached a high stretch of ground, he could see the opposite side of a rocky wash streaked with blue and red and yellow. Behind the mesa dark blue-black thunder clouds spit out streaks of lightning just like the darting tongues of serpents.

Rain began to fall in torrents. It washed away the tracks of the automobile and almost washed away the road itself. The water made deep channels, leaving a terribly high center in the road. Younger Brother followed the road until it forked on top of a steep bank. Below he could see water running in the wash. What had been a dry wash an hour ago, was now a raging torrent coming down from the mountains.

He wondered if his friend had been able to cross. At the forking of the road, Younger Brother turned to the right. He had not gone more than half a mile in the drenching rain before he found the white boy and his car stuck in the sand on the edge of the wash.

Younger Brother was wet to the skin but the white boy was dry. He had sat helpless with a blanket around him, after digging for an hour in the sand. The hind wheels were in mud to the hubs.

168

The white boy was glad to see Younger Brother ride up, and he motioned him to jump in the car out of the wet. There they sat, waiting for the rain to stop.

After a while the sun shone again, just long enough to say good-by, with a flood of orange and magenta light dancing on the rocky cliffs. The boys proceeded to make a fire. Younger Brother's clothes must be dried. That was a problem as he had nothing to wear while they were drying. The white boy loaned him a blanket and as he sat by the little campfire he could see two Navaho horsemen on the opposite bank riding fast and furiously.

They slowed up as they approached the river and consulted about crossing. Then in Navaho fashion they dismounted, and urged their horses into the water to swim across. Each Navaho followed his horse, holding tightly to its tail while it swam. They crossed that way all right. Navahos are not strong on swimming. They let the ponies do it for them.

At the camp they sat down by the fire and joined the boys in a cup of coffee. They talked with Younger Brother and told him the machine might get lost in the night as the flood would get higher. One of the men said:

"What if it does? Then the Pelicano will have to pay us for a pony."

Younger Brother looked at the fellow. He had never met that kind of man before. He didn't like his looks. He had little mean eyes and a cruel mouth.

Younger Brother said nothing for awhile. He just sat, wrapped in the blanket, thinking. He knew the machine must be hauled back onto high ground and the sooner it was done the better. So he told the two men if they would help dig and push, the Pelicano would pay them.

"How much?" asked the wicked-looking one.

169

"One peso," said Younger Brother.

"It is not enough," said the man.

"I think it is enough. It will buy much tobacco."

The white boy was helpless in this situation. He knew it was not safe to leave his car so near the water. He guessed that the men were bargaining so he held up two fingers and said, "Pesos."

One man went to work with the shovel while the other brought sagebrush to fill up the soft muddy ruts. Younger Brother still sat wrapped in his blanket while the white boy jacked up the rear end of the car. After repeated trials of starting the engine and putting more brush in the ruts, the car was finally pulled out and off the road for the night. It was safe from the danger of a flood.

The white boy gave the men a dollar each and more coffee. As they rode away Younger Brother wished they had gone back across the water. He didn't like them and he would feel easier to have a river between himself and the men.

The white boy was in the best of spirits because his car was safe. He thought what a lucky thing it was for him that he met the Navaho boy. It was good to have someone that could talk to the natives for him. He wished he could tell the Navaho that he liked him. Of course Younger Brother knew that he did, but white people always like to talk.

While the tent was being set up for the night, Younger Brother put on his clothes. They were nearly dry and he must attend to his pony, who was grazing a little way off.

170

He called the pony with a low sweet whistling sound. The white boy, busy driving tent stakes, thought he heard a mourning dove calling. He didn't know that Younger Brother had taught the pony to obey that call. It had taken months to teach him but now he always answered.

The pony came up to have the saddle removed. He was a pinto pony marked with big white spots on red. A small white crescent between the eyes was the only mark on his red face.

Younger Brother took the buckskin hobble from the saddle and put it on the pony's flanks. He went off to graze in the sagebrush.

A bucket of water was brought from the wash and left to stand over night. It was so muddy that it would take all night to settle. Everything was as cozy as possible inside the little tent and for the second night the two boys lay down to sleep.

The white boy was still wishing he could talk with the Navaho. There were so many questions to ask about cliff dwellings and arrows and old pottery and hunting. He knew that the boy had a bow and arrows but he hadn't seen him use them yet. They were lying close to him with the bridle and the saddle blanket. The white boy thought the silver bridle was a beauty and he knew his mother would like to own the blanket with the red tassels on the corners.

Younger Brother didn't miss the talking. Being an Indian he found entertainment in just lying still and doing nothing. Besides he was always thinking of the wide water where the Turquoise Woman lived in her turquoise house. He was content because he was headed toward the west. He fell asleep listening to the water roaring down the wash. It too was headed west and would some day lose its red, muddy self in the wide water, where the kind mother of all lived in her turquoise house.

171

PECOS BILL had the strangest and most exciting experience any boy ever had. He became a member of a pack of wild Coyotes, and until he was a grown man, believed that his name was Cropear, and that he was a full-blooded Coyote. Later he discovered that he was a human being and very shortly thereafter became the greatest cowboy of all time. This is how it all came about.

Pecos Bill's family was migrating westward through Texas in the early days, in an old covered wagon with wheels made from cross sections of a sycamore log. His father and mother were riding in the seat, and his father was driving a wall-eyed, spavined roan horse and a red and white spotted milch cow hitched side by side. The eighteen children in the back of the wagon were making such a medley of noises that their mother said it wasn't possible even to hear thunder.

Pecos Bill

BY JAMES CLOYD

BOWMAN

Illustrated by Laura Bannon

Just as the wagon was rattling down to the ford across the Pecos River, the rear left wheel bounced over a great piece of rock, and Bill, his red hair bristling like porcupine quills, rolled out of the rear of the wagon, and landed, up to his neck, in a pile of loose sand. He was only four years old at the time, and he lay dazed until the wagon had crossed the river and had disappeared into the sage brush. It wasn't until his mother rounded up the family for the noonday meal that Bill was missed. The last anyone remembered seeing him was just before they had forded the river.

The mother and eight or ten of the older children hurried

172

back to the river and hunted everywhere, but they could find no trace of the lost boy. When evening came they were forced to go back to the covered wagon, and later, to continue their journey without him. Ever after, when they thought of Bill, they remembered the river, and so they naturally came to speak of him as Pecos Bill.

What had happened to Bill was this. He had strayed off into the mesquite, and a few hours later was found by a wise old Coyote, who was the undisputed leader of the Loyal and Approved Packs of the Pecos and Rio Grande Valleys. He was, in fact, the Granddaddy of the entire race of Coyotes, and so his followers, out of affection to him, called him Grandy.

When he accidentally met Bill, Grandy was curious, but shy. He sniffed and he yelped, and he ran this way and that, the better to get the scent, and to make sure there was no danger. After a while he came quite near, sat up on his haunches, and waited to see what the boy would do. Bill trotted up to Grandy and began running his hands through the long, shaggy hair.

"What a nice old doggie you are," he repeated again and again.

"Yes, and what a nice Cropear you are," yelped Grandy joyously.

And so, ever after, the Coyotes called the child Cropear.

Grandy was much pleased with his find and so, by running ahead and stopping and barking softly, he led the boy to the jagged side of Cabezon, or the Big Head, as it was called. This was a towering mass of mountain that rose abruptly, as if by magic, from the prairie. Around the base of this mountain the various families of the Loyal and Approved Packs had burrowed out their dens.

Here, far away from the nearest human dwelling, Grandy made a home for Cropear, and taught him all the knowledge

173

of the wild out-of-doors. He led Cropear to the berries that were good to eat, and dug up roots that were sweet and spicy. He showed the boy how to break open the small nuts from the piñon; and when Cropear wanted a drink, he led him to a vigorous young mother Coyote who gave him of her milk. Cropear thus drank in the very life blood of a thousand generations of wild life and became a native beast of the prairie, without at all knowing that he was a man-child.

Grandy became his teacher and schooled him in the knowledge that had been handed down through thousands of generations of the Pack's life. He taught Cropear the many signal calls, and the code of right and wrong, and the gentle art of loyalty to the leader. He also trained him to leap long distances and to dance; and to flip-flop and to twirl his body so fast that the eye could not follow his movements. And most important of all, he instructed him in the silent, rigid pose of invisibility, so that he could see all that was going on around him without being seen.

And as Cropear grew tall and strong, he became the pet of the Pack. The Coyotes were always bringing him what they thought he would like to eat, and were ever showing him the many secrets of the fine art of hunting. They taught him where the Field Mouse nested, where the Song Thrush hid her eggs, where the Squirrel stored his nuts; and where the Mountain Sheep concealed their young among the towering rocks.

When the Jack Rabbit was to be hunted, they gave Cropear his station and taught him to do his turn in the relay race. And when the pronghorn Antelope was to be captured, Cropear took his place among the encircling pack and helped bring the fleeting animal to bay and pull him down, in spite of his darting, charging antlers.

Grandy took pains to introduce Cropear to each of the

174

animals and made every one of them promise he would not harm the growing man-child. "Au-g-gh!" growled the Mountain Lion, "I will be as careful as I can. But be sure to tell your child to be careful, too!"

"Gr-r-rr!" growled the fierce Grizzly Bear, "I have crunched many a marrow bone, but I will not harm your boy. Gr-r-rr!"

"Yes, we'll keep our perfumery and our quills in our inside vest pockets," mumbled the silly Skunk and Porcupine, as if suffering from adenoids.

But when Grandy talked things over with the Bull Rattlesnake, he was met with the defiance of hissing rattles. "Nobody will ever make me promise to protect anybody or anything! S-s-s-s-ss! I'll do just as I please!"

"Be careful of your wicked tongue," warned Grandy, "or you'll be very sorry."

But when Grandy met the Wouser, things were even worse. The Wouser was a cross between the Mountain Lion and the Grizzly Bear, and was ten times larger than either. Besides that, he was the nastiest creature in the world.

"I can only give you fair warning," yowled the Wouser, "and if you prize your man-child, as you say you do, you will have to keep him out of harm's way!" And as the Wouser continued, he stalked back and forth, lashing his tail and gnashing his jaws and acting as if he were ready to snap somebody's head off. "What's more, you know that nobody treats me as a friend. Everybody runs around behind my back spreading lies about me. Everybody says I carry hydrophobia—the deadly poison—about on my person, and because of all these lies, I am shunned like a leper. Now you come sneaking around asking me to help you. Get out of my sight before I do something I shall be sorry for!"

"I'm not sneaking," barked Grandy in defiance, "and besides, you're the one who will be sorry in the end."

So it happened that all the animals, save only the Bull Rattlesnake and the Wouser, promised to help Cropear bear a charmed life so that no harm should come near him. And by good fortune, the boy was never sick. The vigorous exercise and the fresh air and the constant sunlight helped him to become the healthiest, strongest, most active boy in the world.

All this time Cropear was growing up in the belief that he was a full-blooded Coyote. Long before he had grown to manhood, he learned to understand the language of every creeping, hopping, walking, and flying creature; and, boylike, he began to amuse himself by mimicking every animal of his acquaintance. He soon learned to trill and warble like a Mocking Bird, and to growl like a Grizzly Bear. He could even yowl like a Wouser and sputter like a stupid Skunk.

The Coyotes didn't much like this mimic language, for they were never sure whether they were hearing a Sage Hen or a Buffalo or a Cricket, or whether it was merely Cropear at his play. But Cropear was so full of animal spirits and healthy mischief that he could never keep long from this sport. In time he became so expert as a mimic that he could confuse even the Rattlesnake or the Field Mouse or the Antelope. He could thus call any animal to himself, assume the rigid pose of invisibility, and completely deceive the cleverest creature alive.

By the time Cropear had become a man, he could run with the fleetest of the Coyotes. At night, he squatted on his haunches

176

in the circle and barked and yipped and howled sadly, according to the best tradition of the Pack.

The loyal and Approved Packs were proud, indeed, that they had made a man-child into a Noble Coyote, the equal of the best both in the hunt and in the inner circle where the laws and customs of the Pack were unfolded. They were prouder still that they had taught him to believe that the Human Race, to a greater extent than any other race of animals, was inhuman. Just what the Human Race was, Cropear never knew, however. For Grandy kept him far away even from the cowboys' trails.

Then one day Grandy went out alone to hunt and did not return; and everyone knew that he had gone down the long, long trail that has no turning.

Not long after Grandy's disappearance, a remarkable adventure befell Cropear. He was, at the time, hunting across the rolling mesa. He had just stopped to examine a stretch of grassy plain where the prairie dogs had built themselves a city. The prairie dogs were making merry as if playing at hide-and-seek in and out of their hidden doorways.

Cropear was lying on the ground stretched out on his stomach and resting on his elbows, his chin in his palms. He suddenly became aware of the dull *tlot, tlot* of an approaching broncho. This was not strange, for he had often met ponies. But now he became conscious of a strange odor. Cropear prided himself on knowing every scent of every animal in his part of the world. This, however, was different; it tickled his nose and was like fire in the wild grasses. It was, in fact, the first whiff of tobacco he had smelled since he was a child, and it awakened in him a vague memory of a world of long lost dreams.

Immediately Cropear became curious and forgot for the

moment the first and most universal law of the Pack—the law of staying put, of sitting so still that he could not be seen. He sat up suddenly and threw his head about to see what this strange smell might be. There, but a few yards distant, the buckskin cow pony and his rider, Chuck, came to a sudden, slithering halt.

Cropear suddenly let out three scared yelps and turned on his heels to run away. Chuck—himself a perfect mimic—repeated the scared yelps. This aroused Cropear's curiosity further. He stopped and let out another series of yelps. These Chuck again repeated. In the Coyote language, Cropear was asking, "Who are you? Who are you?" Chuck was repeating this question without in the least knowing what the yips meant.

Thus began the most amusing dialogue in all the history of talk. Cropear would bark a question over and over, and in reply Chuck would mimic him perfectly.

Cropear kept galloping in circles, curiously sniffing, and wondering when and where it was he had smelled man and tobacco. Chuck kept his hand on his gun and his eyes on the strange wild creature. He couldn't help admiring the sheer physical beauty of this perfect, healthy wild man. Every muscle was so fully developed that he looked like another Hercules.

Cropear was, in fact, as straight as a wagon-tongue. His skin, from living all his life in the open sunlight and wind, was a lustrous brown, covered with a fine silken fell of burnished red hair. Over his shoulders lay the bristling mane of his unshorn locks.

After an hour or two of galloping about, Cropear lost much of his fear, approached nearer, and squatted down on his haunches to see what would happen.

"You're a funny baby!" Chuck laughed.

178

"Funny baby," Cropear lisped like a child of four.

The cowpuncher talked in a low, musical accent; and slowly and brokenly at first, Cropear began to prattle. He was taking up the thread of his speech where he had dropped it years before when he was lost by his family.

For nearly a month Chuck wandered around on the mesa and continued his dialogue with Cropear. Chuck would patiently repeat words and sentences many times. He was forced to use his hands and arms and his face and voice to illustrate all that he said. But Cropear proved such an apt pupil that soon he was saying and understanding everything. What's more, Cropear's speech became far more grammatical than Chuck's own, for only the finest language had ever been permitted among the Coyotes. And Cropear had evolved a combination of the two. The worst he ever said from then on, in cowboy lingo, was just an "ain't" or two.

Chuck was astonished at the speed with which he learned. "He's brighter'n a new minted dollar!" Chuck declared to his broncho.

Over and over Chuck asked Cropear, "Who in the name of common sense are you, anyhow?" Cropear tried his best to remember, yet all he knew was that he was a Coyote. "But who are you?" Cropear asked in turn.

"My real name is Bob Hunt," Chuck laughed, "but the boys all call me Chuckwagon because I'm always hungry—Chuck for short." He drawled his words musically as he swung into an easy position across his saddle. "What are you doin', runnin' around here naked like a wild Coyote, that's what I want to know?"

"I *am* a Coyote," Cropear snapped back.

"Coyote, nothin'! You're a *human*!"

"An accursed *human*! I guess not! I wouldn't belong to

179

that degraded *inhuman* race for anything in the world. Haven't I got fleas? Don't I hunt with the pack and run the fleet prong-horn Antelope and the spry Jack Rabbit off their legs? And don't I sit on my haunches, and don't I have my place in the circle, and don't I howl at night in accordance with the ancient approved custom of all thoroughbred Coyotes? Don't you suppose I know who I am as well as you?" Cropear answered quite out of patience.

"You've just been eatin' of the locoweed and are a little out of your head," laughed Chuck. "Besides, every human in Texas has got fleas, so that's got nothin' at all to do with it."

"I haven't been eating of the locoweed! Only silly cattle and mustangs do a thing like that. I *am* in my right mind—and what's more, I *am* a Coyote!"

"You're loco, or else I am," insisted the smiling Chuck. "Why, you're a *human* just the same as I am. Don't you know that every Coyote's got a long bushy tail? Now, you ain't got no tail at all and you know it."

Strange as it may seem, this was the first time that Cropear had really looked himself over, and sure enough, he saw at once that he had no tail.

Just at this instant, Chuck caught sight of a strange mark on Cropear's upper right arm—a tattooed star, showing plainly through the red fell of hair.

"I'll be locoed if I ain't got one of them, too," he cried, pointing to a similar mark on his own arm.

Cropear looked first at his arm, then at Chuck's. "What does it mean?" he asked, slowly.

"It means you're found. You're my little lost brother Bill. You ain't Cropear and you ain't never been."

Cropear stood stone still. "Your brother?"

"Surest thing you know. Listen. This is how I know. When

180

Dad was travelin' around once with a Patent Medicine Man, he learned how to do this here tattooin'. So when us kids arrived, Mother got the idea it'd be a good thing to have a big star on the arm of each and every one of us. She said she didn't intend any of us ever to forget the Lone Star State we belonged to. And what's more, if any one of us happened to get lost, this star would help find us. So, as usual, Mother was right! You got lost but you're found again. See?"

"Now you sound as if you're the one that's been eating of the locoweed and gone crazy," Cropear replied.

"It's the honest truth, I'm tellin' you. I'd be willin' to stand on a stack of Bibles as high as the moon and repeat every word of it out in public, if you'd but quit your foolish notion that you're a varmint."

"Varmint, indeed!" Cropear snarled. "You're completely locoed. It's the pale-face *inhumans* that are low-down varmints! Coyotes are the noblest of all the earth's creatures!"

Fortunately Chuck was so interested in the story he was just beginning that he did not take time to answer this last insult.

"Honestly, Cropear—Bill, I mean. This is what happened. Our family was goin' along from the Brazos River valley down to the Rio Grande. Dad was drivin' a little east-Texas spotted cow and a little wall-eyed spavined roan horse. They was hitched to an old covered wagon with wooden wheels made from cross sections of a sycamore tree. Mother'd insisted it was gettin' too crowded up there in Texas, and she wanted to be where there was at least elbow room."

"What kind of woman was she, anyway?" Cropear asked curiously.

"Well, judge for yourself. She swept forty-five Indian Chiefs out of her back yard with her broomstick one mornin'

182

before breakfast. You see, she found them prowlin' around, set on doin' mischief, and she sent them flyin' with one swoop and never give it more never mind than as if they was a bunch of sage chickens, or meddlesome porcupines.

"You probably don't remember it, but you cut your teeth on a Bowie knife that Davy Crockett sent our mother as a present when he heard what a brave, wise woman she was."

"Well, that's the kind of mother I have always dreamed I would like. Perhaps I am partly *human,* after all," Cropear now conceded. This mother sounded very fine indeed!

"Well, as we was migratin' in the covered wagon," Chuck continued without noticing the remark, "I guess you jumped overboard right along about here. Half a day passed before the rest of us discovered that you was missin', and then when we come back, we couldn't find you."

"So that was it," Cropear said as in a dream. "But when my mother discovered that I was gone, what then?"

"Well, it was the old story of the 'Ninety and Nine' all over again each day, ever after. Your mother had the whole seventeen of us to feed and look after; but she was often talkin' about her Little Lost Bill. Sometimes she put in the Pecos part, for the last sight she had of you when when she inspected things just before the wagon started to ford this river. She used to wake up in the middle of the night and get to thinkin' the Coyotes and Grizzly Bears was crunchin' your tender bones. And I can hear her yet, at table, sighin' as she looked at your vacant chair. Her last words when she died were, 'Now I'll be seein' Little Bill!' "

"The dear good woman," Cropear sighed, in genuine relief, "but I can never love her as I love Grandy. And what about my father?"

Chuck laughed loud and long. "He was a regular copperas

183

breeches and one gallus kind of man. He had seven dogs, a cob pipe and a roll of home-spun tobacco stuck down his pocket. He would spend more time pokin' a rabbit out of a hollow tree than he would to secure shelter for his family in a storm. He could easily afford to have one or two of his children blow away, but rabbits was too scarce to take the chance of losin' one! You see, he didn't count for much with Mother. A woman who could sweep out forty-five big Indian Chiefs with a single broom-handle couldn't be expected to show much mercy for a mere husband.

"Besides, she'd never have been able to scare the Big Chiefs so easily if she hadn't been practisin' up on her own old man! Fact is, she was the cock of the walk at our ranch. Dad merely took orders. We nicknamed him Moses. But Mother was the God of the Mountain! She wrote her commands on tables of stone and the poor man who received them from her hands was meek. I'm tellin' you, he was meek!"

"Your story begins to sound reasonable, and I do agree that I now see a faint likeness between us. . . . But

I don't want to be an *inhuman*! I don't want to have to wear clothes and ride horses. I want to be free! I want to continue to be strong. I want to be healthy like my brothers, the Bears, the Wolves, and the Coyotes, who are wild and natural and vigorous! I want to live where I can lay me down on a sheet of mist and roll up in a blanket of fog. I want to sleep where I can breathe the clean air and see the countless eyes of all my brother animals peeping down at me as they race across the sky!"

"Don't be a fool, brother. It's high time for you to forget that you was ever called Cropear. It's right and proper for you now to become Pecos Bill. Come with me and I'll take you to the ranch house, where you'll be happier than you've ever been yet."

"But I can't think of going with you today. I've at least got to go back and take my farewell of the Pack."

"Well then, tomorrow. Tomorrow I'll come for you. And I'll say we'll teach you the gentlest of all ancient arts, the art of the ranch. Oh yes, you'll still be right in the great out-of-doors. With your strength like an ox and your spry heels, you'll become the greatest of all the great cowmen the world has ever known."

Chuck's words stirred something deep within Cropear's nature. What it was, he did not know. But he saw clearly in this instant, that come what might, he must go with Chuck. Lifting his head with a gesture of determination, he said solemnly, "Brother Chuck, I hear the call! Today I bid you adieu; tomorrow I join you!"

With these words and without once looking back, Cropear loped easily over the chappiro, across the rolling mesa. He skirted the sagebrush and was soon lost in the haze of the distant mesquite.

BILL Peters was a hustler
From Independence town;
He warn't a college scholar
Nor man of great renown,
But Bill had a way o' doin' things
An' doin' 'em up brown.

Bill driv the stage from Independence
Up to Smoky Hill;
And everybody knowed him thar
As Independence Bill,
Thar warn't no feller on the route
That driv with half the skill.

Bill driv four pair of horses,
Same as you'd drive a team,
And you'd think you was a travelin'
On a railroad driv by steam;
And he'd get thar on time, you bet,
Or Bill 'u'd bust a seam!

He carried mail and passengers,
And he started on the dot,
And them teams o' his'n, so they say,
Was never known to trot;
But they went it in a gallop
And kep' their axles hot.

Bill Peters, the Stage Driver

AMERICAN

FRONTIER BALLAD

Illustrated by

Douglas Gorsline

When Bill's stage 'u'd bust a tire,
Or something 'u'd break down,
He'd hustle round an' patch her up
And start off with a bound;

And the wheels o' that old shack o' his
Scarce ever touched the ground.

And Bill didn't 'low no foolin',
And when Injuns hove in sight,
And bullets rattled at the stage,
He druv with all his might.
He'd holler, "Fellers, give it to 'em!
I ain't got time to fight."

Then the way them wheels 'u'd rattle,
And the way the dust 'u'd fly,
You'd think a million cattle
Had stampeded and gone by;
But the mail 'u'd get thar just the same,
If the horses had to die.

He driv the stage for many a year
Along the Smoky Hill,
And a pile o' wild Comanches
Did Bill Peters have to kill,
And I reckon if he had got luck
He'd be drivin' still.

But he chanced one day to run agin
A bullet made o' lead,
Which was harder than he bargained for
And now poor Bill is dead;
And when they brung his body home
A barrel of tears was shed.

187

OUT where the hand-clasp's a little stronger,
Out where the smile dwells a little longer—
   That's where the West begins.
Out where the sun shines a little brighter,
Where the snows that fall are a trifle whiter,
And the bonds of home are a wee bit tighter—
   That's where the West begins.

Out where the skies
   are a trifle bluer,
Where friendship ties
   are a little truer—
   That's where the West begins.
Out where a fresher
   breeze is blowing,
Where there's laughter
   in every streamlet flowing,
Where there's more of reaping
   and less of sowing—
   That's where the West begins.

Out Where the West Begins

BY

ARTHUR CHAPMAN

Illustrated by

Douglas Gorsline

Out where the world is still in the making,
Where fewer hearts in despair are breaking—
   That's where the West begins.
Where there's more of singing and less of sighing,
Where there's more of giving and less of buying,
And a man makes friends without half trying—
   That's where the West begins.

NO TALE of the spur ever told is more heroic than that of the race of Portuguese Phillips against torture and death in the killing cold of a Wyoming blizzard.

Late December of the terrible winter of 1866 found a little band of American troops isolated at Fort Phil Kearney, Wyoming. There were one hundred and nineteen men, and there were women and children. A few miles from the fort, Red Cloud, at the head of three thousand Sioux warriors, had just destroyed to the last man a detachment of eighty-one soldiers. The victorious warriors now encircled the fort. Destruction seemed certain unless help could be secured. The nearest help was at Fort Laramie, two hundred and thirty-six miles away down the bleak and empty Bozeman Trail.

It was the night of December 21. The thermometer stood thirty degrees below zero. The cold was so intense that the sentries had to be relieved every fifteen minutes. Every hour men shoveled the drifting snow back from the walls of the stockade so that it would

In a Wyoming Blizzard

BY J. FRANK DOBIE

Illustrated by

Lorence F. Bjorklund

not bank up and form a bridge for the Sioux warriors to cross on. Finally the commanding officer in desperation called for a volunteer to go for aid.

Portuguese Phillips answered the call. He had been a trapper with the Hudson's Bay Company. He knew the country like a coyote. He had lived for years among the Sioux and had married one of them. He was now post interpreter; it is said that he was also employed as scout and hunter. Most of the

189

details about him that have come down are uncertain. It is certain that he filled his pockets with dried meat and hardtack, tied a bag of grain on his horse, and about midnight began his perilous journey.

He fully realized that he must take the utmost care in order to get through the Indian lines. Red Cloud would be looking for a messenger to go out. Phillips' plan was to crawl, leading his horse, until he should get past the danger of detection. He had a lariat sixty feet long. His horse was pure white, selected on account of his color as well as mettle, for a white horse against white snow is hard to see—especially at night. A horse carrying an empty saddle is likely to shake himself making considerable noise; to avoid the risk of betrayal by such a noise, Phillips led his horse forth without saddle. He would make the ride bareback.

For hours he crawled, paused, listened, felt his way, led his horse. Then he mounted and struck for Fort Laramie. He knew that the Indians were waylaying the trail; so he avoided it, picking his own route, sometimes miles off the beaten road. The snow on the ground was from three to five feet deep; the blizzard blowing down from the Big Horn Mountains never laid. Each morning at daybreak he took cover in brush; his only chance was to travel in darkness. At dawn of Christmas Day, after four nights of riding, he reached Horseshoe Station, forty miles still from Fort Laramie and a hundred and ninety-six miles from the fort he had left. There he telegraphed. But he did not trust the telegraph, and as soon as darkness fell he rode on.

It was well that he did not trust the telegraph. The line had either been cut or put out of order by the blizzard. At eleven o'clock that night the giant figure of Portuguese Phillips entered "Bedlam." Bedlam was the officers' club house at

190

Fort Laramie, and when the exhausted messenger came through the door, a gay Christmas ball was in full swing. His hands, knees, and feet were frozen, although he was swathed from head to foot in buffalo skin. He was shaggy with snow. His beard trailed icicles. He gasped out that he was a courier with a desperate dispatch. Then he reeled and fell upon the floor.

The besieged folk at Fort Phil Kearney were saved.

Portuguese Phillips was just one of the riders who won the West. The story of his ride is just a detail in a riding tradition that neither automobile nor airplane can ever entirely run away from.

OH, give me a home where the buffalo roam,
Where the deer and the antelope play,
Where seldom is heard a discouraging word
And the skies are not cloudy all day.

Home, home on the range,
Where the deer and the antelope play,
Where seldom is heard a discouraging word
And the skies are not cloudy all day.

Where the air is so pure,
    the zephyrs so free,
The breezes so balmy and light,
That I would not exchange
    my home on the range
For all of the cities so bright.

The red man was pressed
    from this part of the West,
He's likely no more to return
To the banks of Red River
    where seldom if ever
Their flickering campfires burn.

A Home on the Range

AMERICAN COWBOY

BALLAD

Illustrated by

André LeBlanc

How often at night when the heavens are bright
With the light from the glittering stars
Have I stood there amazed and asked as I gazed
If their glory exceeds that of ours.

Oh, I love these wild flowers in this dear land of ours,
The curlew I love to hear scream,
And I love the white rocks and the antelope flocks
That graze on the mountaintops green.

192

Oh, give me a land where the bright diamond sand
Flows leisurely down the stream,
Where the graceful white swan goes gliding along
Like a maid in a heavenly dream.

Then I would not exchange my home on the range,
Where the deer and the antelope play,
Where seldom is heard a discouraging word
And the skies are not cloudy all day.

Home, home on the range,
Where the deer and the antelope play,
Where seldom is heard a discouraging word
And the skies are not cloudy all day.

THE Jungle is in many ways a very good school both for animals and little boys. My father was so convinced of this that he never troubled about any other kind of education until I was much older. "To read and write is a dangerous thing," he would say, "and the learning thereof should not be undertaken before a man is duly fortified by experience." So I was carefully instructed in the ways of the tiger and the leopard before being subjected to the risk of book-learning!

I was taught the ways of the jungle, the meaning of nature and the place of man among his brothers, the creatures below and the gods above. Of course it was not all study and no play because in between studying life and nature we used to go off on tramping trips.

My Education

BY
DHAN GOPAL MUKERJI

Illustrated by

Ernest Crichlow

We went on observing the life of the forest and the more we learned about it, the less we destroyed, for my father said: "There are three laws for man in the jungle: First, he must not kill without warning. Second, he must not kill for food; and Third, he must neither hate nor fear."

To illustrate the first rule, my father told me how once he had gone on a hunting expedition with two young English subalterns. They had set up a shooting platform in a likely place and had tethered a goat near by for a decoy. Soon after nightfall a leopard made his appearance, and possibly because he suspected a trap, he failed to attack the goat. The moonlight fell brilliantly clear and one could plainly see him turn as though about to walk away. One of the Englishmen, impatient and afraid of losing his quarry, was foolish enough to shoot. Considering his haste it was not surprising that he missed. Instantly, my father said, the animal turned about and leaped at the platform. In the dark one could not make out how he reached it so quickly. A flash of moonlight fell across his flank and then on the white fangs of his open jaw, and lo, he was upon them! There was no time for a second shot and no room to take aim. My father leaped to the ground, giving a long piercing wail—the cry of a she-leopard in peril. The creature, startled, turned to look, and in that instant my father shot him through the shoulder. So always, if you cry to an animal or throw a stone at it, for a moment it will pause in surprise and be off guard and you will have your chance to aim at a vulnerable spot. When you give warning you have asserted the superiority of your nerves over your adversary's, and that is half the battle won.

One of the first things my father taught me was how to know in which direction an animal was passing and why. I had to learn by the nature of the tracks and by the odor and by the movements of the undergrowth as an animal passed, what kind of a creature it was that I was likely to meet. Suppose it were a bear? How would I know it by the track I was following? There were many ways but the inevitable one was this. Bears have a great love for eating ants out of an ant-hill. The ants make their hills so that they go in and out of their home through only a hole, and this little aperture is the only source of ventilation for the ant-hill. By a suction started at this hole, all the ants can be drawn out of the ant-hill. So in a jungle infested with bears, I would keep a sharp eye out for ant-hills. I would carefully examine each one I came to in order to make sure whether the bear had passed that way or not. If the ant-hill were empty of ants, that meant the bear had

195

eaten them all and had gone on, and was ahead of me, but if the ant-hill were full of ants, everything was safe; the bear was somewhere far behind. Though the bear does not eat human beings, he does not like the sight of them. No sooner does a bear see a man close than he runs after him and, if he can, scratches him from head to foot with his claws. Several scratches from a bear's claws are apt to be fatal. You must remember there is no escape from a bear by running up a tree, for he too can run up and pursue you from branch to branch until he kills you.

During the rainy season it is very difficult to know where the bears are. Even the tracks are quite impossible to recognize. Between showers, it is easy to discern their footprints but it is altogether hopeless to tell the nature of an animal by examining his footprints after a shower. However, in the rainy

196

season there is one safeguard: the animals are not so apt to attack each other at that season. You would be surprised to know how afraid they are of rain and thunder. Once I was deep in the recesses of the jungle with my father when the rain and the thunder burst upon us. It was two o'clock in the afternoon and suddenly the clouds overcast the sky, the thunder pealed, and the heart of the forest was thick as midnight gloom. By the afterglow of each lightning flash I could see mysterious inquiring eyes coming out at us, as if to ask questions. The wondering, frightened animals that were looking at us did not growl, nor did they wish to attack us; there was no malice in their questioning eyes; they seemed to say, "So you are also in the same danger as we. Some fellows have found a big gun somewhere and are firing it at us, while they shake the heavens with their torches. Well, since we are all likely to be shot, we won't attack you if you don't attack us!" Though the animals are dumb, their eyes tell more stories than we with our continual jabbering. Down came the rain and the darkness like the end of all things. It was very uncanny—that feeling of wet darkness. It was as if a huge black panther, wet to the marrowbone, were rubbing his side against my leg, and when the wind blew through the forest this soaked hide of gloom shivered and every black hair on it stood erect and wet. When the storm was over, however— about half-past four—almost the entire jungle was alight with the afternoon sun, very pale by the time it penetrated the thick depth at the heart of the forest. Suddenly we heard a strange humming sound. It was as if a million bees were swarming somewhere.

"There is a bear ahead of us!" said my father. "He is in quest of honey but he is too early. It will be another fortnight before the combs are well filled. He must be very hungry, or he would wait. Let us go far away!"

The crooning of the bear drew nearer and nearer, and we began to draw away from him in the opposite direction but still he came closer. Suddenly my father said,

"He will be upon us in a minute. We must make haste!"

We moved in the direction of the wind, for we did not want the odor of our presence to be blown toward the bear. Suddenly the bear's decoy cry stopped and we thought we were safe. Then we heard the humming of the bees not far from us. We looked around but could see nothing. We looked up, and behold, there was the bear on a tree above us, eating honey from a comb! The bees were coming home, and their humming grew louder and louder as they approached.

"If we are not killed by the bear," my father said, "we will be stung to death by the bees."

198

So we stealthily moved away. My father began to imitate the sound of humming in order to draw away the bees from the bear, who would not molest us while eating honey, but he did not hum loud enough to attract the bees far in our direction. For a moment he stopped his humming and listened. We heard the bear snarl and we knew that the bees had found him and were tormenting him. Then we climbed hastily into the next tree and watched. In a few minutes the snarling bear fell down to the ground with a thud and ran off into the jungle in an effort to save his snout from the angry swarm. So you see, if you cannot detect the presence of a bear by an ant-hill, you can detect it by examining the honeycombs in the trees, for he will never pass honey without eating it.

My father could imitate many sounds besides the humming of bees which he taught me, and which were very useful to us. For example, we could call to each other by using the cry of the wild peacock. We chose this cry first of all because it was very loud and clear, and secondly, because peacocks were not very numerous, and we were less likely to confuse our own calls with theirs. But things did get mixed up sometimes. Once I called to him from a treetop and instead of my father's answering my summons, a gigantic male peacock came and pranced about looking for his mate. I then cried some more in peacock language. His tail bristled up, he spread his fan and started to look for his antagonist, for apparently I was not giving the call of the female peacock but of the male, the challenge of another male fighting for a mate!

I have spoken at length of bears, for we depended considerably on killing them for our livelihood. Bear skins were greatly in demand in foreign markets. This soon became very easy for my father, for bear hunting to a man of his steady nerves was almost child's play. A bear exposes himself readily

199

to a bullet, standing on his hind legs to attack, while other animals, like the tiger, leap at you too quickly to make an easy mark.

One day we were in the forest wandering about. Suddenly, and not knowing why, we heard a growl and a snarl. We stood back and in the semidarkness of the forest we saw a vast mass of black charging at us. My father told me to stand behind him, which I did, but I bent sideways to have a look at what was going on. It would not have done to shoot at the dark mass because where the bear's hair was so long and so thick the bullet might have glanced off his body; had it been a tiger, on the contrary, one could have shot into his chest or his back, breaking the backbone—in some ways an easier matter. But though we knew by his howl it was a bear, we had to wait until he came nearer, which gave him quite an advantage over us. Very soon we saw the gigantic black creature running at us but my father did not move a muscle. I thought he was petrified with terror. The bear came nearer and nearer. I could feel his hair standing on end in anger. His eyes glowed like

red-brown fire, and from his lolling tongue was falling a stream of foaming, white saliva. His teeth gleamed like knives, and yet my father did not raise a finger to save himself or me. I longed to turn around and run but my feet felt heavier than lead as I stood rooted to the spot in terror, hypnotized by my fright. Suddenly the bear leaped up, as it were. He stood on his hind legs—he seemed to come faster that way than on all fours—and reached out his front paws hardly two yards away from my father's face. I could feel his claws rend the air. He opened his mouth wide, where white saliva foamed in a furnace of red. I almost felt his white-hot breath upon me, when like an electric shock, my father's hands rose up, the barrel of the rifle went into the furnace-mouth, and with a thunder-clap, the shot rang out. Blood spurted into the air, followed by a ghastly wail of pain, the last sound of life. I say "sound of life" because I had closed my eyes: I could see no more, I only heard. I felt my father shaking me. When I opened my eyes he said sweetly, "It is not wise to be afraid, little son. Your fear kills you long before what you fear has come upon you. Look, the bear is almost eight feet long. It is a pity that I cannot save his head. His skull is ruined. We must now flay him. But it is getting dark; let us go up into a tree and wait till morn." The dead bear kept watch for us below while we stayed in the tree all night. Because he stayed there no animals came to the spot at all. Death has a strange effect upon most animals. If an animal's kindred is killed, he does not visit the spot for a long time.

In the morning we got down and flayed the bear. It was surprising to notice that no animal came to eat up the corpse. Apparently the creatures that lived in that part of the jungle never ate bear flesh. For that reason we found the skin quite intact when morning came.

 EARLY one morning Suatsuak came to Oomialik and told her, "I go with Ittuk up to the mouth of the river to spear fish. Will you let Salumo go with us?"

Oomialik gave her permission, then turned to Salumo. "Remember, Salumo," she cautioned, "you are going up to fresh water. Fresh-water ice is dangerous. While it may look thick, it falls away in long strips. Sea ice is tough and will bend, but fresh-water ice is brittle." Salumo knew this was true and nodded his head.

While making preparations to go, Suatsuak discovered that one of his dogs couldn't travel that day on account of his front foot which had been cut on the sharp ice and still hadn't healed. "Let us take my dog, Sokkotuk," said Salumo. "He is a good leader for my puppy team and is old enough to run with the big dogs." So Sokkotuk was harnessed with the others.

Dangerous Ice Pans

BY HELUIZ WASHBURN
AND ANAUTA

Illustrated by Kurt Wiese

"You had better tie shoes on those three dogs of ours," said Suatsuak. "Their feet were bleeding yesterday."

Salumo got the strips of skin and put them on the dogs' feet, slipping the toenails through the little holes and tying the strips around the ankles. As he did so he saw where the sharp ice had cut deep gashes in the flesh, and decided he had better put shoes on Sokkotuk, too. But Sokkotuk had never worn them before and didn't know what to make of the queer things. He cocked his ears and looked at them, sniffed, lay down on his back and kicked his feet, rolled over and rubbed

202

his paws together, doubled up and tried to bite them off. Salumo stood watching his antics and laughing till his sides hurt. Finally he called sharply, "Sokkotuk!" and the dog got up. But when he walked he lifted his feet high and set them down carefully, like an old man.

Even with the shoes on, the poor dogs ran lame. It was not until the skins became wet and the melting snow softened the hard sores that they stopped limping.

Salumo and Ittuk trotted along happily beside Suatsuak, jumping on the sled sometimes for a short ride. The sun shone down on the gleaming whiteness all about them, and glistened on the millions of little ice particles frozen in the snow.

"You had better put on your eye shields, Salumo," said Suatsuak. He and Ittuk had already put on theirs. These strips of skin with narrow slits for the eyes gave welcome protection from the terrible snow glare.

"I didn't bring mine."

"Didn't Oomialik tell you to take them?"

"Ami-lang! But I did not think I would need them."

"Salumo was not wise. He did not know what was best!" said Suatsuak, running on without looking at him.

After awhile Salumo knew he had been very foolish. The glaring whiteness hurt his eyes. He looked up at the blue sky, but was blinded by the sparkling ice drops. Even in the sky he could see them glittering. They seemed to be inside his eyes.

The sun was high when they reached the mouth of the river. Now the dogs lay down to rest. They would wait quietly all day without being fastened. Salumo took off their worn snowshoes, and they began contentedly to lick their poor swollen paws.

In the river the ice was still firm, but at the mouth of the river, where the sun and tides had been at work, the ice had broken into great floating pans which drifted with the current, heaving, bumping, and knocking against each other.

Salumo kept looking at those pans of ice. How he would love to get out there and jump from one to another! He thought of all the times he and Angmak and Supeali had chased each other over the bobbing ice pans. It was exciting!

Suatsuak saw his eyes light up and knew what he was thinking. All the children loved to play on the dangerous ice pans. The danger was half the fun. Hadn't he done it many times himself? But he didn't like the look of them today, and he warned Salumo, "You keep away from those pans! There is too much current. One might break with you. You would be swept under and drowned. Stay away from them."

Salumo listened in silence. He had come here to fish, he knew, and reluctantly he got to work. Suatsuak and Ittuk, fishing spears in hand, were already lying out on the ice peering down through a crack, and lowering their lines. Taking up his own long handled spear, he threw himself down not far away.

For a long time he lay this way, on his left side, dangling his line, his eyes glued to the crack, spear poised. From time to time he thrust, quickly and accurately, the way Oomialik had taught him. When he pulled up his spear there was a plump trout wiggling frantically in the grip of the two curving prongs that were clamped around his middle. Finally he had quite a nice pile of trout. He was tired of lying still. And out there were the ice pans!

Salumo remembered Suatsuak's warning, but the pans looked firm. He tried to keep his mind on the fishing, but instead of watching the fish he looked more often toward the mouth of the river where the big ice blocks were bumping each other, and drifting apart again. "If only I could have a few jumps on them!" he thought, "I would feel more like fishing." He looked at Suatsuak. He was busy with his fishing, and so was Ittuk. Salumo laid his spear on the ice, walked slowly down to the river mouth, and jumped onto one of the large ice pans.

He tingled with excitement as he felt it dip under his weight. This was fun! Just as it went down he leaped quickly to another one, then to another and another. He dared not rest for they sank under him, so he kept hopping from piece to piece. Sometimes the jumps were quite long, and he nearly lost his balance. But that was the thrill he loved.

He was having a fine time till suddenly he had to jump onto a large piece that didn't look too safe. He felt it break with his weight. Then he plunged helplessly into the icy river. Down he went. The water closed over his head and he felt himself being sucked under. When he came up, gasping, he saw that he was being carried to the edge of the firm ice. What was it Suatsuak had said about being swept under it? He threw up his arms just in time to catch hold of the edge of the ice, but the force of the current dragged at his legs. If he was washed under that ice, no one could ever reach him!

He began to shout with all his strength. Would they hear him? Would they come in time? His hands were freezing, his fingers had no feeling. The current tugged at his body, he couldn't hold on much longer. His fingers were slipping. "Aai! Aai!" he screamed.

Just then he saw Suatsuak and Ittuk running toward him. They grabbed his hands and, pulling with all their strength, got him up onto the ice. His heavy fur clothes and boots were full of water. There was no way to get dry ones, so, while Sal-

umo stood there shaking, Suatsuak ran his hands down over his suit, squeezing out as much water as possible, and Ittuk pulled off his boots and emptied them.

"We must start home at once. Hurry!" said Suatsuak. "You'll freeze."

The fish were quickly packed into a sealskin bag and loaded on the sled. The dogs were harnessed, and with a "oo-isht, oo-isht!" from Suatsuak, they started on the run. Often Suatsuak threw out the long line of the dog whip with a quick turn of the wrist, and the lash cracked like a gun shot, making the dogs leap ahead.

There was no night at this time of the year, but the sun went behind the hills and it was bitterly cold, with a strong wind blowing.

Salumo shivered until his teeth rattled. His feet ached with the cold. They were so heavy he could hardly pick them up, for the water from his clothes kept dripping inside his boots and they were caked with ice. When he was too miserable to go a step farther, he climbed on the sled to rest. But each time, Suatsuak shoved him off and made him run. "You'll freeze stiff if you sit there," he said, anxiously.

Salumo knew Suatsuak was right. He knew, too, that now he was paying for his disobedience. But worse than that, what would Oomialik say about this foolishness?

When they reached home Oomialik helped Salumo out of his frozen clothes and into his dry sleeping bag to get warm. He was too tired to tell the day's adventures, but Suatsuak and Ittuk explained the details as they divided up the fish.

Oomialik listened as she puffed her pipe. When she heard that Salumo had not even been fishing when he fell into the water, she shook her head, but didn't say a word. Salumo, sitting over on the furs of the sleeping place, wished Oomialik would scold him instead of just shaking her head like that, for he knew what she was thinking.

Now Salumo was sorry he had not worn his eye shields that day. His eyes were beginning to burn and he couldn't stand the light. He tried to cover them to keep them dark, but this made them hot. Burning tears flowed down his cheeks. Frantic with pain, he crawled into the back of the igloo and hid like a wounded animal. He couldn't see, he couldn't even keep his eyes open; fiery needles seemed to stab them. He lowered his head on his knees and covered them with his arms.

"Why, why can't I ever do as I'm told," he moaned. This snow blindness would last for many days, and no one could help him. He must only wait for the pain to pass. Deeper he buried his head in the darkness between his knees, and the hot tears flowed without stopping.

That night while Salumo was still huddled wretchedly in the back of the sleeping place, Oomialik took up her sewing and began to speak. "I will tell you of a time when my son, Salumo, the brave hunter for whom you were named, was snow-blinded as you are now. It happened while he was on a hunting trip. He groped his way back to his dogs, crawling over lumps of ice, fearing he would fall into some great crack. The dogs finally hauled him home safely. After that, one day followed another and he could not see. He could not go to hunt. There was not much food, and the other families had moved on for better hunting. We were left by ourselves. Our dogs died, and we were weak from hunger.

"It was winter when the big ice is grinding and crashing in the straits and the whales come into the quiet places near shore. For several days I had been seeing them, but had not the strength to throw the spear hard enough or far enough to get one—not the way Salumo could, were he able to see. But he was blind.

"Then one day Salumo told me to guide him to the edge of the firm ice. I did. And he stood there, on the edge, with me beside him. 'Now, when a whale comes up,' he said, 'tell me exactly where he is and I will try to get him!'

"In a short while I saw three white whales bobbing up and

down. I told him where to throw. He missed the first time, drew in his harpoon by the long line and thrust again. This time he got a whale—a little harmless white whale that was just flopping around in play. But we were happy for the meat is tender and good.

"The dart was in him and we wound the line around a lump of rough ice so he couldn't get away. When he came in close enough we darted him with our spears. Then we hauled him up against the ice. He was slick and smooth all over, and white like the snow—and what delicious eating!" Oomialik smacked her lips, remembering it. "We had plenty to eat then, and enough to last till some hunters came with their teams to help us. And that is how my son, Salumo, saved our lives when he was snow-blinded."

Oomialik put down her work and looked at young Salumo. Her story had done what she hoped it would. He had stopped groaning and was sitting up.

Salumo knew why Oomialik had told him this story. Hadn't he been named for Oomialik's son, Salumo, so that he would grow up to be strong and brave like him? When the man, Salumo, was snow-blind, instead of feeling sorry for himself, he had thought of his old mother, and had found a way to keep them from starving. Now Oomialik was trying to give him courage, to help him to be brave, too, like the great hunter.

Salumo shut his poor swollen eyes and began unlacing his boot strings. "Salumo will try to be brave," he said, as he slid into his sleeping bag.

"Ami-lang!" said Oomialik smiling gently. "Your eyes will get well soon. I know they feel like fire now but that will pass. You are my good son."

PART ONE

THE wind was a torrent of darkness
    among the gusty trees;
The moon was a ghostly galleon
    tossed upon cloudy seas;
The road was a ribbon of moonlight over the purple moor;
And the highwayman came riding, riding, riding,
The highwayman came riding, up to the old inn-door.

He'd a French cocked hat on his
    forehead, a bunch of lace
      at his chin,
A coat of the claret velvet, and
    breeches of brown doe-skin;
They fitted with never a wrinkle:
    his boots were up to the
      thigh!
And he rode with a jewelled
    twinkle, his pistol butts
      a-twinkle,
His rapier hilt a-twinkle,
    under the jewelled sky.

The

Highwayman

BY ALFRED NOYES

Illustrated by

John Alan Maxwell

Over the cobbles he clattered
    and clashed in the dark inn-yard;
And he tapped with his whip on the shutters,
    but all was locked and barred;
He whistled a tune to the window,
    and who should be waiting there
But the landlord's black-eyed daughter,
    Bess, the landlord's daughter,
Plaiting a dark red love-knot into her long black hair.

And dark in the dark old inn-yard a stable-wicket creaked
Where Tim the ostler listened;
     his face was white and peaked;
His eyes were hollows of madness, his hair like mouldy hay,
But he loved the landlord's daughter,
     the landlord's red-lipped daughter;
Dumb as a dog he listened, and he heard the robber say—

"One kiss, my bonny sweetheart, I'm after a prize tonight;
But I shall be back with the yellow gold
     before the morning light;
Yet, if they press me sharply, and harry me through the day,
Then look for me by moonlight, watch for me by moonlight,
I'll come to thee by moonlight,
     though hell should bar the way."

He rose upright in the stirrups; he scarce could reach her hand,
But she loosened her hair i' the casement!
     His face burned like a brand
As the black cascade of perfume
     came tumbling over his breast;
And he kissed its waves in the moonlight,
     (Oh, sweet black waves in the moonlight!)
Then he tugged at his rein in the moonlight,
     and galloped away to the West.

PART TWO

He did not come in the dawning; he did not come at noon;
And out o' the tawny sunset, before the rise o' the moon,
When the road was a gipsy's ribbon, looping the purple moor,
A red-coat troop came marching, marching, marching,
King George's men came marching, up to the old inn-door.

They said no word to the landlord, they drank his ale instead,
But they gagged his daughter and bound her
        to the foot of her narrow bed;
Two of them knelt at her casement, with muskets at their side!
There was death at every window;
        And hell at one dark window;
For Bess could see, through her casement,
        the road that *he* would ride.

They had tied her up to attention, with many a sniggering jest;
They had bound a musket beside her,
        with the barrel beneath her breast!
"Now keep good watch!" and they kissed her.
She heard the dead man say—
Look for me by moonlight; watch for me by moonlight;
I'll come to thee by moonlight, though hell should bar the way!

She twisted her hands behind her; but all the knots held good!
She writhed her hands till her fingers
        were wet with sweat or blood!
They stretched and strained in the darkness,
        and the hours crawled by like years,
Till, now, on the stroke of midnight,
        Cold on the stroke of midnight,
The tip of one finger touched it! The trigger at last was hers!

The tip of one finger touched it;
        she strove no more for the rest!
Up, she stood up to attention,
        with the barrel beneath her breast.
She would not risk their hearing; she would not strive again;
For the road lay bare in the moonlight;
        Blank and bare in the moonlight;
And the blood of her veins in the moonlight
        throbbed to her love's refrain.

212

Tlot-tlot; tlot-tlot! Had they heard it?
     The horse-hoofs ringing clear?
Tlot-tlot; tlot-tlot! In the distance?
     Were they deaf that they did not hear?
Down the ribbon of moonlight, over the brow of the hill,
The highwayman came riding, riding, riding!
The red-coats looked to their priming!
     She stood up, straight and still!

Tlot-tlot, in the frosty silence! *Tlot-tlot,* in the echoing night!
Nearer he came and nearer! Her face was like a light!
Her eyes grew wide for a moment;
      she drew one last deep breath,
Then her finger moved in the moonlight,
      Her musket shattered the moonlight,
Shattered her breast in the moonlight
      and warned him—with her death.

He turned; he spurred to the West;
      he did not know who stood
Bowed, with her head o'er the musket,
      drenched with her own red blood!
Not till the dawn he heard it; his face grew grey to hear
How Bess, the landlord's daughter,
      the landlord's black-eyed daughter,
Had watched for her love in the moonlight,
      and died in the darkness there.

Back he spurred like a madman, shrieking a curse to the sky,
With the white road smoking behind him,
      and his rapier brandished high!
Blood-red were his spurs i' the golden noon;
      wine-red was his velvet coat,
When they shot him down on the highway,
      Down like a dog on the highway;
And he lay in his blood on the highway,
      with the bunch of lace at his throat.

And still of a winter's night they say,
      when the wind is in the trees,
When the moon is a ghostly galleon tossed upon cloudy seas,

When the road is a ribbon of moonlight over the purple moor,
A highwayman comes riding, riding, riding,
A highwayman comes riding, up to the old inn-door.

Over the cobbles he clatters and clangs in the dark inn-yard;
And he taps with his whip on the shutters,
        but all is locked and barred;
He whistles a tune to the window,
        and who should be waiting there
But the landlord's black-eyed daughter,
        Bess, the landlord's daughter,
Plaiting a dark red love-knot into her long black hair.

NIGHT came down swiftly over the equatorial forest. There was no lingering of daylight; but, after the snuffing out of the sun, darkness and the bright appearing of stars. No silence came with the darkness, for this was a night alive with song and movement. In the village of the At-mun-shi the people were gathering for their mystic dance that would welcome in the time of herbage, the time for the planting of corn.

Into the center of the clearing surrounded by small conical huts that was the village, a wooden drum had been brought. With solemn reverence Saala, the old wise man of the tribe, approached and began beating it. It was not long the only sound in the darkness. Soon smaller drums in distant parts of the clearing took up a beating. Then wooden flutes joined in from the outskirts of the village. Their sound was muted

Africa, 1725

BY ELIZABETH YATES

Illustrated by

Nora S. Unwin

at first but it grew sharper and higher as the men blowing the flutes came nearer. Joined by the beaters on the drums, the sound quickened in pace and fervor as all gathered in a group around the great drum, coming into time with Saala's rhythmic beating. The moon rose high enough for the light to filter through the heavy foliage. It gleamed on the black bodies of the men, on the faces of the women and children who had been gathering in the clearing, summoned by the music and swaying with it like a field of tall grass before the wind.

When the flutes and the drums ceased, all the At-mun-shi turned and faced the same way, making obeisance to their chief who sat on a raised platform at one end of the clearing,

216

the moon full on him and his children standing beside him. At-mun, the young prince, was tall and powerfully built, though he had seen no more than fifteen summers. He carried his head high and his eyes flashed. Ath-mun, the twelve year old princess, smiled shyly at her tribespeople, then turned to whisper in her father's ear. She leaned against him, hoping to hide the deformed leg that—but for her father's love— would have caused her to have been drowned as an infant. Only the sacrifice of the imperfect to the God of Life could assure protection for the perfect. But the chief had gone against his tribal code and sacrificed his favorite dog to keep his infant daughter and thus far the God of Life had wreaked no vengeance on him. The At-mun-shi were as pagan as all the tribes in Africa, but they were peaceable and they were, as well, intense in their love of freedom.

The chief acknowledged the obeisance of his people and spread his hands before them, palms down, indicating that they might do their own pleasure for the next space of time. The people stood quietly while more and more of the At-mun-shi came in from the jungle to join the group in the clearing. At the outskirts of the village, beyond the circle of conical huts, they laid down their knives and spears. The weapons, lying in their piles without men to hold them, gave back the moonlight's sheen in harmless splendor. This was a night of peace and during it no At-mun-shi would bear anything symbolic of killing. This was the time when the earth was reborn.

Saala commenced beating the great drum again and all the smaller drums followed, but in such unison that it was like single reverberations on the night; then flutes picked up the sound. The dancers gathered themselves together, twelve men well matched in size. Slowly they made their way around the open space in the clearing, shoulders, hips, feet translat-

217

ing the sound of flutes and drums into movement. The music quickened, steps grew longer, and guttural voices uttered the incantation which had been said by their fathers and would be said by their children:

Earth our mother, Sun our father, watch while we plant.
Moon our sister, Rain our brother, aid the seeds to bear fruit
That the harvest may be good, enough for us and our children.

Over and over the words were repeated as family after family of the At-mun-shi joined in until the forest beyond the clearing echoed and re-echoed the chant. Then, at a signal from the chief, the chanting ceased and the dancers fell back, leaving an open space in their midst.

At-mun bowed to his father and with a series of leaps covered the distance from the raised platform at one end of the clearing to the open space. There he stood in his full height, lifting his hands, palms up, to the sky. Then swiftly he knelt, palms down to the earth, bowing his head and pressing his lips to the soil. All that he had, all that he ever would be, he gave to his people. He was their prince, someday to be their chief. He could not do otherwise. Rising, he bounded back to the platform and knelt before his sister. Taking her in his arms, frail and slight of body as she was, he danced with her before the people.

"He is strong," they said to each other, voices hushed like the wind through the bamboo.

"He is beautiful," they said, smiling to each other like the first light of dawn.

"When the time comes he will rule us well," said Saala who had seen many rulers.

An old woman tapped her head, "Not with this will he rule," she said, "but so," and she laid her hand upon her heart. "See how he is with his sister."

218

At-mun danced on, swirling his light burden above the heads of the people, then swinging her low. Always Ath-mun smiled, for with her brother she felt safe. At-mun's expression never changed until the dance was over, then he set the small dark girl down on the platform and stood before his father, head bowed. The chief laid his hand on his son's head in approval. At-mun swung around and faced his people while the smile that flashed from his face might have dazzled the moon itself.

The drums and the flutes began again to build up an air, and the people began again to sway in time with it. At-mun, young, strong, tireless, leapt into their midst, leading the At-mun-shi in a tribal dance until the whole clearing seethed with joyous ecstatic motion. Dawn was still far distant and this was the night of the year when no one would sleep.

Dawn was further off than the invaders creeping silently through the jungle, a hundred black men commanded by three whites. Stealthily they surrounded the village, making sure that their line was within the piles of knives and spears that the At-mun-shi had left. Dropping to their knees at a given signal, they held their guns, took aim and waited, tense and silent, for another signal. One of the white men raised his arm and a hundred muskets blazed into the night. The dancing people stopped and looked skyward. Then they fell to their knees, bewildered, fearful only of one thing, that they had offended the Spirit of the Night. The chief slumped forward. All of the muskets but one had been aimed into the treetops.

At-mun rose to his feet and bounded across the clearing to kneel by his father. Then, in the strange and fearful stillness of the jungle night, he knew what had happened. He stood tall and held out his hands to his people, but no smile flashed from his lips.

There was not time for the At-mun-shi to acknowledge the gesture of their new chief. With cries and shouts, the slavers advanced on the village. Seeing them, the At-mun-shi screamed wildly and ran across the clearing, trying to reach their chief who stood above them in strength and power, symbolizing protection. But the slavers, advancing among them, tossed the At-mun-shi about like leaves in a wind. Seizing the strongest and tallest, they quickly clamped wrist and ankle shackles on them, thrusting aside the old men and women, and the little children.

A white man approached the platform where At-mun was standing, his arm around Ath-mun. The white man uttered a volley of words, sharp as the sound of the muskets had been in At-mun's ears and less meaningful. But At-mun would not lower himself to respond. When the slaver advanced and tried to separate the brother and sister, At-mun's hold only tightened on the girl. The white man hesitated; he had seen fire flashing from the eyes of the tall black youth and he was afraid. A second white man, fully armed, approached from one side and seeing him gave the slaver courage. Stepping forward, he seized Ath-mun and hurled her to the ground. When At-mun reached out to help her the two whites secured his wrists with bamboo withes and threw him down to chain his ankles.

"He's a likely one," the slaver muttered, "and should fetch a good price, but he's dangerous. Tighten those irons."

Dawn came. The At-mun-shi men and some of their women stood in a long line chained together in the clearing surrounded by the conical huts. Those whom the slavers had not wanted cowered together, too stunned for any utterance. Commands were barked out that meant nothing to the At-mun-shi. Then the crack of a lash started the long line moving slowly. Seeing them disappear into the jungle, the old men and women and the little children set up a low wailing. It was so soft at first that it was scarcely audible, but it grew in volume and intensity. Desolate, deprived of their youth, their strength, their leadership, what were a handful of old people and children to do in the jungle?

The line filed slowly on as the best of the At-mun-shi with bowed heads and bowed shoulders stumbled into the unknown. Only a youth at the end of the line still carried his head high. Past the raised platform they went, past the huddled form of a young girl, and only the sound of her weeping let them know that she was alive. Passing her, At-mun suddenly bent low and said something to her, then he raised his head again. The slaver, bringing up the rear, came forward with his lash. At-mun cringed as he felt it, but he uttered no sound, though for the rest of his life his back would bear the marks made on it by the white man's lash.

Ath-mun lifted her head and listened until she could no longer hear the dull thud of footsteps echoing on the jungle floor. She rose to her feet with difficulty, then holding her hands open and outspread as was the custom of her tribe she advanced slowly toward her people. At-mun had reminded her that her birth had made her the servant of her people. He was still a prince, though chains bound him, and she was a princess. Neither one could escape the work they had been born to do.

221

WHEN King Arthur learnt from Merlin that his mother Igraine was still alive, he sent for her in all haste; and the Queen came, and brought with her Morgan le Fay, her daughter, who was as fair a lady as any might be. Igraine had never known what became of the little babe she entrusted to Merlin, for she had never seen the child afterwards, and did not even know what name was given to it. Then Merlin took the King by the hand, saying, "This is your mother." Therewith Arthur took his mother, Queen Igraine, into his arms, and kissed her, and each wept. Then the King commanded a feast to be held that lasted eight days.

One day there came to the Court a squire on horseback, leading a knight before him, wounded to death. He told how there was a knight in the forest who had reared a pavilion by a well, and how he had slain his master, a good knight; and he besought that his master might be buried, and some knight revenge his death.

There was much stir in the Court because of this knight's death, every one giving his advice, and a young squire called Griflet, who was about the same age as Arthur, came to the King, and besought him to make him a knight.

"Thou art full young and tender," said Arthur, "to take so high an order on thee."

"Sir," said Griflet, "I beseech you make me knight."

"Sir, it were great pity to lose Griflet," said Merlin, "for

The Knight of the Fountain

BY MARY MACLEOD

Illustrated by

Henry C. Pitz

222

he will be a passing good man when he is of age, abiding with you the term of his life."

So the King made him knight. "Now," he said, "since I have made you knight, you must give me a gift."

"What you will," said Griflet.

Then the King made him promise that when he had fought with the knight at the fountain he would return straight to the Court without further debate.

So Griflet took his horse in great haste, and got ready his shield, and took a spear in his hand, and rode at a gallop till he came to the fountain. There he saw a rich pavilion, and near by under a cloth stood a fair horse, well saddled and bridled, and on a tree a shield of many colors, and a great spear. Griflet smote on the shield with the butt of his spear, so that it fell down.

With that the knight came out of the pavilion, and said: "Fair knight, why smote you down my shield?"

"Because I would joust with you," said Griflet.

"It is better you do not," said the knight, "for you are but young and lately made a knight, and your might is nothing to mine."

"As for that," said Griflet, "I *will* joust with you."

"I am loath to do it," said the knight, "but since I needs must, I will make ready. Whence be ye?"

"Sir, I am of Arthur's Court."

The two knights ran together, so that Griflet's spear was all shivered to pieces, and therewith the other knight, whose name was Pellinore, smote Griflet through the shield and left side, and broke his own spear, while horse and knight fell down.

When Pellinore saw Griflet lie so on the ground he alighted, and was very sad, for he thought he had slain him. He unlaced his helm, and gave him air, and set him again on his horse, saying he had a mighty heart, and if he lived he would prove a passing good knight. So Sir Griflet rode back to Court, where great dole was made for him. But through good doctors he was healed.

King Arthur was very wrathful because of the hurt to Sir Griflet, and he commanded one of his men to have his horse and armor ready waiting for him outside the city before daylight on the following morning. On the morrow, before dawn, he mounted, and took spear and shield, telling the man to wait there till he came again.

He rode softly till day, and then he was aware of Merlin being chased by three churls, who would have slain him. The King rode towards them, and bade them, "Flee, churls!" They were frightened when they saw a knight, and fled.

"O, Merlin," said Arthur, "here hadst thou been slain, for all thy crafts, had I not been here!"

"Nay, not so," said Merlin, "for I could save myself if I would. And thou art nearer thy death than I am, for thou art going towards thy death, if God be not thy friend."

As they went thus talking they came to the fountain, and the rich pavilion there beside it. Then King Arthur was aware there sat a knight, armed, in a chair.

"Sir Knight," said Arthur, "for what cause abidest thou here, that no knight may ride this way unless he joust with thee? I counsel thee to leave that custom."

"This custom," said Pellinore, "I have used, and will use, despite who saith nay; and whoever is grieved with my custom, let him mend it who will."

"I will amend it," said Arthur.

"I shall prevent you," said Pellinore.

He quickly mounted his horse, adjusted his shield, and took his spear. They met so hard against each other's shields

224

that their spears shivered. Thereupon Arthur at once pulled out his sword.

"Nay, not so," said the knight, "it is fairer that we twain run once more together with sharp spears."

"I will, readily," said Arthur, "if I had any more spears."

"I have enough," said Pellinore.

A squire came and brought two good spears, and again the knight and the King spurred together with all their might, so that both the spears were broken off short. Then Arthur set hand on his sword.

"Nay," said the knight, "ye shall do better. Ye are a passing good jouster as ever I met withal, and for the love of the high order of knighthood let us joust once again."

"I assent," said Arthur.

Then two more great spears were brought, and each knight took one, and they ran together, so that Arthur's spear was all shivered. But Pellinore hit him so hard in the middle of the shield that horse and man fell to the earth. Then Arthur eagerly pulled out his sword, saying, "I will assay thee, Sir Knight, on foot, for I have lost the honor of horseback," and he ran towards him with his sword drawn.

When Pellinore saw that, he too alighted, for he thought it no honor to have a knight at such disadvantage, for himself to be on horseback, and the other on foot. Then began a strong battle with many great strokes, both hacking and hewing, till the field was wet with blood. They fought long, and rested, and then went to battle again. At last they both smote together, so that their swords met evenly, but Pellinore's sword smote Arthur's in two pieces, wherefore the King was much grieved.

Then said the knight unto Arthur:

"Thou art in danger whether I choose to save thee or to slay thee; and unless thou yield thee as overcome and recreant

225

thou shalt die."

"As for death," said King Arthur, "welcome be it, when it cometh; but to yield me unto thee as recreant, I had rather die than be so shamed." And with that he leapt unto Pellinore, and threw him down, and tore off his helm.

When the knight felt this he was sorely frightened, though he was a very big and mighty man; but he quickly got Arthur underneath, and raised off his helm, and would have smitten off his head.

But up came Merlin, and said:

"Knight, hold thy hand, for if thou slay that knight thou puttest this realm in the greatest damage that ever realm was in. For this knight is a man of more honor than thou art aware of."

"Why, who is he?" said Pellinore.

"It is King Arthur."

Then Pellinore would have slain himself, for dread of his wrath, and lifted up his sword. But Merlin cast an enchantment on the knight, so that he fell to the earth in a great sleep.

After throwing Pellinore into an enchanted sleep, Merlin took up King Arthur, and rode forth on Pellinore's horse.

"Alas!" said Arthur, "what hast thou done, Merlin? Hast

226

thou slain this good knight by thy crafts? There lived not so worshipful a knight as he was; I would rather than a year's income that he were alive."

"Do not be troubled," said Merlin, "for he is less hurt than you. He is only asleep, and will wake within three hours. There liveth not a greater knight than he is, and he shall hereafter do you right good service. His name is Pellinore, and he shall have two sons, that shall be passing good men—Percival of Wales, and Lamerack of Wales."

Leaving Sir Pellinore, King Arthur and Merlin went to a hermit, who was a good man, and skilled in the art of healing. He attended so carefully to the King's wounds, that in three days they were quite well, and Arthur was able to go on his way with Merlin. Then as they rode, Arthur said, "I have no sword."

"No matter," said Merlin, "near by is a sword that shall be yours if I can get it."

So they rode till they came to a lake, which was a fair water and broad; and in the midst of the lake, Arthur saw an arm, clothed in white samite, that held in its hand a beautiful sword.

"Lo," said Merlin, "yonder is the sword I spoke of."

With that they saw a damsel rowing across the lake.

"What damsel is that?" said Arthur.

"That is the Lady of the Lake," said Merlin, "and within that lake is a rock, and therein is as fair a place as any on earth, and richly adorned. This damsel will soon come to you; then speak you fair to her, so that she will give you that sword."

Presently the damsel came to Arthur, and saluted him, and he her again.

"Damsel," said Arthur, "what sword is that which yonder

the arm holdeth above the water? I would it were mine, for I have no sword."

"Sir Arthur, King," said the damsel, "that sword is mine; the name of it is Excalibur, that is as much as to say *Cut-Steel*. If you will give me a gift when I ask you, ye shall have it."

"By my faith," said Arthur, "I will give you what gift ye shall ask."

"Well," said the damsel, "go you into yonder barge, and row yourself to the sword, and take it and the scabbard with you, and I will ask my gift when I see my time."

So King Arthur and Merlin alighted, and tied their horses to two trees, and went into the barge, and when they came to the sword that the hand held, Arthur lifted it by the handle, and took it with him. And the arm and hand went under the water; and so they came to the land, and rode away.

Then Arthur looked on the sword, and liked it passing well.

"Which like you the better, the sword or the scabbard?" asked Merlin.

"I like the sword better," replied Arthur.

"You are the more unwise," said Merlin, "for the scabbard is worth ten of the sword. While you have the scabbard upon you, ye shall never lose any blood, be ye ever so sorely wounded. Therefore keep well the scabbard always with you."

So they returned to Camelot, where King Arthur's knights were passing glad to see him. When they heard of his adventures they marvelled that he would so jeopardy himself alone. But all men of honor said it was merry to be under such a chieftain who would put his person in adventures as other poor knights did.

228

IT WAS three o'clock of a summer day. The low hills inclosing the valley of the Meuse were streaked with shadows cast by fluffy clouds. In the silence, pierced only by the faint tinkle of cowbells from distant meadows, the little village seemed asleep. Cottages of green-gray stone, a little church with its cross sparkling in the sun, thatched sheepfolds circling garden patches—all these seemed to dream together in the soft air.

Suddenly in the dusty lane, which was the main street of the village, appeared a group of children. Although their bare feet made no sound, their voices were shrill with merry haste, and as they scampered along they waked the place to life.

From a window overlooking the street a withered face leaned out. "Hush thy noise, little pigs! My daughter is ill!" cried a cracked treble.

Across the way a woman in gray homespun kirtle and petticoat stood still with fat arms akimbo to watch them pass. A

A Shepherdess of Domrémy

BY JEANETTE EATON

Illustrated by

Frederick T. Chapman

few steps farther on they were passing into the shadow of two gnarled tree trunks, when suddenly out sprang a figure in a black cassock with two arms spread to catch unwary ones. Screaming with laughter, the children dodged and tried to flee. "Father Fronte! Father Fronte!" they shouted.

Two of the smaller ones, unable to escape, were collared and held fast. "Now then," boomed the jovial priest, in mock sternness, "little Mengette, and thou, Pierre Colin, must an-

229

swer for the rest! Where art thou going in such haste and with such a clack of tongues?"

Mengette piped up gaily, "Why, father, we're going to find Jeanne—Jeanne d'Arc."

"That's good, that's excellent!" The curé bent and kissed her rosy cheek. "Jeanne will see that you behave." He patted Colin's head, waved his hand to the others, and made off down the dusty street.

Pellmell the children hastened on to the cottage next the church. They dipped around the corner of the house, pattered through the barnyard, and brought up before the door. "Jeanne! Jeanne!" they called.

Through the opening where flies buzzed lazily a girl sat at her spinning-wheel. At the sound of her name a bare foot left the treadle and came down on the earthen floor. The busy hands laid by the distaff. She stood up and came to the doorway, a tall girl of thirteen.

"What would you?" she asked, smiling. Her big gray eyes, her strong white teeth, even her black hair, glistening in the sunlight like a starling's wing, lent radiance to that smile.

"Oh, come and watch the fight! All the boys of Maxey came out on the bridge an hour ago to shout for Burgundy, and all our boys that could leave their cattle have gone over to fight for the king and the Armagnacs!"

Jeanne's eyes grew big and her nostrils quivered. "I would I could fight for the Dauphin!" she cried. Then her face sobered. "But I fear there will be bloody noses this afternoon, and that I like not. It is to no purpose. For look you, the boys of Domrémy would never cheer for Burgundy even if they lost the day, and they will never make Maxey cheer for the Armagnacs. That will not be till the Dauphin comes riding at

230

the head of his troops and takes the town—takes all the towns that swear allegiance to false Burgundy and the English king!"

For an instant the children stared at her flashing eyes. Then Michel Lebuin said, quickly: "We're going over to cheer for Domrémy, in any case. Come with us at once! I see thy father walking hither from the meadows. Let us go, or he will give thee some task to do."

Jeanne's face fell. "Ah, yes. He's come for me to mind the sheep. I was to take my brother's place at the fifteenth hour."

"Then hurry, while there is yet time to escape!" Off skipped the youngsters. Around the cabbage-patch and the stack of yellow straw and so to the fields they streaked like rabbits.

The girl, however, did not follow them. Quietly she walked down the sloping grass, leaped the brook, and joined her father. Sunburnt and strong looked Jacques d'Arc in his leathern doublet and long homespun stockings. He was a man of substance and held the office of dean of Domrémy—which meant that he collected the taxes for its lord and represented the village in money matters.

"I was just coming, father." Jeanne held out her hand for the crook her father carried.

"Thou art late," he grumbled. "Idling here with those lazybones! Let me tell thee, my girl, these are no days to leave the beasts unguarded. Thou didst hear what that traveler said last night when he stopped for a cup of wine? Lately a raid was made near Gondrecourt."

The man stared toward his house and rubbed his forehead with a great brown fist. "A murrain on these skinners! Would to God they could be rounded up and forced to fight the English instead of laying this land to further waste! It's hard

231

enough for poor folks to pay the taxes without being robbed and utterly destroyed."

Soberly the girl went on her way. All afternoon her heart had been full of peaceful thoughts of the Blessed Margaret, once a shepherdess herself. But now as she looked about the great rolling stretches of long grass it was with a frightened sense of insecurity.

Terrible stories she had heard from wayfarers coming north to Paris or southwest to Besançon—stories that made her quake for all peasants everywhere. Barns and houses burned, cattle carried off, fathers and mothers slain in their own dooryards and little children left to die of hunger. Hadn't the husband of her own godmother been carried off a prisoner once, and brought back half dead with fear and hunger when the ransom was paid? What if these dreadful men should fall on Domrémy?

Jeanne d'Arc never had been to school. She could neither read nor write. Yet she knew much of her country's sufferings all these years until now in 1425. She knew that after Charles the Sixth, the king, went mad, all his uncles began to quarrel,

232

and that the hatred between two of them—the Duke of Burgundy and the Duke of Orléans—was dividing all France into two camps of war. Since the young Duke of Orléans had married the daughter of Count Armagnac, however, his party was called the party of the Armagnacs.

If you were a Burgundian in those days, you did not necessarily live in the province of Burgundy. But wherever you lived you had to pay tribute to the great duke, and you dared not show any enmity to the English. Indeed, you had to acknowledge the English king as your liege lord. If you were an Armagnac you swore faith to Charles the Seventh, the young and uncrowned king of France. Also, you tried to get towns and provinces back from Burgundy and England. Only, alas for the Armagnacs! they were not nearly so strong nor so well banded together as the Burgundians.

For an instant Jeanne stopped her reflections to run and bring back one of her wandering sheep. When she returned to her flock it was to see a group of village boys crossing the bridge from Maxey. She called to them and waved her crook. Presently they came near enough to shout: "They would not fight! They ran away!"

Hot and weary from the long walk and from hurling names at their neighbors, the boys came to fling themselves on the grass near the shepherdess. Soon there arose among them all a great wag of tongues.

"How can this be answered?" asked one of the boys. "They say in Maxey that Orléans and the Armagnacs were just as much to blame for bringing the English across the Channel as the party of Burgundy. Is it true?"

"Mayor Aubritt says it's true," replied Jeanne. "Whenever Burgundy got too strong they called on the English, and then the other way around. Because they didn't have a strong king to check them, these great dukes only thought of themselves and never of their country's good. You all know that when the Duke of Orléans was murdered by Burgundy five years before I was born the Armagnacs did not rest until they murdered Duke Jean of Burgundy in his turn. That was three years ago. No good comes of such wickedness."

"Very true," chimed in another lad, named Francois, "for after that Burgundy was closer friend than ever to the English and now they are gobbling up the country—north, east, and west."

"Then why are we Armagnacs, if they are so wicked?" asked the first boy. "That is what is so strange."

Jeanne stood looking down at the group. "I know," she said, gravely, and there came a ring into her voice. "It's because now the Armagnacs are fighting the English tooth and claw, and theirs is the party of the Dauphin. He is with them in the south—all that remains of France. Our hope lies in him. One day the Dauphin will rise and make Burgundy and the English captains bow the knee and there will be peace in the kingdom."

"Why don't you call Charles the Seventh king, Jeanne? He is the king since his father's death."

Stubbornly the girl shook her head. "He is not king till he has been crowned at Rheims, where all the kings of France are crowned. When the sacred oil which baptized King Clovis has been placed upon his head, then will Charles be truly king. In God's name, I would rather that be done than anything. But Rheims is held by Burgundy and the bishop has fled away."

Francois kicked his heels in the long grass. "I punched the nose of the great Thomas over in Maxey a month gone when he said King Charles was but a weakling and a fool. I think

234

he's only sad, and he's so young—only twenty-two. I'd fight for him with a right good will if I could join the company of La Hire. La Hire! There's a greater captain than any who serve Burgundy!"

"Well, why doesn't he fight then and save France?" cried out another lad. Mengette, who long ago had come back to tend her cows, had been slowly strolling toward them through the fields. The last few speeches she had heard, and now drew near to say, "France will have to wait for that maid of the prophecy to save her."

"What prophecy is that, little Mengette?" asked François, rolling over to look up at her and smile.

At this every voice rose in protest: "Why, everybody knows that prophecy! A virgin will come forward to save the country from its foes."

"Yes," asserted Mengette, gravely, "Father Fronte says it is an old saying, but that only a little while ago it was voiced again by a lady in Avignon, a lady named Marie. She said France would be lost by a woman and saved by a woman."

"Aye," replied a boy behind François. "And it *has* been lost by a woman. When Queen Isabel gave her daughter in marriage to the king of England, she furnished him with a new reason for claiming our throne. Would that the maid who is to save us would make haste. For all the barons and counts fight among themselves and robber bands rove through the country unchecked!"

Instinctively, at the mention of robbers, the children turned their heads in the direction of a small fort called the Castle which stood on an island between two arms of the river Meuse. It belonged to the lord of Bourlemont along with the lands of Domrémy. To him the villagers paid a heavy tax. In return, Jacques d'Arc, the dean, had made the lord rent his people

235

this stronghold, where they could drive their cattle in time of raid.

"Look!" suddenly cried a lad. "There's a watcher on the tower! Could it be that news of danger has come in?"

A chill of foreboding struck through Jeanne. The boys scrambled to their feet and strained their eyes, first toward the fortress, then toward the horizon. Jeanne's lips murmured, "Blessed Saint Catherine, Saint Margaret, and glorious Michael, protect us now." In the midst of her prayer the great bell on the tower began to ring.

"An alarm!" The children stood rigid in terror. They were coming down—armed men—upon the village! It was Domrémy's turn now. Oh, what would happen to them?

"Quick!" shouted Jeanne d'Arc. "Drive in all the beasts!"

With hoarse cries, the children scattered over the meadows to collect the cattle. As Jeanne ran and called and herded her placid sheep, she caught glimpses of people hurrying from the village. She made out her father and her brothers, the mayor and other men, carrying bags of grain and flour. Behind them

trooped a long line of women. Even at this distance she faintly heard their lamentations. Father Fronte came last of all, bearing in his arms a baby.

What confusion of fear! What desperation of haste! At last they were all within the gates. The castle yard was one seething mass of frightened animals, screaming infants, men and women with awful dread in their eyes. And now, riding down the village street, came the robber band. The sun caught their lances, the breeze tossed the plume on the leader's hat. Wild and fierce they looked. Some wore mail and carried crossbows. Others were armed with axes and short swords. Jeanne covered her face with her hands. Would they burn the village— kill them all?

Presently she heard the sound of loud commands: "Open the gates! Open or you are all dead men!"

Faintly she caught the sound of a reply. She guessed it came from her father, Mayor Aubritt, and Father Fronte. Then she had to stoop to rescue a lamb which had been swept off its feet in the rush, and after that she tried to comfort little Mengette, sobbing there beside her. It seemed an eternity that they stood there in the heat and terror of the crowd.

Suddenly the herds of sheep began to move. The press grew less. Jeanne's heart nearly burst her bodice. The gates must have been opened! What would these fierce men do? Was it the end of everything? Rough voices still were shouting, but they were farther away. The girl pulled Mengette forward, and now she could see. The robbers were driving away the poor beasts. They forced them toward the road with crack of whip and prick of lance—all, all! Not one was left behind.

Jeanne ran to her father, who leaned upon the gate like a man of wood. He raised dumb, tragic eyes. And then above the wailing and the din was lifted the curé's ringing voice.

237

"Let us give thanks, my children. Ourly has promised not to burn the village and to harm no one. He and his men wanted only the flocks and herds!"

Only the flocks and herds! It was the entire wealth of Domrémy. Without them the villagers would starve. Slowly, in the silence of despair, they crept back to their houses. True, at sunset they dispatched a messenger to take the tidings to the nearest member of the House of Bourlemont, Joanna of Joinville. But there was little hope of help from her and gloom filled every home.

Nevertheless, aid was forthcoming. The lady of Bourlemont sent for succor to her kinsman, the Count of Vaudemont. He was one of the powerful lords of Lorraine and at once he sent his men after Ourly and Ourly's roving band. They were routed in short order and one fine day the flocks and herds were driven back again to Domrémy. Ah, how the bells rang out for joy that evening! Mayor Aubritt invited his neighbors in to eat roast pig and make merry, and Father Fronte held a special service of thanksgiving in the little church next Jacques d'Arc's cottage.

Fortunately, the memory of dreadful things is short. Not many weeks after Ourly's raid the children were as full of pranks and gaiety as if beyond their meadows lurked never a threat. And livelier than any other was Jeanne of the gray eyes, the red cheeks, the laughing voice.

"Let's race to the fairy tree!" she cried, one afternoon.

More than a dozen boys and girls were down in the meadows. It was a gray day, a little chill for summer, and the clouds hung low. They almost seemed to Jeanne to touch the top of the great beech tree there beyond the brook, the one the children called the fairy tree. On Fountain Sunday in mid-Lent they hung garlands on its massive trunk, and in its great pool

238

of shade they ate boiled eggs and little rolls. Many people thought that on moonlight nights the fairies came to dance around the tree. Indeed, Dame Beatrix, Jeanne's godmother, declared she'd seen them once. But although Jeanne only laughed at such stories, she loved the tree as all the children did.

Now as they heard that challenge for a race, all the boys and girls threw down their crooks and staves. "Yes, yes! A race to the fairy tree!" Mengette hurried forward to be the judge. Her flowers just now picked would be the prize.

Off they started. Heads thrown back, they swept forward in a rush. But Jeanne was fleetest. Laughing and panting, she took the bouquet and waved it in triumph at having won.

"Why, Jeannette, your feet scarcely seem to touch the ground!" So the losers praised her without grudging. "Come on, let's race back again!"

But the victor had turned away. With drooping head she wandered off. "Jeanne!" her companions shouted. "Come back and play!"

She did not hear them. She suddenly felt strange. Her dreaming feet had taken her nearly to the river's brink when her misty eyes were dimly aware of a shepherd boy near by. She thought she heard him say, "Jeanne, your mother wants you."

That whirled her around. Her mother wanting her in mid-afternoon, with no one else to mind the sheep? Something must be wrong. Swift as a deer she ran through the grass the whole long distance to her own barnyard. Panting, she reached the door.

From within came the smell of fresh loaves of bread. She saw her mother's arms busy at the oaken table. Then the good, familiar face looked out upon her, astonished and disapprov-

ing. "Why have you left your sheep, child? Run back at once! They may wander away."

The girl looked at her in bewilderment. Her mother had not wanted her, then. It was a joke. Which boy had told her that and made her run? She turned back slowly.

And then at one stroke the world as she had known it changed forever. Everything familiar vanished from her sight. Something utterly new and not of the earth at all was taking place. Terror such as she had never imagined filled her being —the terror of the unknowable. It was as if the grassy meadows, the hills and trees, the river—all that she could see, all that she had ever touched—were but an outer shell. That shell held something else more real than these. Before her now it had opened suddenly and she could look inside. What she beheld was a bright, cloudlike form. What she heard was a Voice. Yet it was neither hearing nor seeing, but quite different.

Some time afterward, sunk to her knees there on a grassy plot in the garden, Jeanne d'Arc felt the commonplace gradually close around her once again. "This is I," she thought, "and this is my father's garden in Domrémy." Her ear caught the tinkle of cowbells. Her cheek felt the stir of a wind that promised rain. And now she became aware of what the Voice had said.

That she must change her course of life; that she had been chosen by the King of Heaven to do marvelous deeds and aid the King of France! A man's dress should be hers, and a lance in her hand, and she should lead armies on to victory.

Trembling from head to foot, she slowly rose from the ground. It was the prophecy! And she, Jeanne d'Arc, had been appointed to fulfill it. She was the maid who was destined to save France.

241

THE are seven men in Moy Castle
    And merry men this night;
There are seven men in Moy Castle
    Whose hearts are gay and light.

Prince Charlie came to Moy Castle
    And asked for shelter there,
And down came Lady M'Intosh,
    As proud as she was fair.

"I'm a hunted man,
    Lady M'Intosh—
A price is on my head!
If Lord Loudon knew
    thou'dst sheltered me,
Both thou and I were sped."

"Come in! come in,
    my prince!" said she,
And opened wide the gate;
"To die with Prince Charlie Stuart,
    I ask no better fate."

Moy Castle

FOLK BALLAD

Illustrated by

Alexander Dobkin

She's called her seven trusty men,
    The blacksmith at their head:
"Ye shall keep watch in the castle wood,
    To save our prince from dread."

The lady has led the prince away,
    To make him royal cheer;
The seven men of M'Intosh
    Have sought the forest drear.

242

And there they looked and listened,
  Listened and looked amain;
And they heard the sound of the falling leaves,
  And the soft sound of the rain.

The blacksmith knelt beside an oak,
  And laid his ear to the ground,
And under the noises of the wood
  He heard a distant sound.

He heard the sound of many feet,
  Warily treading the heather—
He heard the sound of many men
  Marching softly together.

"There's no time now to warn the prince,
  The castle guards are few;
'Tis wit will win the play tonight,
  And what we here can do."

He's gi'en the word to his six brethren,
  And through the wood they're gone;
The seven men of M'Intosh
  Each stood by himself alone.

"And he who has the pipes at his back,
  His best now let him play;
And he who has no pipes at his back,
  His best word let him say."

It was five hundred Englishmen
  Were treading the purple heather,

Five hundred of Lord Loudon's men
    Marching softly together.

"There's none tonight in Moy Castle
    But servants poor and old;
If we bring the prince to Loudon's lord,
    He'll fill our hands with gold."

They came lightly on their way,
    Had never a thought of ill,
When suddenly from the darksome wood
    Broke out a whistle shrill.

And straight the wood was filled with cries,
    With shouts of angry men,
And the angry skirl of the bagpipes
    Came answering the shouts again.

244

The Englishmen looked and listened,
　　Listened and looked amain,
And nought could they see through the murky night,
　　But the pipes shrieked out again.

"Hark to the slogan of Lochiel,
　　To Keppoch's gathering cry!
Hark to the rising swell that tells
　　Clanranald's men are nigh!

"Now woe to the men that told us
　　Lochiel was far away!
The whole of the Highland army
　　Is waiting to bar our way.

"It's little we'll see of Charlie Stuart
    And little of Loudon's gold,
And but we're away from this armed wood,
    Our lives have but little hold."

It was five hundred Englishmen,
    They turned their faces and ran,
And well for him with the swiftest foot,
    For he was the lucky man.

And woe to him that was lame or slow,
    For they trampled him on the heather!
And back to the place from whence they came
    They're hirpling all together.

Lord Loudon's men, they are gone full far,
    Over the brow of the hill;
The seven men of M'Intosh,
    Their pipes are crying still.

They leaned them to a tree and laughed,
    'Twould do you good to hear,
And they are away to Moy Castle
    To tell their lady dear.

And who but Lady M'Intosh
    Would praise her men so bold?
And who but Prince Charlie Stuart
    Would count the good French gold?

There are seven men in Moy Castle
    Are joyful men this night;
There are seven men in Moy Castle
    Whose hearts will aye be light.

IT WAS a calm, still night in the autumn of the year 1307. The waters of Lake Lucerne lay silvery in the moonlight, and from the glittering tops of the snow-covered mountains shining slopes ran down to the shadowy pasture lands below. Everything was very quiet and peaceful. The time was long past midnight, and the whole world seemed asleep.

A sound of many footsteps on the mountain paths broke the silence. Dim forms began to gather on the little grassy plateau at the foot of the Seelisberg mountain. More and more came softly along the winding path until there were three bands, each of ten men and their leader, standing still and resolute in the shadow of the rocky height. They came from the three forest cantons of Uri, Schwyz, and Unterwalden, and they were all hardy mountaineers, men who had been born and bred within a few miles of that place.

William Tell

BY AMY CRUSE

Illustrated by Hans A. Mueller.

The three leaders stepped forward. One was an old, white-bearded man, upright and stately. His face was mild and benevolent, though just now it looked very stern and resolute. This was Walter Fürst, the wealthiest and most respected man in the canton of Uri. The next was a dark-haired, dark-eyed man of middle age, sturdy and powerful; the third was younger, taller, and slighter, with glowing eyes and quick, eager movements. These two were also men of mark in their cantons; their names were Arnold von Melchthal and Werner Stauffacher. All three wore the plain and simple dress of Swiss peasants—a tunic with a broad leather belt, a colored hunting shirt, and high boots.

"We are met here," said Walter Fürst, "to confirm the resolve we made when last we talked together of our country's wrongs. Each of us since then has held secret converse with the men of his canton. I myself have gone about through Uri, and I have found all willing and eager to rise against the tyrant. Since the Austrians sent Gessler to rule over us things have gone from bad to worse, and the men of Uri have sworn that they will bear no longer with his cruelty and oppression. What say their brothers of the other two forest cantons?"

"Every man in Schwyz will fight to the death!" cried von Melchthal; and Stauffacher shouted, "Unterwalden can scarce wait for the call to the battlefield."

"Think of Rollin, a fugitive among the mountains, hunted like a wild beast, parted from his wife, his children, and his home merely because he struck down the man who had foully insulted his wife," cried Arnold von Melchthal, turning to the men who stood at a little distance from their leaders.

"Aye, and think of poor old Undern, with his eyes put out, shut up in a loathsome dungeon, because his son lifted a hand against the bailiff's man who, without claim or right, unyoked his oxen and drove them off, saying with taunts that his master had need of them," cried the fiery Stauffacher.

"We do think of them," came the answer from many voices, "and we will avenge them." Strong hands gripped bows and hunting knives, and there were loud and angry murmurs. "We will fight!" "We will throw down the tyrants!" "Down with the Austrians!" "We will be free!"

The calm, deep voice of Walter Fürst stilled the rising tumult.

"Swear, then," he said, "swear to be true to the cause and to fight to the death to free your country from the tyrant. Our

248

motto shall be, 'One for all and all for one.' Swear that you will bear it always in your minds and in your hearts."

The three leaders joined their left hands in a firm grasp, and raised their right hands, with three fingers lifted, toward heaven.

"We swear!" they said solemnly; and from their followers there came a fervent response, "We swear! One for all and all for one."

"On the first day of the new year, then," said Walter Fürst, "be ready. Till then, silence and secrecy."

The dawn was breaking as the men went down the mountain paths toward their homes. Among them was a man tall and strong and agile, with a noble face and clear, fearless eyes. He had been in the band that followed Walter Fürst, who was his father-in-law, and he had joined quietly but very fervently in the response to the oath which the leaders had taken. Now he went toward his home, a cottage at Bürglen, among the mountains, with a firm, quick step, treading lightly and easily over difficult places, and scarcely noting where he went, so deep was he in thought. But he never missed the way, or took a false step, for he knew the mountain paths so well that he could walk them as easily in that dim morning light as in full day. He was the best climber and the boldest hunter in the three cantons, and his name was William Tell.

A few weeks after the midnight meeting William Tell went one day, taking with him his seven-year-old son, to the little town of Altdorf, which was near his home. The two went happily along together until they came to the market place; but to the little boy's disappointment scarcely a person was to be seen. There was no pleasant stir and bustle such as had delighted him on former visits, and he looked round curiously to

see if he could discover the cause.

All was as usual except that in the middle of the market place a great pole was stuck up, and on the top of the pole was a hat—a very grand hat with a feather and a gold buckle. Four Austrian soldiers stood on each side of the pole.

William Tell, holding his little son by the hand, walked straight across the square, taking no notice of the hat or of the soldiers who guarded it. But he had gone only a few steps past them when they rushed out upon him.

"Throw him into prison!" they cried. "He has not bowed to Gessler's hat which stands there as a sign of the might of Austria. Gessler has commanded that all who pass by shall do it reverence, and this man has not even glanced toward it."

They seized William Tell roughly, while the frightened child clung closely to him. With flashing eyes Tell pushed them

250

away, and stood looking so fiercely on them that for a moment they hung back. People came running into the market place from the houses and streets round about and a great commotion arose. Tell was well known in the town, and many voices were raised to explain to him what was going on.

The hated Gessler had placed the hat in the square that morning. Some few of the inhabitants of Altdorf had bowed before it, but most had kept out of the market place. Those who had been obliged to pass that way had gone to the priest and begged him to stand by the pole, holding the Holy Sacrament in his hands; then when they had bowed they had said they had done it in reverence to the Holy Sacrament, and the soldiers could not take them, for they had, in fact, bowed before the pole.

While the men of Altdorf were pouring out this story to William Tell, Gessler himself rode into the market place. He saw who it was that his soldiers had taken prisoner, and a smile of satisfaction came upon his dark, cruel face. He knew Tell well and hated him—hated him for his proud and fearless spirit, for the glance of scorn which had often told the tyrant how he was despised and detested, though the man's tongue was silent; hated him, too, for his strength and courage and skill which helped to make him a leader among his fellows.

When Tell saw the governor he cried out boldly, "I appeal for justice. Bid these men let me go. I have done no wrong."

Gessler got down from his horse and came toward the excited group. The people drew back from him with dark and sullen looks and angry murmurs. He looked round on them with the cruel smile of satisfaction still on his face.

"You shall have justice," he said; "more than justice. You shall have a chance to win your pardon for this disobedience. Men say that you have wonderful skill as an archer." He turned to his soldiers. "Take an apple," he commanded, "and put it on this child's head. Then let him stand under yonder linden tree, and let the father shoot at the apple. If he hits it he shall go free."

Tell caught the hand of his son, who through all the disturbance had clung closely to him, then turned, and looked at Gessler. He did not speak, but the people round about—there was a great crowd now—made a loud, angry murmuring, and some of them raised their hands as if to strike down the Austrians. But the little boy laughed happily. This, he thought, was an easy thing to do. He had seen his father hit smaller marks than an apple, at a distance greater than this to the linden tree, which could not be more than a hundred and fifty paces. It would be all right, and they would soon be free; and the people, Gessler, and his Austrians, and all, would see how well his father could shoot.

He pulled his hand from his father's and took the apple the soldier had brought. Then he ran over to the linden tree, laughing joyously.

"Shoot now, Father," he cried, placing the apple on his head. "I will stand quite still."

Very slowly Tell took his bow. The people were very quiet, except the Austrian soldiers who were laughing rudely.

"He will not do it," said Gessler with a sneer; "these Swiss dogs are cowards and no marksmen, though they boast so loudly of what they can do."

Tell took two arrows from his quiver, put one inside the bosom of his tunic, and with the other took careful aim at the apple. It pierced the fruit, and the two halves fell to the ground.

The little boy, radiant with pride and delight, picked up the pieces and ran with them toward the group of Swiss and Austrians who were standing in astounded silence.

252

"See what my father has done!" he shouted. "Here is the apple."

Then the others found their voices. The Swiss cried out in triumph; the Austrians muttered angrily. Gessler's face was very dark.

William Tell stood silent in the midst, showing neither joy nor triumph. He lifted the little boy and kissed him. As he set him down Gessler spoke.

"Why did you take two arrows when you were to shoot only one?" he asked.

Tell looked at him steadily. "I meant the second one for you," he said, "if with the first I killed my son."

Then Gessler fell into a terrible passion. "Take this man," he shouted, "and throw him into the boat that is waiting for me on the lake. He shall not be killed, since I promised to spare his life, but he shall never again see the light of the sun or moon, for he shall remain in a dungeon under the ground where serpents shall devour him alive."

The little boy screamed at these dreadful words, and the people around cried out in horror. But the Austrian soldiers ruthlessly tore the child from his father. They seized Tell, bound him with strong cords, carried him down to the lake, and threw him into the waiting boat.

Pitying friends carried the heart-broken little boy back to his home at Bürglen, and told his mother the terrible news. Quickly it spread through the canton, and there were few who dared to hope that William Tell would ever be seen in Uri again, for they knew what happened to prisoners who were shut up in Austrian dungeons. They had lost one on whom their hopes had rested, a man strong and fearless, loyal to the cause; he would be terribly missed when the three cantons rose against their tyrants. But the loss filled them with rage, not dismay; and the leaders hurriedly made plans to hasten their rising that they might try to rescue Tell before the Austrian dungeon had done its fatal work.

That night Tell's wife was sitting sadly in her cottage, while the little boy, worn out with grief and terror, slept on a bed in the corner of the room. The door opened softly, and Tell himself came in. His wife cried out in joy and astonishment, scarcely able to believe her eyes. Her husband took her in his arms and kissed her tenderly, assuring her that he was safe and unharmed; then they both sat down, and, speaking softly so as not to awaken the exhausted child, he told her what had happened after he had been thrown into Gessler's boat.

"They rowed out over the lake," he said, "but very soon a storm such as we sometimes have came up, with a great wind and rain and darkness. The boat was driven about wildly, so that the men were frightened, and besought Gessler to unloose my bonds that I might guide the boat, since I alone had the skill and knowledge that could save them. So they unbound me, and I steered toward a place I knew where there is a piece of rock on which a man may land, though with danger, for the foothold is difficult and the water there is very deep. When we came near this place I leapt suddenly on shore and none dared follow me. They shouted threats and curses at me

as I sped away over the rocks, but they could not stop or harm me.

"I hid myself in the Hohle Gasse, the narrow way you know of between the mountains, for I knew that if Gessler and his men managed to reach the land they must pass that way homeward. And they did. After many hours I saw them coming, so I placed myself behind a rock and shot an arrow straight and true to the tyrant's heart."

His wife cried out in terror. "Oh, what will become of you? They will surely find you and kill you for this deed."

"Nay, fear not," he answered, "the tyrant is dead, and I am here, safe among friends. Soon our country shall be free from all tyrants. This deed of mine doth but hasten by a little the day of vengeance. For know, my wife, that the men of the forest cantons have sworn to rise on the first day of the new year and take arms to throw off the yoke of their oppressors. I did not tell you before, for I feared that it might trouble you, but now you shall know all."

Then he told her of the midnight meeting, and how her father and the other two leaders had vowed to fight to the death that their country might be free; and how they had taken for the motto of their rising, "One for all and all for one."

"So it shall be," he said, "and before men thus united the Austrians will not be able to stand. Our preparations have gone on steadily, and though it is now only the end of November, in a few days we shall be able to take the field. The news of Gessler's death will spread among the people, and they will rise joyfully and fight like the noble Switzers that they are."

So it fell out. Before the next evening all the men of the forest cantons knew that their tyrant was dead, and that Tell was free. Full of joy and hope, they thronged to the appointed

256

meeting places, and their leaders decided that the time had come for the great blow to be struck.

All the might of the tyrants could not prevail against these hardy, fearless mountaineers. In each of the three cantons the power of the Austrians was broken, the governors killed, and the rule of the Swiss set up. The land was free.

When the rising was over and the victory won, William Tell went back to his cottage and lived there as simply and quietly as he had done before. He did not care for power or position; it was enough for him to know that he had helped to make his country free. He could roam over the mountains he loved, hunt in the forests, fish in the streams, sail over the beautiful lake without interference from the hated stranger. He saw his countrymen as free and happy as himself. This was what he had fought for, and he was content.

So he lived for many years. Then on a bleak winter day a child fell into one of the rushing mountain streams near his home. Tell was an old man by this time, but at once he plunged into the ice-cold water to rescue the child. He went home chilled and shivering, and in a few days he was dead.

Switzerland has never forgotten William Tell, and holds him as the chief of her heroes. A great statue of him has been set up in the market place of Altdorf on the spot where he shot the apple from the head of his son. A chapel has been built on the place where he leapt to shore from Gessler's boat; another on the spot where Gessler fell, slain by the patriot's arrow; a third on the site of the cottage at Bürglen where he lived. Countless songs and stories have been made about him, and the famous drama of the German poet Schiller has kept his name in remembrance far beyond the borders of his own country.

IT WAS in the spring of the year 1241 that rumors began to travel along the highroad from Kiev in the land of Rus that the Tartars of the East were again upon the march. Men trembled when they heard that news and mothers held their children close to their breasts, for the name "Tartar" was one that froze folks' blood in their veins. As the weeks went on, the rumors grew thicker and there began to come through to Poland, our land of the fields, the news that the country lands of the Ukraine were ablaze. Then it was heard that Kiev had fallen, then Lvov, the city of the Lion, and now there was naught between the savage band of warriors and the fair city of Krakow, save a few peaceful villages and fertile fields.

The Tartars came through the world like a horde of wild beasts. They left not one thing alive nor one green blade of wheat standing. They were short, dark men of shaggy beards and long hair

The Broken Note

BY ERIC P. KELLY

Illustrated by

Angela Pruszynska

twisted into little braids, and they rode on small horses which they covered with trophies that they had gained in war. Brave they were as lions, courageous they were as great dogs, but they had hearts of stone and knew not mercy, nor pity, nor tenderness, nor God. On their horses they carried round shields of leather and iron, and long spears often trailed from their saddles. About their shoulders and thighs they wore skins of animals. Some decorated their ears with golden rings—here and there one wore a gold ring in the nose. When they traveled, the dust rose high into the sky from beneath the hoofs of their little horses, and the thunder of the hoofbeats could be heard

258

many miles away. They were so numerous that it took days for the whole horde to pass any one given point, and for miles behind the army itself rumbled carts bearing slaves, provisions, and booty—usually gold.

Before them went always a long, desperate procession of country people driven from their humble homes by the news of the coming terror; they had already said farewell to the cottages where they lived, the parting from which was almost as bitter as death. So it has always been in time of war that the innocent suffer most—these poor, helpless peasants with their carts and horses and geese and sheep trudging along through the dust to escape, if God so willed, the terrible fate which would befall them were they left behind. There were old people in that procession too feeble to be stirring even about a house, mothers nursing children, women weak with sickness, and men broken-hearted at the loss of all that a lifetime of labor had brought. Children dragged themselves wearily along beside them, often bearing their pets in their arms.

To this company Krakow opened her gates, and prepared for defense. Many of the nobility and rich citizens had, in the meantime, fled to the west or taken refuge in monasteries far to the north. The brothers of the monastery at Zvierzyniec, a short distance outside the city, took in all the refugees that the building could accommodate, and then prepared to stand siege. But the great, weary, terror-mad mob that had fled ahead of the band of Tartars was content enough to make the city itself its destination. And once within its walls all turned their faces toward the south. For there, in the south of the city, towering on its rocky hill high over the Vistula River, was the great, irregular, turreted mass that was the Wawel—the fortress and castle of the kings of Poland from the time of Krakus, the legend king, and the home of the dukes and nobles who formed the king's court.

It had been decided to make no attempt to defend the city outside the castle gates, since that would entail a great loss of life; and so for several days the city dwellers who remained and these refugees from all the country about poured into the fortification and were housed inside its walls. The old castle gates which were then on Castle Highway opposite the Church of St. Andrew were at last shut and barricaded, and the walls were manned with citizen soldiery prepared to give their lives for the protection of the city and their families.

The Tartars fell upon the city in the night and, after burning the outlying villages, pillaged the districts that lay about the churches of St. Florian, St. John, and the Holy Cross. The whole night long was one of hideous sounds—the crackling and fury of flames, the snarling and yelling of the enemy when they found that the prey had fled, their roars of triumph when they came upon gold and treasure.

As morning dawned the watchers from the Wawel looked out over the town and saw but three churches not already in flames. These were the Church of Our Lady Mary near the great market, the Church of St. Andrew with its stalwart towers at the Castle Gate, and the Church of St. Adalbert in the market place. Already a colony of Jews in the Black Village had perished, also those refugees and town dwellers who had not rushed inside the walls of defense. There remained but one man—or rather a youth—still alive in the midst of all that destruction.

He was the trumpeter of the Church of Our Lady Mary, and he had taken solemn oath to sound the trumpet each hour of the day and night from a little balcony high up on the front of the church. As the first golden rays of the sun changed the Vistula from a dark line to a plash of dancing gold, he mounted this balcony to sound the Heynal—the hymn to Our Lady which every trumpeter in the church had in the past sworn to

260 .

play each hour of the day and night—"until death." He felt with a strange joy the glow of the sun as it fell upon him that morning, for the night had been very dark with its own shadow and with the gloomy blackness of men's ruthlessness.

About his feet, down in the town highway, stood groups of short, fierce men gazing up at him curiously. Here and there the roof of a house was shooting upward in flames and belching forth clouds of black smoke. Hundreds of dwellings lay charred and ruined by the conflagration. He was alone in the midst of a terrible enemy—he might have fled on the previous day and gained the castle with the refugees and the town dwellers, but he had been true to his oath and remained at his post until he should be driven away. Now it was too late to retreat.

He was a very young man, perhaps nineteen or twenty, and wore a dark cloth suit that was caught at the knees with buckles, like the knickerbockers of a later generation; dark, thick hose extended from the knees to the tops of his soft, pointed sandals, and a short coat falling just below the waist was held together in front by a belt. The head covering was of leather and something like a cowl; it fell clear to his shoulders and ran up over the head in such a way that only his face and a bit of hair were visible.

"My mother and sister are safe," he thought. "May God be praised for that! They are gone these ten days and must be now with the cousins in Moravia."

It came to him then what a sweet thing life is. The sun over the Vistula was now reflected in the windows of the Cathedral of the Wawel where the priests were already saying mass. At the tops of all the gates he could see guards in full armor upon which the sunlight flashed. A banner with a white eagle hung in the air above the gate at the great draw.

"Poland lives," he thought.

And then it came to him, young as he was, that he was part
of the glorious company of Polish men that was fighting for all
Christendom against brutal and savage invaders. He had not
seen much of death before that minute—he had heard of it
only as something vague. And now, he himself was perhaps

going out to meet it, because of his oath, because of his love for the Church, because of his love for Poland.

"I shall keep my word," he mused. "If I die it shall be for that. My word is as good as my life."

Had a painter caught his expression then, he would have caught only the expression of a very great peace—an expression that signified somehow that God was very close. There was no moment of weakness, no faltering, no suffering even— for he did not think of what might come after his duty was performed. The sand in the hourglass already marked the hour for the trumpet to sound.

"Now, for Poland and Our Lady I will sound the Heynal," he said, and raised the trumpet to his lips.

Softly he blew at first—then, thrilled with a sense of triumph, he felt in his heart a joy that was almost ecstatic. He seemed to see in a vision that though he might now die alone and for naught save what perhaps some scoffing ones might call a foolish honor, still that bravery was to descend as a heritage to the people to whom he belonged, and was to become a part of their spirit, their courage, their power everlasting—all this that moment brought.

A Tartar below crouched to his bow and drew back the arrow as far as he could draw. The string whirred. The dark shaft flew like a swift bird straight for the mark. It pierced the breast of the young trumpeter when he was near the end of his song—it quivered there a moment and the song ceased. But still holding to the trumpet the youth fell back against the supporting wall and blew one last glorious note; it began strongly, trembled, and then ceased—broken like the young life that gave it birth, and at that moment those below applied the torch to the wooden church and it, too, rose in flames to Heaven, with the soul of the youth among them.

MYLES FALWORTH was but eight years of age at that time, and it was only afterwards, and when he grew old enough to know more of the ins and outs of the matter, that he could remember by bits and pieces the things that afterwards happened; how one evening a knight came clattering into the courtyard upon a horse, red-nostrilled and smeared with the sweat and foam of a desperate ride— Sir John Dale, a dear friend of the blind lord.

Even though so young, Myles knew that something very serious had happened to make Sir John so pale and haggard, and he dimly remembered leaning against the knight's iron-covered knees, looking up into his gloomy face, and asking him if he was sick to look so strange. Thereupon those who had been too troubled before to notice him, bethought themselves of him, and sent him to bed, rebellious at having to go so early.

Men of Iron

BY HOWARD PYLE

Illustrated by

Lorence F. Bjorklund

He remembered how the next morning, looking out of a window high up under the eaves, he saw a great troop of horsemen come riding into the courtyard beneath, where a powdering of snow had whitened everything, and of how the leader, a knight clad in black armor, dismounted and entered the great hall doorway below, followed by several of the band.

He remembered how some of the castle women were standing in a frightened group upon the landing of the stairs, talking together in low voices about a matter he did not understand, excepting that the armed men who had ridden into the courtyard had come for Sir John Dale. None of the women paid any attention to him; so, shunning their notice, he ran off down the winding stairs, expecting every moment to be called back again by some one of them.

A crowd of castle people, all very serious and quiet, were gathered in the hall, where a number of strange men-at-arms lounged upon the benches, while two billmen in steel caps and leathern jacks stood guarding the great door, the butts of their weapons resting upon the ground, and the staves crossed, barring the doorway.

In the anteroom was the knight in black armor whom Myles had seen from the window. He was sitting at the table, his great helmet lying upon the bench beside him, and a quart beaker of spiced wine at his elbow. A clerk sat at the other end of the same table, with inkhorn in one hand and pen in the other, and a parchment spread in front of him.

Master Robert, the castle steward, stood before the knight, who every now and then put to him a question, which the other would answer, and the clerk would write the answer down upon the parchment.

His father stood with his back to the fireplace, looking down upon the floor with his blind eyes, his brows drawn moodily together, and the scar of the great wound that he had received at the tournament at York—the wound that had made him blind—showing red across his forehead, as it always did when he was angered or troubled.

There was something about it all that frightened Myles, who crept to his father's side, and slid his little hand into the palm that hung limp and inert. In answer to the touch, his father grasped the hand tightly, but did not seem otherwise to notice that he was there. Neither did the black knight pay any attention to him, but continued putting his questions to Master Robert.

Then, suddenly, there was a commotion in the hall without, loud voices, and a hurrying here and there. The black knight half arose, grasping a heavy iron mace that lay upon the bench beside him, and the next moment Sir John Dale himself, as pale as death, walked into the antechamber. He stopped in the very middle of the room. "I yield to my lord's grace and mercy," said he to the black knight, and they were the last words he ever uttered in this world.

The black night shouted out some words of command, and swinging up the iron mace in his hand, strode forward clanking towards Sir John, who raised his arm as though to shield himself from the blow. Two or three of those who stood in the hall without came running into the room with drawn swords and bills, and little Myles, crying out with terror, hid his face in his father's long gown.

The next instant came the sound of a heavy blow and of a groan, then another blow and the sound of one falling upon the ground. Then the clashing of steel, and in the midst Lord Falworth crying, in a dreadful voice, "Thou traitor! thou coward! thou murderer!"

Master Robert snatched Myles away from his father, and bore him out of the room in spite of his screams and struggles, and he remembered just one instant's sight of Sir John lying still and silent upon his face, and of the black knight standing above him, with the terrible mace in his hand stained a dreadful red.

It was the next day that Lord and Lady Falworth and little Myles, together with three of the more faithful of their people, left the castle.

His memory of past things held a picture for Myles of old Diccon Bowman standing over him in the silence of midnight with a lighted lamp in his hand, and with it a recollection of

266

being bidden to hush when he would have spoken, and of being dressed by Diccon and one of the women, bewildered with sleep, shuddering and chattering with cold.

He remembered being wrapped in the sheepskin that lay at the foot of his bed, and of being carried in Diccon Bowman's arms down the silent darkness of the winding stairway, with the great black giant shadows swaying and flickering upon the stone wall as the dull flame of the lamp swayed and flickered in the cold breathing of the night air.

Below were his father and mother and two or three others. A stranger stood warming his hands at a newly-made fire, and little Myles, as he peeped from out the warm sheepskin, saw that he was in riding-boots and was covered with mud. He did not know till long years afterwards that the stranger was a messenger sent by a friend at the King's court, bidding his father fly for safety.

They who stood there by the red blaze of the fire were all very still, talking in whispers and walking on tiptoes, and Myles' mother hugged him in her arms, sheepskin and all, kissing him, with the tears streaming down her cheeks, and whispering to him, as though he could understand their trouble, that they were about to leave their home forever.

Then Diccon Bowman carried him out into the strangeness of the winter midnight.

Outside, beyond the frozen moat, where the osiers stood stark and stiff in their winter nakedness, was a group of dark figures waiting for them with horses. In the pallid moonlight Myles recognized the well-known face of Father Edward, the Prior of St. Mary's.

After that came a long ride through that silent night upon the saddle-bow in front of Diccon Bowman; then a deep, heavy sleep, that fell upon him in spite of the galloping of the horses.

When next he woke the sun was shining, and his home and his whole life were changed.

From the time the family escaped from Falworth Castle that midwinter night to the time Myles was sixteen years old he knew nothing of the great world beyond Crosbey-Dale. A fair was held twice in a twelvemonth at the market town of Wisebey, and three times in the seven years, old Diccon Bowman took the lad to see the sights at that place. Beyond these three glimpses of the outer world, he lived almost as secluded a life as one of the neighboring monks of St. Mary's Priory.

Crosbey-Holt, their new home, was different enough from Falworth or Easterbridge Castle, the former baronial seats of Lord Falworth. It was a long, low, straw-thatched farmhouse, which once, when the church lands were divided into two holdings, was one of the bailiff's houses. All around were the fruitful farms of the priory, tilled by well-to-do tenant holders, and rich with fields of waving grain, and meadow-lands where sheep and cattle grazed in flocks and herds; for in those days the church lands were under church rule, and were governed by church laws, and there, when war and famine and waste and sloth blighted the outside world, harvests flourished and were gathered, and sheep were sheared and cows were milked in peace and quietness.

The Prior of St. Mary's owed much if not all of the church's prosperity to the blind Lord Falworth, and now he was paying it back with a haven of refuge from the ruin that his former patron had brought upon himself by giving shelter to Sir John Dale.

I fancy that most boys do not love the grinding of school life—the lessons to be conned, the close application during study hours. It is not often pleasant to brisk, lively lads to be so cooped up. I wonder what the boys of today would have thought of Myles' training. With him that training was not only of the mind, but of the body as well, and for seven years it was almost unremitting. "Thou hast thine own way to make in the world, sirrah," his father said more than once when the boy complained of the grinding hardness of his life, and to make one's way in those days meant a thousand times more than it does now; it meant not only a heart to feel and a brain to think, but a hand quick and strong to strike in battle, and a body tough to endure the wounds and blows in return. And so it was that Myles' body as well as his mind had to be trained to meet the needs of the dark age in which he lived.

Every morning, winter or summer, rain or shine, he tramped away six long miles to the priory school, and in the evenings his mother taught him French.

269

Myles, being prejudiced in the school of thought of his day, rebelled not a little at that last branch of his studies. "Why must I learn that vile tongue?" said he.

"Call it not vile," said the blind old lord, grimly; "belike, when thou art grown a man, thou'lt have to seek thy fortune in France land, for England is haply no place for such as be of Falworth blood." And in after-years, true to his father's prediction, the "vile tongue" served him well.

As for his physical training, that pretty well filled up the hours between his morning studies at the monastery and his evening studies at home. Then it was that old Diccon Bowman took him in hand, than whom none could be better fitted to shape his young body to strength and his hands to skill in arms. The old bowman had served with Lord Falworth's father under the Black Prince both in France and Spain, and in long years of war had gained a practical knowledge of arms that few could surpass. Besides the use of the broadsword, the short sword, the quarter-staff, and the cudgel, he taught Myles to

270

shoot so skilfully with the long-bow and the cross-bow that not a lad in the countryside was his match at the village butts. Attack and defense with the lance, and throwing the knife and dagger were also part of his training.

Then, in addition to this more regular part of his physical training, Myles was taught in another branch not so often included in the military education of the day—the art of wrestling. It happened that a fellow lived in Crosbey village, by name Ralph-the-Smith, who was the greatest wrestler in the countryside, and had worn the champion belt for three years. Every Sunday afternoon, in fair weather, he came to teach Myles the art, and being wonderfully adept in bodily feats, he soon grew so quick and active and firm-footed that he could cast any lad under twenty years of age living within a range of five miles.

"It is main ungentle armscraft that he learneth," said Lord Falworth one day to Prior Edward. "Saving only the broadsword, the dagger, and the lance, there is but little that a gentleman of his strain may use. Neth'less, he gaineth quickness and suppleness, and if he hath true blood in his veins he will acquire knightly arts shrewdly quick when the time cometh to learn them."

But hard and grinding as Myles' life was, it was not entirely without pleasures. There were many boys living in Crosbey-Dale and the village; yeomen's and farmers' sons, to be sure, but nevertheless, lads of his own age, and that, after all, is the main requirement for friendship in boyhood's world. Then there was the river to bathe in; there were the hills and valleys to roam over, and the wold and woodland, with their wealth of nuts and birds' nests and whatnot of boyhood's treasures.

Once he gained a triumph that for many a day was very sweet under the tongue of his memory. As was said before, he had been three times to the market town at fair-time, and upon the last of these occasions he had fought a bout of quarter-staff with a young fellow of twenty, and had been the conqueror. He was then only a little over fourteen years old.

Old Diccon, who had gone with him to the fair, had met some cronies of his own, with whom he had sat gossiping in the ale-booth, leaving Myles for the nonce to shift for himself. By-and-by the old man had noticed a crowd gathered at one part of the fair-ground, and, sniffing a fight, had gone running, ale-pot in hand. Then, peering over the shoulders of the crowd, he had seen his young master, stripped to the waist, fighting like a gladiator with a fellow a head taller than himself. Diccon was about to force his way through the crowd and drag them asunder, but a second look had showed his practised eye that Myles was not only holding his own, but was in the way of winning the victory. So he had stood with the others looking on, withholding himself from any interference and whatever upbraiding might be necessary until the fight had been brought to a triumphant close. Lord Falworth never heard directly of the redoubtable affair, but old Diccon was not so silent with the common folk of Crosbey-Dale, and so no doubt the father had some inkling of what had happened. It was shortly after this notable event that Myles was formally initiated into squirehood. His father and mother, as was the custom, stood sponsors for him. By them, each bearing a lighted taper, he was escorted to the altar. It was at St. Mary's Priory, and Prior Edward blessed the sword and girded it the lad's side. No one was present but the four, and when the good Prior had given the benediction and had signed the cross upon his forehead, Myles' mother stooped and kissed his brow just where the priest's finger had drawn the holy sign. Her eyes brimmed bright with tears as she did so. Poor lady! perhaps she only then and for the first time realized how big her fledgling was growing for his nest. Henceforth Myles had the right to wear a sword.

ALONG South Street, New York, the wharves stretched out into the East River like the fingers of a hand. From below Wall Street, as far up as Market and Pike streets, a forest of masts lifted tall and straight against the sky. If you were seaman enough to be able to tell one ship from another, you could have made out brigs, barques, barkentines, clippers, East Indiamen, packets of the famous Black Ball Line, sturdy whalers out of Nantucket, Flemish luggers, and French corvettes. The eager thrust of their bowsprits, pointing up across the street, all but raked the shuttered windows of the warehouses. Ships from every harbor of the world, lading their cargoes of cotton and potash and flour or disgorging their chests of fragrant tea, bales of Chinese silks, hogsheads of sugar, and puncheons of rum.

South Street belonged to the sea. The signs of the ship chandlers swung in the breeze. Windows displayed quadrants, compasses and barometers, and all manner of seagoing gear. There were sail lofts, and the houses of the underwriters, merchants, and auctioneers. Thus the commerce of the continent met the trade of the ocean in a bustle of activity that deafened the ear and confused the eye.

Pier 20 was a blackened wharf whose cobbles rumbled with drays, horses, barrows, and toiling men. Here lay a ship whose masts towered out of proportion to wise practice. The

The Unforeseen Happens

BY

ARMSTRONG SPERRY

Illustrated by

Armstrong Sperry

sun shone smartly on her yards and gleaming brightwork; on the lines of pins in the pinrails; on the gold of the figurehead growing out of the upward curve of her stem. Her hull was charged with the lean tension of a greyhound, and from her foremast a canvas tarpaulin flaunted the legend:

FOR SAN FRANCISCO
CLIPPER FLYING CLOUD
APPLY GRINNELL, MINTURN & COMPANY

while at the maintruck the swallow-tailed house flag of red, blue, and yellow fluttered in the ocean-wandering breeze. From somewhere about her decks a man's voice was singing:

O! A sailor's life is the life for me!
A gallant barque and a roarin' sea!
Ho—my bullies, yo ho!

A clipper had arrived that morning from the Orient, the first of the season's China tea racers. The smell of her cargo lay fragrant on the air; tea of the first picking it was, from Whampoa. Merchants were swarming around her like flies about a honeypot. Bids were soaring. The finest teas had a way of molding in the salt air of a long sea voyage; hence the first and swiftest clipper home fetched top prices for her cargo.

A Chinese mandarin, passenger on the newly arrived ship, drew his brocaded robes about him and disappeared in a lurching carriage. Sailors ashore rubbed elbows with sea captains; country folk, in to see the sights of the great city, gazed with like astonishment at coolies and crimps and boarding-house runners. A restless place was South Street in 1851, I can tell you; as humming with industry as a beehive. Manhattan was an island which had its business with the sea; there was no question about that.

My eyes took in every detail of the scene, as a hungry man might look upon a table laden with good food. The ring of the chanteys and the click-click of capstan were music to my ears. A polyglot of ship smells that every sailor knows struck me like a blow; made up it was of Stockholm tar and bilge and rotting fruit and moldering cargo, cut through by a reek of fish. Yet it was as sweet as the perfumes of Araby! The harbor at East Boston had a like smell, and it made me, for the moment, less homesick.

My sea chest, brass-bound and nautical as you please, lay in a humble room of the Seaman's Rest. It held my purchases of duck pants, woolen underwear, oilskins, sea boots, my precious spyglass, together with sundry incidentals that the clerk had persuaded me that Jack always took to sea.

That morning in the Grinnell offices, producing the letter from Donald McKay that was the opening wedge, I had signed

my Indentures, thereby agreeing faithfully to serve my employers for a period of two years; to discharge my duties to the best of my meager ability; to obey my officers; not to embezzle my ship's goods; not to frequent saloons or play at games of chance! In consideration for which service, the shipowners did contract to teach the "undersigned Apprentice the whole business of being a seaman . . . and to provide same with sufficient food and drink . . . ."

I'm sure you've known all along, my good reader, that I was to sail on the Flying Cloud. Well—I did. It came about like this: Two weeks after the Ajax had towed the Cloud out of Boston Harbor, Donald McKay had stopped before my drafting table one morning and remarked:

"What's ailin' ye, laddie? Ye're as uneasy as a bear on a hot griddle."

"Why—nothing, sir."

"Nothin', eh? I'll wager I could mak' a sharp guess! Couldna' by any chance be the Cloud, could it?"

I glanced up to see him looking at me with a shrewd twinkle in his eye.

"Is there news of her, sir?" I cried. "Has she arrived in New York? When is she sailing?"

He sat down opposite me then, and it struck me that I had seldom seen him unbend to this degree.

"Aye, she's arrived, right enough," he assented. "Berthed up snug as a bug at Pier 20. They're stowin' her for the trip around the Horn to California and thence to China." Donald McKay leaned across the table. "An' how would ye like tae sail aboord her, laddie? Afore the mast?"

The question was a quiet one but it struck my ear like a pistol shot.

"Muckle ye ken aboot ships now," the man continued, "but

277

it's a' theory. Ye can name every inch o' cordage, but I'll warrant ye'd hae a deal o' trouble picking them oot in the teeth o' a nor'easter. There's but one way to know ships, laddie, an' that's tae sail them. Yer friend Cap'n Clarke would fall in wi' that, albeit he doesna' hold wi' a lot o' my views."

Sail on the Cloud! I could scarce breathe for the feelings that whirled through me.

"I've talked wi' Grinnell's aboot ye," the man was saying, "an' if ye mak' a favorable impression they will sign ye on. Likewise I spoke wi' yer guid mother an' explained tae her that if ye would be a fine shipbuilder ye've got tae come up through the hawsepipe an' not in the cabin window. She has confidence in me and gi'ed her consent."

"My mother—consented?"

Donald McKay nodded. He stood up then and laid his hands on my shoulders with firm grip.

"Think weel before ye mak' yer decision. An' sleep on it, too," he warned. "I would ne'er advise any man tae tak' up a seafarin' life save as a means tae an end. Hard it is, an' cruel an' dangerous; small pay in it an' smaller future. Yer womenfolk will wring oot their hearts wi' weepin' for ye. Aye, a hard school, an' no mistake! So think aboot it, lad, an' if ye decide upon this step, yer wages can be paid each month tae yer mother, an' yer mind can be at ease aboot her."

"There's nothing I would rather do than sail aboard the Cloud, sir," I managed finally.

He chuckled. "I had an idea 'twas so! Talk it over wi' yer mother, laddie, an' mak' up your mind. An' if ye should decide the way I think ye will, may God go wi' ye."

When I reached home, I found my mother in the parlor with old Messina sitting to one side of the stove, drawing on his pipe. There was an air of expectancy, as if portentous

278

things were about to happen. My mother looked up as I entered and I saw that her eyes were bright. She dropped her needlework and crossed to my side.

Before I could speak, she exclaimed: "You are going to sea in the Flying Cloud! My dear son, how glad I—am!" She kissed me, and if her heart was nigh to breaking, her voice was soft and sure.

Messina Clarke rose with creaking bones and came over to me. "You've the makin' of a deep-sea sailor in you, lad," he said huskily, putting his hands on my shoulders, "and so I've been a-tellin' your mother. I've watched you ever since you was a little tyke buildin' ships out o' seegar boxes and riggin' 'em with string, and sailin' 'em in every puddle 'twixt here and Bunker Hill. The sea's the place for the likes o' you. Contrary to that McKay upstart, you'll ne'er spend your days in any office when once you've felt the lift of a deck under your feet! 'Tis the only life fit for a man. Blast me, if I wasn't so blamed rusty in the j'ints, I'd ship aboard the Cloud myself. She'll need a proper salt-water sailor on her with her bows blown inside out thatways!"

"If only he were a little older," sighed my mother.

"Older?" queried Messina testily. "He's fifteen, ain't he? The sooner a man gets started about his business in life the better, I say."

"I couldn't speak, for the life of me. I glanced around the room at the familiar objects that I had lived with all my life and never really seen until this moment: the hair flowers under a glass protector on the mantel; the framed sampler worked by my mother when she was a child—Abigail Winthrop, Aged Seven; a painting of the ill-starred Empress of Asia; silhouettes and whatnots . . . Now that I was leaving, they had a meaning.

So it was settled. I was to drive by coach to New York, an event that under ordinary circumstances would have been a big adventure; but with a passage around the Horn in the Flying Cloud in the offing, it seemed little enough.

The next few days sped by like a dream. When an evening came that the coach drew up to the door, my carpetbag was packed in readiness with a few belongings: a fresh shirt, underwear, a muffler of thickest wool knitted by my mother (though the month was May)—"for the weather you will meet off Cape Horn," she said—a brass spyglass from Messina Clarke, his best one, too, and lastly, a box of sandwiches and my favorite cakes.

I kissed my mother good-by, and she clung to me. Her lips whispered against my ear, "God keep you, my son, and bring you home."

I threw up my head, for I was a sailor and I was going to sea.

Old Messina gripped my arms. "Remember, boy," he muttered, "When you're down there off the Horn: one hand for yourself and one for the ship. Never forget! One hand for yourself and one for the ship!"

Good old Messina. Little did I suspect that when a day came that I should be in East Boston once more, you would be gone. Rest in peace, old friend, in Fiddler's Green where the ghosts of all good sailormen keep their watch below. But for you, how different would the course of my life have run.

I was past speech and must have looked mighty glum, for old Messina cried, "Brail up, lubber!" and fetched me a crack on the back, then came about and blew his nose violently. I stumbled across the sidewalk to the waiting coach. The door banged behind me. A whip cracked—the horses strained forward in their harness. Then the darkness shut down and I remember only the lurching, lurching of the coach on the highway to New York.

The Flying Cloud was to sail with the afternoon tide. Stevedores struggled up one gangplank to descend by another. They had finished lading the lower hold, and a diminishing pile of cargo on the wharf showed that their work 'tween-decks was almost done. The mates were standing over them, bawling orders. A ticklish business, this stowing of cargo, since the Cloud was as yet an untried ship and the lading must balance her sail plan.

By twelve noon I went aboard my ship with the sea chest aperch my shoulder. My lubber's clothes were stored in the bottom of it against the day—who knew when—I should step back once more upon native soil. In my new rig I felt that I would pass muster as an old sea dog: blue shirt, duck trousers tight around the midriff and falling loose about the feet; a varnished hat with its dangling "admiral's pennant"; a black silk neckerchief, and lastly a nautical-looking knife slung with importance to my belt. Little did I realize that complexion and walk removed me at a glance from confusion with the seasoned sailormen who swung down the decks with bronzed cheek and rolling gait. I lowered my brass-bound sea chest and looked about. How the long sweep of familiar deck gladdened my eye! I glanced up at the spidery maze of rigging and felt a glow of satisfaction and pride and gratitude, as one feels in close familiar things. It was like coming home.

Perhaps a man's fate is written when he is born—and a ship's too . . . "I knew that it was my fate to cross your wake, Flying Cloud! You didn't think you could clear for China without me, did you? I can hear the water chuckling about your forefoot and the song of the ropes running through your blocks. What are you telling me? That the wind blows fresh, and there are spice islands on the other side of the—"

"Ahoy, lad! What might you want?" A big man in a blue peajacket bore down upon me.

"I'm an apprentice, sir."

"Now whoever would ha' guessed that! Well, I'm the second mate. Mister Andrews to the likes o' you. See that you step smart when I speak or there'll be trouble 'tween you and me." He pointed fo'ard along the deck. "Half deck's up there. Stow yerself and yer gear, and brisk about it, too!"

The half deck is the apprentices' quarters. It may be anywhere on a ship except under the foc'sle head. In the Flying Cloud it was placed well for'ard and its dignified name gave small indication of its appearance. To the eye it was no more than a scuttle, seen from the deck side. Once below the scuttle you would have found two small boxlike rooms, one of which was fitted with four bunks, the other with six. I turned into the "Box" on the starboard side, and by the light that filtered in through the small port I could distinguish four bunks, two on each wall. This, unless something unforeseen changed the course of planned events was to be my home for the next two years.

The room was half filled with a clutter of ropes, sailcloth, kindling, pots and pans, and general rubbish. It appeared to be a repository for any odd thing that no other place could be found for. It was completely cheerless. I cleared a space large

282

enough to set down my sea chest, then I sat upon it and took
in my surroundings with a dejected eye. I thought of old
Messina and his friendly study, of my mother, and in that
moment I was no stouthearted sailorman, I can tell you. But
my bleak thoughts were broken by the door banging open. A
young lad about my own age bounded into the room.

"My name's Archie Warner," he threw at me by way of
greeting. "What's yours?"

I told him. "Are you an apprentice, too?" I queried.

"Aye, and there's two more of us to come in here. Ever
been to sea before?"

"No."

"Ho! A proper landlubber, eh? It'll be keelhauling for you,
my bucko."

"Well, I can name every line and stay and plank aboard,"
I bragged.

"Humph!" he grunted. "Bet I can turn a quicker splice than
you can!"

"Prove it!"

In no time we were at it, and that's how we became friends.
He could turn a quicker splice then I, for I have always been
clumsy at the trick, but I could beat him all to hollow on the
topmast rigging. He was a New Yorker by birth, and the only
sailing he had ever done was around the harbor and neighbor-

ing waters. He was as tall as I and as hard as a hickory nut; his face was a mask of freckles and his hair as red as a brick. Indeed, that's the name he was soon known by—Brick Warner.

The third and fourth occupants of our cabin appeared. Brick and I examined them with interest. Having been established in our quarters for some fifteen minutes, we felt their seniors and superiors. Their names were Tad Lancraft and Jake Whittlesy; names which were quickly shortened to Lanny and Whit, and as such they were known thereafter.

Lanny was a big lad of sixteen, a full fathom tall. His hands protruded to some length from the ends of his sleeves. In fact the whole impression of him was of being too big for his clothes. He had an open friendly face and was as fair as a Swede.

Whit, on the other hand, was shorter, of a height with Brick and me. He was as dark as Lanny was light, serious too, and —it was my guess—unleavened by humor.

The newcomers set down their duffels and tossed a copper for bunks. A few tentative questions and answers began to get us acquainted. Little did we know then that we four were to become close friends, sticking together through fair fortune and ill, aye, even unto death, since death was to claim one of us when the time came. Whit took leadership in the half deck, for his was the prestige of having served one year of his apprenticeship in the clipper Fair Haven.

"And under Mister Jones, the blasted first mate of the Flying Cloud, too," he explained. "May the devil fry him in his own fat!"

A whistle shrilled above our heads.

"That means us!" cried Whit, leaping for the ladder. We tumbled up after him.

On deck men and rigging boxes and barrels were all mixed

284

up together. There was running and shouting and a confusion of activity that bewildered me. If, in my conceit, I had prided myself that I knew the name and location of every line on the ship, I could not in that moment have picked one from the other. No human being is more helpless than the landsman who takes to sea. Although my interest in ships dated from earliest childhood, I had never sailed in anything larger than a dory. I found that a ship laid out on the floor of a mold loft is one thing; at sea, something else. We apprentices got in one another's way, fell over the sheets, and were generally useless.

There was a medley of orders half pronounced and unintelligible to our ears. Fortunately a first voyage apprentice is expected to know nothing and we fully lived up to expectation. We could only stand by stupidly or fall on the end of a rope where men were pulling. The wharf was filled with an excited crowd of spectators. Flags were flying; bunting lent the dingy dock a festive look. People had come from all over the city, even from New Jersey and Long Island, attracted by the fame of the Flying Cloud, as well as by that desire that lies dormant in every human breast, to see a ship take to sea.

A brougham drawn by two spanking bays pulled up with a flourish. From it descended two stylish young ladies accompanied by their father, Mr. Moses H. Grinnell, the owner of the Cloud. Captain Josiah Perkins Creesy, master of the ship, appeared, balancing his chronometers, his clearance papers bulging in his pocket. "Perk" Creesy he was, to his intimates, The Old Man, to us. He was a Marblehead skipper who had won his reputation in the China tea trade as master of the Oneida. He greeted young Mr. Minturn, who would accompany the pilot as far as Sandy Hook, and the two men came aboard together through a lane of admiring bystanders.

The last of the barrels and cases had vanished from the

285

wharf into the capacious belly of the vessel. She was loaded to the bolts of her chain plates. The stevedores, pocketing their wage, laid a course for the nearest saloon. Their work was done. The Flying Cloud could go to the bottom, for all of them!

On the wharf the crowd surged and shouted. A band was puffing out the strains of "Lost on the Bosom of the Deep." Funny thing to be playing, thought I, with a swallow. Whit had invested his last dollar in a formidable-looking accordion, urged upon him by a peddler. Brick Warner called his farewells to a rosy-cheeked sweetheart. Lanny laid in a supply of cinnamon balls and a fathom of Irish Twist tobacco. I had sent ashore three letters for the post: one for Donald McKay, one for my mother, and one for Messina Clarke.

Now we were moving . . . Cries and cheers and good-bys reached us across a widening gap of water. The Ajax, puffing like a porpoise out of water, was nosing the Cloud out between the pierheads, lining her up to stem the running tide. We were straining at the capstan bars with:

> *Our anchor's a-weigh and our sails they are set,*
> *Good-by, fare ye well! Good-by, fare ye well!*
> *And the gals we are leaving we leave with regret,*
> *Good-by, fare ye well! Good-by!*

All the sails had been shaken from their harbor gaskets. A favorable wind was hauling out of the north. Men jumped to set jib and spanker. The yards on the foremast were braced so that the wind would catch the sails aback and thus swing the head off to starboard; while the yards on the main and mizzen were braced in the opposite direction so as to force the ship ahead as soon as her bow canted enough for these sails to draw. There came a hiss of water thrown back from the bows

286

as the Flying Cloud heeled to the wind and moved down the river toward Governor's Island and the Lower Bay. Proud she was, like a lady decked out in a new dress, conscious of her beauty and of the admiration she attracted; preening, showing off a bit.

The windows of the buildings along the waterfront were filled with people, waving, shouting, crying, wishing Godspeed to us. I stood in the bows by the knightheads, watching Manhattan drop away. A heavy hand was upon me, for I was leaving the only land I knew, and my people. But the ship was aquiver with life, eager for what lay ahead, and I was aboard her. And feeling this, I knew a sudden lift of the spirit. Ah, it was good to be young, with the world before me!

Ships slipped past, their crews cheering; gulls swooped low at the masthead. The Battery was left behind . . . The hills of Staten Island . . . the desolate line of Coney . . . The Flying Cloud took her first lift to the grounding swells. Beyond the rim of the ocean a new world beckoned.

". . . Winds blow fair for you, Flying Cloud! Fine freights swell your hold! Deep harbors wait for you . . ."

Sea-Wash

BY CARL SANDBURG

THE sea-wash never ends.
The sea-wash repeats, repeats.
Only old songs? Is that all the sea knows?
     Only the old strong songs?
     Is that all?
The sea-wash repeats, repeats.

CADMUS found the balloon camp in a small opening in the woods, about a half mile behind the lines. But he hadn't come to make any preliminary visit. He was going to go right up. And perhaps that was a good thing in a way, for he hadn't had time to get more than just about scared to death.

At six o'clock that morning he had been brought orders to report to General Johnston's headquarters. There Major Ghett had supplied him with a notebook, pencils and a powerful pair of glasses. "We want you to mark down all the enemy troops you can see. Take your time, and identify them by organization, if possible. Estimate the numbers. Also mark down any moving troops, and any new batteries. You'll want to go high enough to get a look back as far as Howard's Bridge and Deep Creek." He dropped a hand on Cadmus's shoulder. "I'm sorry to call on you so suddenly. But you ought not to have any difficulty with signals and things. The crew has had experience. It would be a good idea though to keep the strap of those glasses round your neck all the time. They're valuable."

He shook hands.

"They'll be expecting you out there. Good luck, Mr. Henry."

It was an almost idyllic spot for a camp—that is, if you were camping there. The fine running spring, the stand of pine trees that left the ground free of underbrush and the good

Cadmus Henry

BY WALTER D. EDMONDS

Illustrated by

Manning deV. Lee

green grass meant nothing to Cadmus. All he saw was the apparatus that used up most of the open space.

It consisted of a long iron flue resting on bricks. One end of the flue was bent up and passed into the mouth of the balloon, while the bag, like the dead body of a slovenly monster, enclosed in the net of cordage, sprawled out on the grass beyond. A rope was attached to the cordage, from which it reached to an enormous windlass; it made several turns round the windlass and then continued off into the woods in coil after coil. To Cadmus's desperate eyes it did not seem possible that so much rope could exist in the world, let alone in the Confederate States of America.

The balloon crew must have heard him coming, for one of them was building a fire under the flue, while a round-shouldered Negro brought up pine knots and turpentine. Two other men were standing near the windlass and they, with a fifth man, who appeared to have charge of the crew, watched Cadmus ride up.

The fifth man was a gangling individual with an intermittent flutter in his left eye. He was wearing what might have passed for a military cap at some earlier stage of its career.

"You Mr. Henry?" he inquired in a soft, slow voice.

Cadmus allowed he was.

"The boys will have her ready right quick," he said. "My name's Norment, Blaney Norment, Mr. Henry. I'm glad to be of service any time." His eyelid nearly closed and then slowly and fascinatingly fluttered open. "Mebane," he shouted, "you come here and take Mr. Henry's horse."

A second Negro came shuffling out of the woods, a little man with grizzled hair and a thin line of whiskers. When he saw the brown mare, his hands cupped a little, and he made a humming sound. The mare, who usually was leery of strangers,

290

dropped her nose and made a faint whickering over the little man's head. When he led her off into the woods she went as slow and shuffling as he did.

"Something about Mebane," Norment said. "Horses like it. I don't know what it is."

Cadmus said something polite, but he didn't know what. He was watching the way the big Negro had begun slinging turpentine at the growing fire. The flames almost exploded upward and the roar of burning found an echo in the iron flue, as if the flames had hands to beat it with. He was conscious of the speculative stares of the men, but he didn't pay much attention. He was finding it hard to make his knees keep upright.

"That's a lot of rope, Mr. Norment," he said, because he had to say something.

"Maybe half a mile. It has good long splices. Mink makes good splices. He was a sailor."

The big Negro lifted his head. He looked at Cadmus briefly, and then threw another armful of knots on the fire. The man who had started the fire now came over to where Cadmus and Norment stood together. He looked like an Irishman and somewhere he had picked up a Zouave's red hat.

"She ought to start swelling pretty soon now, the danged old beast," he said, glancing at Cadmus from the corners of his eyes. "Will I get the gentleman the flag?"

"Yes," said Norment.

Neither he nor Cadmus had anything to say while the Irishman went for the flag. Cadmus wondered momentarily whether it was a Confederate flag, to be attached to the balloon. His attention was absorbed by a sudden swelling of the bag, just beyond the point where the flue entered it. It made no sound; or if it did, the roar of the fire covered it. He watched while the swelling grew. The fabric began to lift un-

291

certainly, the center of heat shifting slightly as the draught through the flue gained or lost momentum. Whenever the last seemed to be the case, the Negro, Mink, threw on turpentine.

As the bag distended, Cadmus observed that it was made up of a great number of irregular pieces of cotton cloth, originally of varying colors, but now faded into an approximate uniformity. The cotton had been coated with some sort of waterproofing to make it airtight, but in places the coating had cracked, and the entire contrivance looked pretty dubious to Cadmus.

The Irishman returned with a small square of red bunting tacked onto a short stick. The man Norment took it from the Irishman.

"Here's the flag," he said. "When you want to go up, you wave it up. When you want to go down, you wave down. It's easy to remember."

"How can you tell which way I'm waving?" Cadmus asked.

"Oh, we can figure it out," said Norment. "When a man wants to come down, he leans farther over the edge. Hooley, here, has good eyesight. Now when you're going up or going down either one, and you want us to hurry up, you shake the flag. The more you want the boys to hurry, the harder you shake it. When you want us to leave off whatever we're doing, you wave."

Cadmus said, "I should think it would be plainer if you had two flags of different colors. That would tell you everything. Red to come down, blue to go up."

"We had a yellow one."

"What did you do with it?"

"Nothing. It got lost." Norment regarded him with a thoughtful expression. Suddenly his eyelid fluttered.

292

Cadmus looked away. The bag of the balloon was increasing enormously. Nearly free of the ground, it had definitely formed its spherical shape. Printed in huge letters around the side was the name PIZZINI.

Seeing that Cadmus was looking at the name, Norment looked at it also.

"Was my brother," he explained. "That was his professional name. Professor Pizzini. He dropped the flag and tried to grab it."

Hooley said, "What goes up must come down." He studied Cadmus out of the corners of his eyes.

Cadmus looked away. His feet didn't feel right. They could have walked out from under him and he wouldn't have known it.

Norment said, "I never sent up a balloon on this kind of business. Only for my brother Pizzini, to make a civilized ascent. Likely they'll shoot at you, Mr. Henry. Those Union people over there, they shoot at anything. Shoot, shoot, shoot, all day and all night till I get tired. But there's one thing about it, they can't shoot only so high, so when you get up far enough, they can't touch you. That's one thing about it, all right."

Cadmus tried to grin.

"But you have to come back down through it."

"What goes up must come down," Hooley said again.

"You shut your mouth with that business," Norment told him, in an utterly toneless voice. He walked over to the windlass, and then back along the coils of rope. "You boys got the end of that rope around something?"

They said no.

"You, Mink," Norment ordered, "you go tie that rope around a tree. Can't never be sure about anything in ballooning unless you're tied down to earth somewhere," he said to Cadmus. "Suppose a cannonshell dumped in here and killed us all when she was still skin-full and hot—that rope would ravel through that windlass like a tax collector's soul. And the man up there wouldn't know a thing about it till he found himself riding in the hand of God. We don't want that to happen, Mr. Henry. There's a time for all things. I guess the old bag's about ready for you."

Cadmus saw that it was so. The two men over by the windlass had laid hold of the handles and now the balloon had drawn free of the flue, and swung suddenly straight above the windlass, picking up its cords as it went. It poised there, a great sphere blotting out half the woods, a monstrous thing to grow in a quiet place, swinging a little, the cords slatting loosely together.

Norment respectfully touched his elbow.

"You want to get in right quick, Mr. Henry. The quicker you do that, the more hot air you've got to lift you."

"When will I know it's getting too cold?" Cadmus asked. "So I can signal you."

"You don't need to worry about that; we'll know."

"Yes," said Hooley, with his sidelong glance. "We'll know."

The Negro, Mink, came up to them. "Mist' No'ment, you all ready fo' de bahskit?" There was a peremptory note in his deep voice.

"When Mink says it's time to go, it is," Norment told Cadmus.

The suspension lines that connected the basket with the concentration ring tightened as the men at the windlass eased up on the brake handle. It seemed to Cadmus that he could see a tremor in the rope. He was conscious of the big Negro's glance, which was almost contemptuous. Mink's eyes seemed to take in everything, and it occurred to Cadmus that he probably had more to do with the actual management of the balloon than Norment.

"All right," he said. "I'm ready."

Mink turned a serious glance on him.

"Dat's good," he said. He steadied the basket with his great hands as Cadmus climbed in.

Cadmus stood holding onto one of the suspension lines with one hand, and grasping the small red flag in the other. He looked around on the good green grass and the line of woods from the shade of which the horses were watching him. The sunlight had a fine warmth. There was hardly a cloud in the sky. But he could feel the tremor in the great envelope as it came down through the net of cords into the suspension line his hand had hold of. He looked up and saw it over his head, looming against the blue sky like the belly of eternity. Underneath, the appendix, by which the hot air had entered this vastness, dangled incongruously, like an elephant's tail.

A slight jerk made him turn to see what the men at the windlass might be up to. But instead of the men, he saw the middle branches of the trees. The balloon was rising, and Cadmus was shocked to realize that he would have to look down if he wanted to see the clearing. The men at the windlass were working the handles. Norment had moved back, resting his hand on his narrow posterior and arching his back to look upward. His mouth was open. Hooley stood off to one side by himself and Mink was watching the uncoiling of the rope. It all seemed very simple and easy, now that he was underway. In fact, Cadmus thought, as he straightened himself in the narrow basket, there was practically nothing to it. He felt almost casual as he glanced out across the treetops.

Lee's house looked closer than he would have imagined. The line of the Warwick River came quickly into view. He made out the dams, the two mills and the Union earthworks on the far side. He could see the troops moving about behind them, the dark blue uniforms almost black, and the men standing on the ends of their shadows. Then he picked out a battery in a meadow beyond Dam No. 2. The guns were placed in a close line with the caissons close up. He could even see the battery teams in an elbow of the meadow, behind some trees. It gave him a curious feeling of detachment to look down on the enemy, as they went about their morning chores, oblivious of his eyes.

But then he noticed that men had started running to their guns. They looked to him like a smart outfit; and they must have had a serious alarm to react so sharply. He wondered what his own people might be up to. He couldn't see any signs of activity in the nearer woods, however, and he looked back at the battery to find an officer busily elevating one of the guns. The muzzle rose and kept on rising, and then it stopped, and Cadmus was seized by a horrid comprehension of the battery's excitement. They had seen the balloon. They were about to shoot at him.

A puff of smoke leaned out of the gun's muzzle and drew to one side, and in the same instant, it seemed to him, a shell burst on his left side. In the next instance the entire surrounding sky was filled with bursting shells. They kept on bursting. He felt completely naked there, and tried instinctively to crouch down behind the basket rim; but the basket was made too small for that. He could neither sit nor kneel.

Then he remembered the red flag. It was still in his hand. Reaching out, he signaled frantically for speed and then ducked back again as a shell passed, cutting a kind of whistle out of the air. He shut his eyes and started praying and heard a thunderous explosion somewhere below. Then another, also below; and still another; and gradually he realized that all the bursts were below him. But he couldn't get up or even open his eyes. He kept crouched as he was, with his heart hammering and a drenching sweat all over him.

A moment later the firing stopped entirely. He felt silence sweep over him, and when finally he opened his eyes, he was surrounded by the sky. Without looking down, he waved the flag from side to side to stop the ascent, and for a little he stayed still, just staring at the blue sky or at the bag over him, with its ridiculous, restless appendix. He had a strange and fanciful impression that the balloon was suspended from some tackle in the sky. He could feel a stir of the air passing him. It was a little like resting in a fabulous swing.

His confidence came back to him with a rush. There was nothing those blue people could do to him now. As he thought

297

of it, he came to the conclusion that none of their shells had burst anywhere really close. So he hoisted himself slightly and looked over the edge of the basket.

The Peninsula now lay like a cloth in gray and green and earth color, stitched and seamed with roads and rivers and fences. It was a clear and beautiful day. The lower waters of the James and the York were blue as the sky itself and to the east he saw the wide shine of the Bay.

All over the land below, and back toward Big Bethel, he made out units of enemy troops: some moving along the roads with what seemed infinite slowness; others in tented villages new-white on the green meadows. Houses and farm buildings cast bold shadows; and the shingled roofs of Yorktown were black and white. Three crows went by below, cocking their heads at him and raucously discussing this phenomenon of a man in the sky; and he had a sudden notion that perhaps they regarded his presence as a usurpation of the rights of crows. It made him grin. He pulled out his notebook and glasses and got to work.

298

It was a more difficult job than he had supposed, for no sooner had he started sketching in the Union positions, than the balloon, with a kind of comic perversity, started slowly to revolve; and Cadmus would no sooner have the line of a field work started than it would have slipped past the orbit of his vision. The basket was too narrow for him to keep continually shifting, so that he had to wait till the continuing revolution brought him around again. But he had good eyes, and the crudely sketched map began to fill up rapidly with the letters I or C or A, to indicate the branches of the service, and the numerals beneath them indicating Cadmus's estimate of their strength.

He had begun with the battery that had fired at him and worked outward and eastward from that point. When finally he finished his work, he turned his glasses back to it again, and saw with a feeling of complete horror that the Yankees had practically filled the field with guns. There must have been three complete batteries brought up while he was working, and more guns were struggling through the roads for neighboring vantage points.

He leaned way over to look down at the balloon camp, which now seemed very far away. He could not identify the men from that distance, except for the Irishman, Hooley, whose red cap stood out against the grass. But when he turned the glasses on them, he saw all of them looking upward, and the Irishman made a gesture with one hand, as if he repeated his favorite phrase.

He had to go down, whether he liked to or not, for the balloon would not retain its buoyancy indefinitely. He unfurled the red flag and waved it.

Long before he reached the danger zone, single guns had begun feeling out the range. The moment the balloon came low enough, the Yankees opened with all their batteries. The shells came in salvos: four, six and eight guns firing at once. Cadmus thought he could hear the shells rumbling from the instant of leaving the cannon's mouth until they burst. They burst in one continual, uninterrupted and enormous blast.

The balloon, which had started down with what had seemed to him a suicidal quickness, now hung floating with tantalizing and vagarish slowness. He had once heard a minister with the preaching gift deliver what Great Uncle Eppa had pronounced a mighty sermon on the gaping jaws of hell. To Cadmus, the sounds and agonies described by that preacher were a trifle to what he was now passing through himself. He kept on signaling for more speed, and he said prayers at the top of his voice. And then, miraculously, he had passed through the thunder; he was behind the shelter of the trees; and the bombshells were passing overhead.

The balloon crew stood as they were, just staring at him, as if they didn't believe the evidence of their own eyes. The two men last at the windlass continued leaning on the handles. One of these was the Negro, Mink. His bowed shoulders were drenched with sweat and his chest labored heavily. But there was a kind of pride in his face as he looked at Cadmus, as if he now had a share in his existence.

"He wouldn't give up his handle, once you got in among them bombshells," Norment explained. "But the other boys took turns on the other one."

When Cadmus climbed out, the earth shifted under him and he had to hang onto the rim of the basket. A shivering was coming down the suspension lines. Looking up, he saw a puckering in the under side of the patchwork bag, as if the balloon, too, shared in the general exhaustion. Then abruptly the Yankees gave up shooting. Silence blanketed the clearing,

300

and through the silence, shuffling slowly towards them and mumbling some kind of jargon about the Promised Land into her attentive ear, Mebane came, leading the brown mare.

It was easier for Cadmus in the saddle. He looked down into the men's blank faces and tried to find some words to say to them. But he couldn't.

The flutter in Norment's eyelid was translated to the envelope of the balloon. It began to settle.

"We all wish you luck, Mr. Henry. Maybe we'll see you again some time. But it won't be this place, I reckon."

Norment looked regretfully round their comfortable camp site.

Cadmus tried to sound casual.

"I probably won't be going up again. But what makes you think you'll have to move?"

"Them Yankees," Norment said drearily. "Now they've missed the balloon, they'll be bound to try and hit us in this camp. Shoot, shoot, shoot. It makes me tired."

As if to second him, a Hotchkiss shell howled gaudily across the trees and exploded with a sudden thump a hundred yards or so back in the woods.

THE first day we passed at sea was Sunday. As we were just from port, and there was a great deal to be done on board, we were kept at work all day, and at night the watches were set, and everything was put into sea order. When we were called aft to be divided into watches, I had a good specimen of the manner of a sea-captain. After the division had been made, he gave a short characteristic speech, walking the quarter-deck with a cigar in his mouth, and dropping the words out between puffs.

"Now, my men, we have begun a long voyage. If we get along well together, we shall have a comfortable time; if we don't, we shall have hell afloat. All you have got to do is to obey your orders, and do your duty like men—then you will fare well enough; if you don't, you will fare hard enough—I can tell you. If we pull together, you will find me a clever fellow; if we don't, you will find me a bloody rascal. That's all I've got to say. Go below, the larboard watch!"

Two Years before the Mast

BY RICHARD HENRY

DANA, JR.

Illustrated by

Alexander Dobkin

I, being in the starboard or second mate's watch, had the opportunity of keeping the first watch at sea. Stimson, a young man making, like myself, his first voyage, was in the same watch, and as he was the son of a professional man, and had been in a merchant's counting-room in Boston, we found that we had some acquaintances and topics in common. We talked these matters over—Boston, what our friends were probably doing, our voyage, &c.—until he went to take his turn at the lookout, and left me to myself. I had now a good opportunity for reflection. I felt for the first time the perfect silence of the sea. The officer was walking the quarter-deck, where I had no right to go, one or two men were talking on the forecastle, whom I had little inclination to join, so that I was left open to the full impression of everything about me. However much I was affected by the beauty of the sea, the bright stars, and the clouds driven swiftly over them, I could not but remember that I was separating myself from all the social and intellectual enjoyments of life. Yet, strange as it may seem, I did then and afterwards take pleasure in these reflections, hoping by them to prevent my becoming insensible to the value of what I was losing.

But all my dreams were soon put to flight by an order from the officer to trim the yards, as the wind was getting ahead; and I could plainly see by the looks the sailors occasionally cast to windward, and by the dark clouds that were fast coming up, that we had bad weather to prepare for, and I had heard the captain say that he expected to be in the Gulf Stream by twelve o'clock. In a few minutes eight bells were struck, the watch called, and we went below. I now began to feel the first discomforts of a sailor's life. The steerage, in which I lived, was filled with coils of rigging, spare sails, old junk, and ship stores, which had not been stowed away. Moreover, there had been no berths put up for us to sleep in, and we were not allowed to drive nails to hang our clothes upon. The sea, too, had risen, the vessel was rolling heavily, and everything was pitched about in grand confusion. There was a complete "hurrah's nest," as the sailors say, "everything on top and nothing at hand." A large hawser had been coiled away on my chest; my hats, boots, mattress, and blankets had all fetched away and gone over to leeward, and were jammed and broken under the boxes and coils of rigging. To crown all, we were allowed no light to find anything with, and I was just beginning to feel strong symptoms of seasickness and that listlessness and inactivity which accompany it. Giving up all attempts to collect my things together, I lay down on the sails, expecting every moment to hear the cry, "All hands ahoy!" which the approaching storm would make necessary. I shortly heard the raindrops falling on deck thick and fast, and the watch evidently had their hands full of work, for I could hear the loud and repeated orders of the mate, trampling of feet, creaking of the blocks, and all the accompaniments of a coming storm. In a few minutes the slide of the hatch was thrown back, which let down the noise and tumult of the deck still louder, the cry of "All hands ahoy! tumble up here and take in sail," saluted our ears, and the hatch was quickly shut again. When I got up on deck, a new scene and a new experience was before me.

The little brig was close-hauled upon the wind, and lying over, as it then seemed to me, nearly upon her beam ends. The heavy head sea was beating against her bows with the noise and force almost of a sledge hammer, and flying over the deck, drenching us completely through. The topsail halyards had been let go, and the great sails were filling out and backing against the masts with a noise like thunder; the wind was whistling through the rigging; loose ropes were flying about; loud and, to me, unintelligible orders constantly given, and rapidly executed; and the sailors "singing out" at the ropes in their hoarse and peculiar strains.

In addition to all this, I had not got my "sea legs on," was dreadfully seasick, with hardly strength enough to hold on to anything, and it was "pitch dark." This was my condition when I was ordered aloft, for the first time, to reef topsails.

305

How I got along, I cannot now remember. I "laid out" on the yards and held on with all my strength. I could not have been of much service, for I remember having been sick several times before I left the topsail yard, making wild vomits into the black night, to leeward. Soon all was snug aloft, and we were again allowed to go below. This I did not consider much of a favor, for the confusion of everything below, and that inexpressible sickening smell, caused by the shaking up of bilge water in the hold, made the steerage but an indifferent refuge from the cold, wet decks. I had often read of the nautical experiences of others, but I felt as though there could be none worse than mine; for, in addition to every other evil, I could not but remember that this was only the first night of a two years' voyage. When we were on deck, we were not much better off, for we were continually ordered about by the officer, who said that it was good for us to be in motion. Yet anything was better than the horrible state of things below. I remember very well going to the hatchway and putting my head down, when I was oppressed by nausea, and always being relieved immediately. It was an effectual emetic.

This state of things continued for two days.

Wednesday, August 20th. We had the watch on deck from four till eight, this morning. When we came on deck at four o'clock, we found things much changed for the better. The sea and wind had gone down, and the stars were out bright. I experienced a corresponding change in my feelings, yet continued extremely weak from my sickness. I stood in the waist on the weather side, watching the gradual breaking of the day, and the first streaks of the early light. Much has been said of the sunrise at sea; but it will not compare with the sunrise on shore. It lacks the accompaniments of the songs of birds, the awakening hum of humanity, and the glancing of the first beams upon trees, hills, spires, and house-tops, to give it life and spirit. There is no scenery. But, although the actual rise of the sun at sea is not so beautiful, yet nothing will compare for melancholy and dreariness with the early breaking of day upon "Old Ocean's gray and melancholy waste."

There is something in the first gray streaks stretching along the eastern horizon and throwing an indistinct light upon the face of the deep, which combines with the boundlessness and unknown depth of the sea around, and gives one a feeling of loneliness, of dread, and of melancholy foreboding, which nothing else in nature can. This gradually passes away as the light grows brighter, and when the sun comes up, the ordinary monotonous sea day begins.

From such reflections as these, I was aroused by the order from the officer, "Forward there! rig the head-pump!" I found that no time was allowed for day-dreaming, but that we must "turn to" at the first light. Having called up the "idlers," namely, carpenter, cook, and steward, and rigged the pump, we began washing down the decks. This operation, which is performed every morning at sea, takes nearly two hours; and I had hardly strength enough to get through it. After we had finished, swabbed down decks, and coiled up the rigging, I sat on the spars, waiting for seven bells, which was the signal for breakfast. The officer, seeing my lazy posture, ordered me to slush the mainmast, from the royal masthead down. The vessel was then rolling a little, and I had taken no food for three days, so that I felt tempted to tell him that I had rather wait till after breakfast; but I knew that I must "take the bull by the horns," and that if I showed any sign of want of spirit or backwardness, I should be ruined at once. So I took my bucket of grease and climbed up to the royal masthead. Here the rocking of the vessel, which increases the higher you go from the foot of the

mast, which is the fulcrum of the lever, and the smell of
the grease, which offended my fastidious senses, upset my stomach again, and I was not a little rejoiced when I had finished my
job and got upon the comparative *terra firma* of the deck. In
a few minutes seven bells were struck, the log hove, the watch
called, and we went to breakfast. Here I cannot but remember
the advice of the cook, a simple-hearted African. "Now," says
he, "my lad, you are well cleaned out; you haven't got a drop
of your 'long-shore swash aboard of you. You must begin on
a new tack—pitch all your sweetmeats overboard, and turn
to upon good hearty salt beef and ship bread, and I'll promise
you, you'll have your ribs well sheathed, and be as hearty as
any of 'em afore you are up to the Horn." This would be good
advice to give to passengers, when they set their hearts on the
little niceties which they have laid in, in case of seasickness.

I cannot describe the change which half a pound of cold
salt beef and a biscuit or two produced in me. I was a new
being. Having a watch below until noon, so that I had some
time to myself, I got a huge piece of strong, cold salt beef
from the cook, and kept gnawing upon it until twelve o'clock.
When we went on deck, I felt somewhat like a man, and could
begin to learn my sea duty with considerable spirit. At about
two o'clock, we heard the loud cry of "Sail ho!" from aloft, and
soon saw two sails to windward, going directly athwart our
hawse. This was the first time that I had seen a sail at sea. I
thought then, and have always since, that no sight exceeds it
in interest, and few in beauty. They passed to leeward of us,
and out of hailing distance; but the captain could read the
names on their sterns with the glass. They were the ship Helen
Mar, of New York, and the brig Mermaid, of Boston. They
were both steering westward, and were bound in for our "dear
native land."

Thursday, August 21st. This day the sun rose clear; we had a fine wind, and everything was bright and cheerful. I had now got my sea legs on, and was beginning to enter upon the regular duties of a sea life. About six bells, that is, three o'clock P.M., we saw a sail on our larboard bow. I was very desirous, like every new sailor, to speak her. She came down to us, backed her main topsail, and the two vessels stood "head on," bowing and curveting at each other like a couple of war-horses reined in by their riders. It was the first vessel that I had seen near, and I was surprised to find how much she rolled and pitched in so quiet a sea. She plunged her head into the sea, and then, her stern setting gradually down, her huge bows rose up, showing the bright copper, and her stem and breasthooks dripping, like old Neptune's locks, with the brine. Her decks were filled with passengers, who had come up at the cry of "Sail ho!" and who, by their dress and features, appeared to be Swiss and French emigrants. She hailed us at first in French, but receiving no answer, she tried us in English. She was the ship La Carolina, from Havre, for New York. We desired her to report the brig Pilgrim, from Boston, for the northwest coast of America, five days out. She then filled away and left us to plough on through our waste of waters.

There is a settled routine for hailing ships at sea: "Ship a-hoy!" Answer, "Hulloa!" "What ship is that, pray?" "The ship Carolina, from Havre, bound to New York. Where are you from?" "The brig Pilgrim, from Boston, bound to the coast of California, five days out." Unless there is leisure, or something special to say, this form is not much varied from.

This day ended pleasantly; we had got into regular and comfortable weather, and into that routine of sea life which is only broken by storm, a sail, or the sight of land.

309

MANY navy operations are secret, so I cannot tell you the name of the test pilot who flew the *Skyrocket* in November 1947. We'll call him John Bennett.

John Bennett pushed open the door of the Airport Restaurant. He walked over to the lunch counter, and climbed on a stool.

"Hi, Pete," he said to the counterman.

"Hi," said the counterman, polishing his shiny counter. "What'll it be?"

"Two cups of coffee, and some of that pie—and some doughnuts. I can drink one cup of coffee while the other is cooling," he explained efficiently.

Pete filled up the thick cups and pushed them across the counter, then lifted the glass domes that covered the pie and doughnuts.

"Going up this morning?"

"Yes, going up," the flier said. "Push over that sugar bowl, will you?" He splashed a glistening white stream into his cup. "Plane's all ready," he said. As if his own words reminded him of the need for speed, he drank down his coffee fast and swallowed the doughnuts and pie.

Then he took his wallet from his pocket, looked for a moment at the picture of his girl smiling through cellophane, and took out a dollar bill which he handed to Pete.

"You can keep it," he said.

"Thanks," said Pete, pulling the empty cups back across the counter.

The Explorer

BY

KATHERINE B. SHIPPEN

Illustrated by

Raymond Lufkin

The Douglas-built Navy D-558-2 *Skyrocket* stood in the middle of the field. It was a little thing, not much more than thirty-five feet long, but powerful, for it was equipped with both rocket and jet power plants. Its nose was needlepointed like the head of a hummingbird, its wings and tail swept back, and its fuselage was slimly tapered. The name *Skyrocket*, painted in gold, glistened against its shiny white side.

A group of aircraft engineers and Navy officials were standing beside the little plane. John Bennett saluted as he came up to them.

"Everything's ready, Bennett," the Commander said.

"Yes, sir," Bennett answered, climbing into the G-suit which two mechanics held for him.

When the suit had been properly inflated and the padded headpiece and collar put in place, he climbed clumsily up to his seat in the plane. The suit made him move awkwardly like a diver at the edge of the sea. But he was glad to have it—it would keep him from "blacking out" with the impact of the fast-moving air that could drag the blood down from his head with its enormous pressure.

"So long," he called to the men around him, closing his visor.

Then the mechanics pulled the top over the cockpit and carefully fastened it, John waved to the men on the ground, the motors roared, and the *Skyrocket* was off.

Up through the air the *Skyrocket* flew. In great wide circles like a soaring hawk she mounted. Now she had reached a layer of filmy clouds, now she was lost in their whiteness, now she had left them behind—soaring up.

Inside the cockpit the big instrument board with its fifty dials was a lighted pattern of black and white. John Bennett, at the controls, sat with his eyes on the dials. There were no

311

landmarks along the way he was going, but the dials could tell him all he needed to know.

Inside the cockpit the air was fresh and moist, the temperature at 70°. There was no need to wear an oxygen mask, not even if you climbed into outer space—at least that was what they said. This was a pressurized cabin. The air was drawn into it and kept exactly at twelve pounds a square inch. Of course if anything pierced the cabin, the air would rush out of a man's lungs so fast his lips would flap together. But there was nothing up here to pierce it.

If anything went wrong, they had provided for that too. There was a button in the wall of the cabin that John Bennett didn't want to push. The button provided for a new kind of emergency exit—different from the red-lighted doors in the movie houses, John Bennett thought to himself. Ordinarily when anything went wrong in an airplane you could just bail out. But you couldn't do that at this altitude. If you did you'd be killed in no time at all by air friction. Nobody could bail out here, you couldn't possibly use a parachute.

That was why they had put in that button. If you pressed it, an explosive charge under the cockpit would shoot the whole nose of the plane free. The nose of the plane would be tossed into empty space with him inside it. And when the thing fell near enough to earth where a man could breathe— then he would use his parachute. John didn't want to try that business.

He examined a gauge to see how the fuel was holding out.

"Plenty," he said. "Motor's running sweet."

"All O.K.," he radioed to the ground.

It was getting cold outside. Sixty-seven degrees below zero, according to the thermometer on the panel board.

312

"Forty-five thousand feet," he radioed to the ground.

He flew on, comfortable, in the still cold, watching the dials.

Once Columbus had left Portugal with three flimsy little ships, daring to cross the gray wastes of the ocean water. Once Magellan had tried to sail around the globe. Water had borne their ships, and they had known a good deal about tides and ocean currents, for many sailors had supplied them with information. But John Bennett knew hardly anything at all about this ocean of air he was navigating. No one had ever been up there before.

"Fellows like us will have to go up and find out what it is like," he said. "Nobody can tell us. We'll just have to go and see."

The hand of the altimeter moved on. Forty-seven thousand feet, it registered.

He still had more than two hundred gallons of fuel for the jet engine, and not much under twenty-five hundred pounds of fuel for the rocket engines.

"O.K.," he said to himself, and switched on the radio again to report to the ground.

The world's altitude record was held by some Italian, wasn't it? Wasn't it in 1938 that that bird had got up to fifty-six thousand feet? What was his name? What was the matter with his memory? Was the altitude getting him? Not in this pressurized cabin, boy.

The finger on the dial pointed to 51,600 now; to 51,750; to 51,800.

How long since he had left the runways? An hour and a half?

"All O.K.," he reported down.

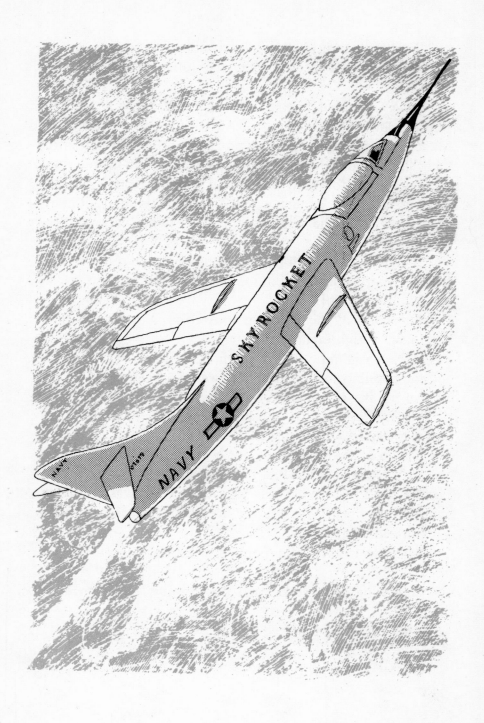

The needle said 51,850, 52,000 . . . 53,000 . . . 54,000 . . . 55,000 . . . 56,000.

And then, at last, it was 56,046.

A smile broke across John's tense features. He leaned back in his seat.

"Record broken—56,046 feet," he reported into the radio transmitter; "56,046 feet—56,046 feet—56,046 feet."

That was enough. He had gone high enough. The record was broken. Better come down now.

For a moment the little white *Skyrocket* seemed to hang still in the cold air. For a moment John Bennett paused in a place where no man had ever been, explorer of a region that no man had ever known before. If all the spheres were singing, as it has been told, he could not hear them, his cockpit being stoutly built of reinforced metal, air-conditioned, qualified to keep out pressure changes, air and sound.

"56,046 feet—56,046 feet," he kept reporting lest there should be some mistake, although the record of the altimeter was sealed, and there could be no mistake when he got back to the ground.

It was only an instant that he hung there. Then he started on the long glide back to the earth. Down through the clear, still regions of the upper atmosphere, down to the clouds and winds, down to the level of the mountain peaks, to the places where the birds flew, to the busy airplane lanes, to the warm earth, to the airport's smooth runways.

At the Airport Restaurant, Pete was still polishing up the counter when John Bennett swung open the door.

"Two more cups of coffee, Pete—and push over the sugar bowl, will you?"

Pete grumbled, and pushed the half-empty sugar bowl across the counter. "You fliers," he said.

315

WE WERE schooner-rigged and rakish,
    with a long and lissome hull,
And we flew the pretty colors
    of the crossbones and the skull;
We'd a big black Jolly Roger
    flapping grimly at the fore,
And we sailed the Spanish Water
    in the happy days of yore.

We'd a long brass gun amidships, like a well-conducted ship,
We had each a brace of pistols and a cutlass at the hip;
It's a point which tells against us, and a fact to be deplored,
But we chased the goodly merchantmen
    and laid their ships aboard.

Then the dead men fouled the
    scuppers and the wounded
        filled the chains,
And the paint work all was spat-
    terdashed with other
        people's brains,
She was boarded, she was looted,
    she was scuttled till she sank,
And the pale survivors left us
    by the medium of the plank.

A Ballad of John Silver

BY JOHN MASEFIELD

Illustrated by

Susanne Suba

Oh! then it was (while standing by the taffrail on the poop)
We could hear the drowning folk
    lament the absent chicken coop;
Then, having washed the blood away, we'd little else to do
Than to dance a quiet hornpipe as the old salts taught us to.

Oh! the fiddle on the fo'c's'le, and the slapping naked soles,
And the genial "Down the middle, Jake,
    and curtsey when she rolls!"
With the silver seas around us and the pale moon overhead,
And the lookout not a-looking and his pipe bowl glowing red.

Ah! the pigtailed, quidding pirates
    and the pretty pranks we played,
All have since been put a stop-to
    by the naughty Board of Trade;
The schooners and the merry crews are laid away to rest,
A little south of the sunset in the Islands of the Blest.

I HAD scarce gained a position on the bowsprit, when the flying jib flapped and filled upon the other tack, with a report like a gun. The schooner trembled to her keel under the reverse; but next moment, the other sails still drawing, the jib flapped back again, and hung idle.

This had nearly tossed me off into the sea; and now I lost no time, crawled back along the bowsprit, and tumbled head foremost on the deck.

I was on the lee-side of the forecastle, and the main-sail, which was still drawing, con-cealed from me a certain portion of the after-deck. Not a soul was to be seen. The planks, which had not been swabbed since the mu-tiny, bore the print of many feet; and an empty bottle, broken by the neck, tumbled to and fro like a live thing in the scuppers.

Suddenly the Hispaniola came right into the wind. The jibs behind me cracked aloud; the rudder slammed to; the whole ship gave a sickening heave and shudder, and at the same moment the main-boom swung inboard, the sheet groaning in the blocks, and showed me the lee after-deck.

There were the two watchmen, sure enough: Red-cap on his back, as stiff as a handspike, with his arms stretched out like those of a crucifix, and his teeth showing through his open lips; Israel Hands propped against the bulwarks, his chin on his chest, his hands lying open before him on the deck, his face as white, under its tan, as a tallow candle.

I Strike the Jolly Roger

BY ROBERT LOUIS

STEVENSON

Illustrated by C. B. Falls

For a while the ship kept bucking and sidling like a vicious horse, the sails filling, now on one tack, now on another, and the boom swinging to and fro till the mast groaned aloud under the strain. Now and again, too, there would come a cloud of light sprays over the bulwark, and a heavy blow of the ship's bows against the swell; so much heavier weather was made of it by this great rigged ship than by my homemade, lop-sided coracle, now gone to the bottom of the sea.

At every jump of the schooner, Red-cap slipped to and fro; but—what was ghastly to behold—neither his attitude nor his fixed teeth-disclosing grin was anyway disturbed by this rough usage. At every jump, too, Hands appeared still more to sink into himself and settle down upon the deck, his feet sliding ever the farther out, and the whole body canting towards the stern, so that his face became, little by little, hid from me; and at last I could see nothing beyond his ear and the frayed ringlet of one whisker.

And at the same time, I observed around both of them, splashes of dark blood upon the planks, and began to feel sure that they had killed each other in their drunken wrath.

While I was thus looking and wondering, in a calm moment, when the ship was still, Israel Hands turned partly round, and, with a low moan, writhed himself back to the position in which I had seen him first. The moan, which told of pain and deadly weakness, and the way in which his jaw hung open, went right to my heart. But when I remembered the talk I had overheard from the apple barrel, all pity left me.

I walked aft until I reached the mainmast.

"Come aboard, Mr. Hands," I said ironically.

He rolled his eyes round heavily; but he was too far gone to express surprise. All he could do was to utter one word, "Brandy."

It occurred to me there was no time to lose; and, dodging

319

the boom as it once more lurched across the deck, I slipped aft, and down the companion-stairs into the cabin.

It was such a scene of confusion as you can hardly fancy. All the lock-fast places had been broken open in quest of the chart. The floor was thick with mud, where ruffians had sat down to drink or consult after wading in the marshes round their camp. The bulkheads, all painted in clear white, and beaded round with gilt, bore a pattern of dirty hands. Dozens of empty bottles clinked together in corners to the rolling of the ship. One of the doctor's medical books lay open on the table, half of the leaves gutted out, I suppose, for pipelights. In the midst of all this the lamp still cast a smoky glow, obscure and brown as umber.

I went into the cellar; all the barrels were gone, and of the bottles a most surprising number had been drunk out and thrown away. Certainly, since the mutiny began, not a man of them could ever have been sober.

Foraging about, I found a bottle with some brandy left, for Hands; and for myself I routed out some biscuit, some pickled fruits, a great bunch of raisins, and a piece of cheese. With these I came on deck, put down my own stock behind the rudder-head, and well out of the coxswain's reach, went forward to the water-breaker, and had a good, deep drink of water, and then, and not till then, gave Hands the brandy.

He must have drunk a gill before he took the bottle from his mouth.

"Aye," said he, "by thunder, but I wanted some a' that!"

I had sat down already in my own corner and begun to eat.

"Much hurt?" I asked him.

He grunted, or rather I might say, he barked.

"If that doctor was aboard," he said, "I'd be right enough

320

in a couple of turns; but I don't have no manner of luck, you see, and that's what's the matter with me. As for that swab, he's good as dead, he is," he added, indicating the man with the red cap. "He warn't no seaman, anyhow. And where mought you have come from?"

"Well," said I, "I've come aboard to take possession of this ship, Mr. Hands; and you'll please regard me as your captain until further notice."

He looked at me sourly enough, but said nothing. Some of the color had come back into his cheeks, though he still looked very sick, and still continued to slip out and settle down as the ship banged about.

"By-the-bye," I continued, "I can't have these colors, Mr. Hands; and, by your leave, I'll strike 'em. Better none than these."

And, again dodging the boom, I ran to the color lines, handed down their cursed black flag, and chucked it over-board.

"God save the king!" said I, waving my cap, "and there's an end to Captain Silver!"

He watched me keenly and slyly, his chin all the while on his breast.

"I reckon," he said at last, "I reckon, Cap'n Hawkins, you'll kind of want to get ashore, now. S'pose we talks."

"Why, yes," said I, "with all my heart, Mr. Hands. Say on." And I went back to my meal with a good appetite.

"This man," he began, nodding feebly at the corpse— "O'Brien were his name—a rank Irelander—this man and me got the canvas on her, meaning for to sail her back. Well, he's dead now, he is—as dead as bilge; and who's to sail this ship, I don't see. Without I gives you a hint, you ain't that man, as far's I can tell. Now, look here, you give me food and drink, and a old scarf or ankecher to tie my wound up, you do; and I'll tell you how to sail her; and that's about square all around, I take it."

"I'll tell you one thing," says I: "I'm not going back to Captain Kidd's anchorage. I mean to get into North Inlet, and beach her quietly there."

"To be sure you did," he cried. "Why, I ain't sich an in-fernal lubber, after all. I can see, can't I? I've tried my fling, I have, and I've lost, and it's you has the wind of me. North Inlet? Why, I haven't no ch'ice, not I! I'd help you sail her up to Execution Dock, by thunder, so I would."

Well, as it seemed to me, there was some sense in this. We struck our bargain on the spot. In three minutes I had the Hispaniola sailing easily before the wind along the coast of

Treasure Island, with good hopes of turning the northern point ere noon, and beating down again as far as North Inlet before high water, when we might beach her safely, and wait till the subsiding tide permitted us to land.

Then I lashed the tiller and went below to my own chest, where I got a soft silk handkerchief of my mother's! With this, and with my aid, Hands bound up the great bleeding stab he had received in the thigh, and after he had eaten a little and had a swallow or two more of the brandy, he began to pick up visibly, sat up straighter, spoke louder and clearer, and looked in every way another man.

The breeze served us admirably. We skimmed before it like a bird, the coast of the island flashing by, and the view changing every minute. Soon we were past the high lands and bowling beside low, sandy country, sparsely dotted with dwarf pines, and soon we were beyond that again, and had turned the corner of the rocky hill that ends the island on the north.

I was greatly elated with my new command, and pleased with the bright, sunshiny weather and these different prospects of the coast. I had now plenty of water and good things to eat, and my conscience, which had smitten me hard for my desertion, was quieted by the great conquest I had made. I should, I think, have had nothing left me to desire but for the eyes of the coxswain as they followed me derisively about the deck, and the odd smile that appeared continually on his face. It was a smile that had in it something both of pain and weakness—a haggard, old man's smile; but there was, besides that, a grain of derision, a shadow of treachery, in his expression as he craftily watched, and watched, and watched me at my work.

Sea Fever

BY JOHN MASEFIELD

Illustrated by Hans A. Mueller

I MUST go down to the seas again,
        to the lonely sea and the sky,
And all I ask is a tall ship and a star to steer her by,
And the wheel's kick and the wind's song
        and the white sail's shaking,
And a grey mist on the sea's face and a grey dawn breaking.

I must go down to the seas again,
        for the call of the running tide
Is a wild call and a clear call that may not be denied;
And all I ask is a windy day with the white clouds flying,
And the flung spray and the blown spume,
        and the sea-gulls crying.

I must go down to the seas again to the vagrant gypsy life,
To the gull's way and the whale's way
        where the wind's like a whetted knife;
And all I ask is a merry yarn from a laughing fellow-rover,
And quiet sleep and a sweet dream when the long trick's over.

324

P. S.

IN preparing this volume, the editors have selected stories and excerpts from complete books, and in those cases where the text of a book is reprinted in its entirety, only a few of the many delightful illustrations from the original have been used. For the benefit of those who would like to read and enjoy the complete books, the following list is given.

Subject Index

Illustrators

Index

331

332

A Vagabond Song The Highwayman

A Ballad of John Silver I Strike the Jolly Roger

The Explorer

A Home...

...st Stand

In a Wyomi...

Men o... Boat!

The Knight of t...

Bill...

...ns

...t Begins

Date Due